UNBREAKABLE

SKYE CALLAHAN

VINCI
BOOKS

By Skye Callahan

Vinci Books

vinci-books.com

Published by Vinci Books Ltd in 2025

1

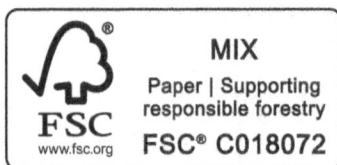

FSC
www.fsc.org

MIX
Paper | Supporting
responsible forestry
FSC® C018072

Printed and bound in Great Britain by Clays Ltd, Elcograf S.p.A.

Chapter One

ALIVE

"HOW MANY WOMEN did you have sex with while you were there?"

This was the third time Dr. Combs had asked me that question. And for the third time, I wanted to avoid it.

I had just gotten out of that hell, and I still had the bullet hole in my chest to prove it, but that didn't stop my boss from pushing the psychiatric evaluation. What he expected it to accomplish right now, I had no clue—I was tired, cranky, and I didn't give a damn about getting my old job back.

Dr. Combs cleared her throat, and I clenched my jaw, still trying to block her out. Some things were left unspoken —better suited to the imagination of nightmares and horror movies than to be discussed openly with any other living person.

I didn't even want to admit the number of women to myself; even though I could see every one of the girls in my mind.

Kat, the red-headed braggart who thought she owned every man who walked into the Retreat.

Gabby, the indignant curly haired brunette.

Raini, a gorgeous but frail girl who was transferred in right after I went undercover. I had feared that one more night in Ross's bed would kill her before her first week was up.

Alley, a blond sweetheart who belonged to Miles, my unconventional friend.

Silver, the girl who simultaneously ruined and saved me.

She was the only reason I was alive, and the only reason I had what was left of my soul—except she wasn't real. Like my undercover alias, Kirk, she was forged from necessity and determination. Now she was gone, and that missing piece was more painful than the hole the bullet had ripped through my side.

That crazy, obstinate woman wouldn't back down. During the raid on the "sex retreat", Ross had turned the gun on me, but she knocked him off balance and I ended up with a graze along my left side rather than a hole through my heart. The bullet splintered two ribs in the process, and left a long and bloody gash, but they'd managed to clean it up in surgery, and so far it was healing without complications.

Now, somewhere out there Rose was learning to live her own life again.

At least that's what I hoped. The day after I was shot, my superiors had me transferred to another hospital and put under protective custody until they were sure I was "safe".

I was fairly positive they were more concerned that any real threat to my life would come from me since there were very few people who knew of my undercover involvement in the operation.

The only company I had been allowed since then was Dr. Combs, my new shrink. I didn't want a shrink. I wanted the woman who saved me—the only person who stood a chance of bringing me any kind of peace.

The woman I could never have.

All I wanted to do was close my eyes and wait for the doctor to leave. But that would put me in a worse situation since she'd just report me for being difficult.

One fucking week.

I still had a hole in my fucking side for Christ sake.

"I want to talk to Trent—this no visitor thing is bull shit."

"It's for your own safety, and we can't do anything until you cooperate."

"Don't preach to me about cooperating." One of the machines next to me screeched and a stabbing pain radiated through my arm, but I'd felt much worse. "I gave up my life to do what was asked of me and I succeeded."

"You need to relax," she warned, reaching a hand toward me.

I shook it off as best as I could in my current condition. I didn't fucking want to relax. I wanted what little I had of my life back.

And, most of all I wanted someone I had no right to want.

"James."

She was just going to stand there and keep yammering.

"With all due respect, Doctor, fuck off."

"I'll have to compile my preliminary evaluation before we can move forward. That'd go much smoother if you'd help me out."

Help. I guess as far as not listening—even for my own supposed good—I could give Silver a run for her money. I waited in silence as a nurse adjusted and silenced the beeping machine. Quiet moments of solitude ticked away— my respite from being expected to answer questions, but it didn't last.

"I don't want to talk about the women," I said when the door closed again. The steady stream of medication weighed down my body and softened my voice, so I didn't sound as menacing as I intended. "I don't much feel like talking about anything, but can we just skip the women and the fucking?"

"All of the women?" Dr. Combs asked, with her usual flat exaggerated calm. "Or is there someone in particular you don't want to discuss?"

I figured pointing out that she was still talking about what I'd asked her not to—regardless of my answer—would be a waste of breath. "You know there is. How about you let me talk to her and I'll answer any damn question you like?"

I didn't even have to glance over to know she was scowling. They wouldn't let me see Trent, my best friend and contact during the investigation, I knew they sure as hell wouldn't let me see Silver… Rose. I didn't even know what the hell I was supposed to call her. She'd made it perfectly clear the few times I'd pressed about her past or used her real name that I had no role in that life.

"She's fine," Dr. Combs assured me. "But I don't think it would be in the best interest of either of you to see each other. You put yourself in a dangerous situation with her."

Put myself? Last I checked I wasn't the one to drag her into the Retreat. "I kept her alive and slightly less broken than she would have otherwise been."

"The two of you adapted to a horrible situation, found comfort in each other—"

I didn't want to hear it.

Stockholm Syndrome.

I wondered if the captor could get it too. Was I even the captor? It seemed like I'd lost control of the situation long ago.

But I'd still been the one to beat her, rape her, bend her will.

Just like she'd bent mine.

I wanted her back so badly I couldn't breathe. The more we talked about it, the worse it got. The harsh reality of it all forced me to face the possibility that I had to walk away if I wanted to do what was in her best interest.

"How long until I can talk to Trent?" I tried again, drawing back a modicum of control by changing the course of the conversation.

Dr. Combs sighed and snapped her portfolio closed. "If it'll get you to talk, I'll make the arrangements on one condition."

I'd already sold my soul, there weren't many more concessions I had left to give.

"I need to know you're not going to try to reach out to Rose—or anyone else."

Did that mean there was a chance she'd see me? Or was Dr. Combs convinced I'd stalk and abduct her anyway? That was quite a laughable possibility, but some sick-as-fuck part of me considered it. "How long are you going to dictate who I can talk to?"

"As long as it's in your best interest. You and Rose need time to heal—being together puts you at a higher risk to continue your relationship based on circumstances that are not ideal. You have to separate yourself from what you became and the things you did in order to survive."

Kirk and Silver no longer exist—she didn't have to outright say it. James and Rose were strangers.

"Four weeks," Dr. Combs said. "Give it at least that long before we discuss the possibility of you two communicating. And even then, you have to face the possibility that it's better for you both to move on separately."

"I know," I growled. It was a tough pill to swallow, but I wasn't going to force myself on her. Again. "And if that's what she wants, I'll give it to her."

"Because you'd give up just about anything to make sure she's safe and happy?"

There was a trap in that question, and even hyped up on whatever the doctors and nurses were feeding me, I wasn't stupid enough to fall for it. There wasn't a right answer. Just like there hadn't been a right answer when I'd found Silver in the basement with Gabe and his group of clods.

"I'll agree to your conditions."

"Are you going to be staying with Trent when you're released?"

"That's a stupid question considering your refusal to let me talk to anyone." I had somewhat of a plan—not one set in stone, but I had given up my apartment, left my belongings in storage and my car with Trent. I knew I'd be coming back to nothing. "I have a cousin nearby."

"Family would be good for you."

"That's only a possibility if no one is coming after me. The last thing I'll do is put my family in danger." Especially since they had a two-year-old living there, too.

"Lucky for you, they all think Kirk is dead. Bled out on the operating table."

"Lucky me," I said drowsily. Kirk *was* dead. He was staying that way.

But Dr. Combs assurance only really told me one thing —they were keeping me isolated because they didn't trust me, not because they were afraid of someone coming after me.

———

AS PROMISED, Trent came in the next morning, and my visitor restrictions were lifted—to an extent. The doctor's new rules still only allowed for Trent and close family members.

I rubbed the exhaustion from my eyes—running a marathon was less tiresome than laying in a bed for days on end, and the meds didn't help. "Fucking hospitable of them to finally let me have visitors the day before I'm supposed to be released."

"I hear you've been quite the agreeable patient, too. It's no wonder they won't let you talk to anyone, they probably want to keep you around." He wheeled over the tall stool from the corner and took a seat next to me. It was nearly eight in the morning, and no surprise, he was already dressed in his suit and tie—all ready for work. I think the thing he liked most about suits was the shocked expression he usually got when people saw below the layers of fabric. He had more tattoos than me, and I wouldn't have been surprised to hear about a few new ones since the last time we'd actually been able to sit down and have a chat in person.

Tattoos weren't what I cared about though, and happy as I was to see my best friend, first I had to address the issue niggling at my mind.

"Have you talked to Rose?"

Trent grunted and sat back in a chair, propping his feet up on the bed frame. "Just jumping right to the point, eh? I'm not playing double operative for either of you."

"I'll interpret that as a yes."

He glared back at me, but he'd given me enough to keep me sated for a while. I assumed that Dr. Combs had already informed him of the agreement.

"I told Evan you're allowed to have visitors," Trent said, "he's coming in as soon as Katie gets off work to stay with Jack."

Jack, my cousin's two-year-old son. I couldn't even imagine how much he'd grown since I'd gone under. "Why do I get the feeling I'm about to become a live-in babysitter."

"You're good with children—dare I even say—"

"Don't." It was difficult, if not impossible, to be intimidating when covered in wires and tubes.

So, of course, he didn't listen. "You like them."

Sure, as long as they belonged to someone else. Living with them was entirely different. But my other possibility was staying with Trent, dealing with his inconsistent work schedule, and sleeping on his couch, which in my current condition didn't sound appealing. Evan at least had a bed, and a quite nice bed as far as I remembered. And since I had a bullet hole in my chest, no one really wanted me staying by myself too long.

Apparently I might fall apart without warning.

I wasn't going to complain yet. Aside from the locked up storage container, I didn't have much of my own left, and time with my cousin—the only close family I had left—was an easy concession. Having his kid also around meant I wouldn't be asked too many questions. Eventually, I figured

I'd get tired of the attention, but for a little while having some things catered couldn't be so bad.

Trent sat forward, his shoes squeaking as his feet landed against the floor. "Was the opportunity to ask about Rose the only reason you wanted to see me?"

"No, I also wanted to see a face that didn't belong to a doctor or nurse, and who, hopefully, wouldn't ask prying questions."

"I think I know as much as I need to at the moment. Until you're able to file all of your reports anyhow."

"No getting out of that?" They already knew what they needed as far as I was concerned, but all of their questions made me wonder if I was now surrounded by sadists.

"Just like there's no getting out of talking to Dr. Combs," he said coolly.

I grunted and dug my head into the pillow. It wasn't enough that she was in my head, now the doctor was recruiting my friends. "How much is she paying you to say that?"

Trent shook his head and shrugged one shoulder. His gaze dropped and he straightened the cuffs on his sleeves. "You've been thinking about not coming back, haven't you?"

That was probably the sanest idea on my mind at the moment. "I'm thinking that I don't have much left to lose and wondering where I should draw the line."

"You have time to figure it out. And—" he blew out a breath. "Don't worry about Rose—I won't play messenger or double agent, but I'm looking in on her."

Much as it pained me that it was him and not me, I couldn't think of anyone else I'd want taking care of her. "Does she also know you're looking in on me?"

"That's only fair, but I gave her the same deal. I'm here

for you because you're my best friend, and I'm there for her because I'm still involved with the case. Never the twain shall meet."

"Now who's the one with dual lives?" I asked with as much of a smirk as I could muster.

He cocked his head. "How long before they clear you for physical activity?"

"I don't know—when I no longer have the possibility of leaking like a sieve out of my chest, I'd assume."

"Good. Heal up. I need my partner and sparring buddy."

Sparring buddy. Trent and I had started Kendo when we were eleven. This was the longest I'd ever gone without practicing. Right before I'd gone under, we'd both been preparing to test for yon-don—my fourth-degree black belt. "It'll be a while."

"Then, I'll test for yon-don without you."

I scoffed. "I'd assumed you already had."

"That wouldn't have been any fun."

"Right, and it'll be so much fun watching my rusty ass fail." Even though he hadn't tested to rank higher than me, he was more in practice than I was, and I had no doubt that it'd take me a long while to catch up.

"At least it'll give you something to do."

Trent's phone sounded, and he peeked down at the display. "I have to head in. Call me if you need anything."

Chapter Two

WIN, LOSE, OR DOMINATE

DR. COMBS RETURNED in the afternoon for her daily session of torture and spared me no peace by jumping straight to the worst topic possible.

"Tell me about Silver." The statement rolled off her tongue like an innocent "good afternoon," except she didn't wish a *good* anything.

"That's what you're going to lead with?" The one thing she knew I didn't want to talk about. My muscles tensed, but it only sent a radiating pain across my side until I relaxed.

"The first day she showed up, what happened?" She had no idea what she was asking. Her calm voice a drastic contrast to the mental images conjured by every word she spoke.

"Doesn't matter." It was like fighting off a lion that already had a taste for my blood.

"Did you force her to have sex with you?"

My hands clenched at my sides twisting and curling the thin hospital sheets. "Not then."

I tried to think about anything else, but my mind betrayed me and jumped straight to that night. My heart went into overdrive, fueling the anger that already tainted my blood and sending it to the deepest part of my brain.

That first day. It seemed like it had happened years ago, only because so much had changed since the day I'd first seen her in the basement of the Retreat.

"When? Another day—or night," Dr. Combs continued prying.

"Second night—only because it would've been Ross if not me."

"How did she react to that?"

I blew out a puff of air. "I got her off if that's what you'd like to know."

Dr. Combs scowled.

"See there," I said, laying my arm over my eyes. "You don't really want to hear about it anymore than I want to talk about it."

"Be crude all you want. I'm not judging—"

I slammed my hand down on the bed to stop her lie. "Don't fucking give me that. I was there. There is no fucking way in hell anyone hears about the things I did without some kind of opinion. I'm the bastard, the abuser, rapist, villain, liar, thief—and I get away with it all as far as the law and any official judgment are concerned. I'd be utterly convinced that I'm guaranteed a spot in the deepest pit of Hell if I wasn't holding on to the slim hope that the time I've already spent there was enough to burn away my sins—at the very least it might have burned away my soul, in which case it won't matter much once I die because there won't even be anything left."

She smiled—of all the fucking reactions in the world, she smiled at that?

"Finally getting an honest reaction. I do believe that's the most you've said all week."

I scowled, the distasteful sting of bile assaulted my mouth. "You're a gem, you know that?"

"Back to the topic. Tell me what happened."

"When?" I was done fighting, only because the smile told me that she was quite possibly more sadistic than me.

"Pick a night."

———

I HAD BEEN TRYING to type out a report on my throw-away phone—my only real connection to the outside world —when a call came in on my other phone. I put the second phone to my ear, trying to finish my report as I listened.

"You might want to have a look in the basement."

"Why?" I growled at the person on the line. I could only send my update to Trent if I stayed out of sight until I hid the phone again.

"Gabe," was the only answer I got and all I needed to know that it was going to be bad. Gabe had had it in for me since I started this assignment.

Although he didn't know it was an assignment—to Gabe I was some fresh crook off the streets who had stepped in the way of his upward mobility nearly a year ago. The idiot was also too self-consumed to realize that even if not for me, he wasn't going anywhere. He was even too hotheaded to be a good criminal.

Luckily, I had acting the part of a good criminal down pat. I canceled the message, stuffing the throw-away cell into the ventilation of my apartment's living room.

From the ninth floor, it was usually just as fast to take the busy and often crowded elevator as it was to take the stairs, but I opted for nine flights of quiet.

I could hear the ruckus before I even reached the basement doors, and I knew I was in for a long day—if not a full-on physical altercation before lunch.

Crazy thing is. I would have gone for it. I was jonesing for a release.

I wished Gabe would give me a reason to punch him square in the face.

I shoved open the door and stepped out on the catwalk that overlooked the dank concrete basement.

Oh God, it's a girl. Not one of our girls—Gabe and his corrupt Neanderthals had abducted and brought someone in. "What the hell breed of trouble are you lot causing?"

I tried to keep my eyes from falling on her, it'd give too much away. Instead, I focused on the men—the greedy bastards who'd taken it under their own gumption to kidnap, torture, and rape.

Ross appeared at my side, and I cursed. Keeping my steely death glare aimed right at Gabe. He'd dragged her in, but I had about as much a chance of getting her out as finding a wild polar bear in the desert.

Gabe blathered on about his reasoning, his stupid, idiotic excuses for putting everything in jeopardy.

On a daily basis, I'd faced down the women—the sex slaves—Milo traded around like chattel. They were women who'd been in this mess for years. It didn't make things any better—they surely didn't deserve it, but I made solace— relative solace—by making sure our girls were taken care of as much as I could. Luckily, I had Miles to side with me on that. There was never a shortage of girls, which also made it easier for us to enforce the rules about not bringing new ones in.

We could pass it off as too dangerous—not worth the risk—and as long as we appeared to be protecting Ross's assets, he was all for the plan. The people with the most to lose could be surprisingly easy to swindle.

This was different. I was watching a girl lose everything in an instant. It had already been done; caught on our security cameras, noticed by the guards—there was no sneaking her back out and covering the whole thing up. My stomach churned at the thought of what this girl had been dragged into.

Ross would order her death before he'd ever let her walk out, but luckily he left me to clean up the mess, going back upstairs—probably to tend to his own "slave".

Death. For a moment, I almost considered that'd be the merciful choice.

Then, I looked into her pale green eyes, and damned myself for even considering it.

I damned myself for considering the only other viable option as well—keeping her until I could secure her a way out.

By keeping her, I'd condemned her to pain and degradation.

She'd hate me, she'd probably fight me, but she'd be alive.

I descended the stairs, as Gabe continued on his rant about never having any fresh girls to mess with—the only reason he liked new girls was because he liked to be the one to break them. He liked the mind-fuck of it all. For him, all sex was a mind-fuck.

Gabe's second, a tall, gangly man named Benjamin, jumped in to defend his friend. He kept his body relaxed, eyes on me as if that would keep me from noticing his twisting hold on the girl's arm. "It's been months since we've had any fun breaking a new girl, so Gabe picked her up."

So much for defense—at least he was kind enough to throw Gabe right under the bus. Gabe growled, and the girl screeched in pain. Before I could take action against Benjamin, Gabe's glare pushed him away from the table. Everyone except Gabe stood back, but their eyes were on her, not me.

I leaned over the head of the table, staring down into tear-filled green eyes. The tears didn't spill over. In an instant, I felt every emotion possible, but I let the anger simmer to the surface—hatred toward the situation I'd been put in, and the men who'd thrown me there. She dropped her gaze away, and I was momentarily free again.

"There's a reason it has been a while," I kept my words slow and deliberate, squeezing Gabe's hand until he released the girl. "You all are sloppy and when you break the rules, we end up with women that are of no use to us."

"We can't release her," Gabe growled, but his self-pleased expression didn't match his bite. "So just go back upstairs to your work and let us have our fun."

I heard her gasp. Face to face with fate—one that neither of us could escape now.

"You're right," I said. "Why the hell should you be rewarded for breaking the rules? Remember how things work. You make a mess, I have to clean it up—I'd rather start now than wait for the mess to get bigger."

"How things work…." Gabe chuckled and looked around at his crew. "Seven against one is how things currently work, or are you counting on two for your side? She is feisty."

Even as the group of men prepared to move toward me, I smirked and went right for Gabe's jugular—which he kept nailed to his ego. "You're right, Gabe, she is feisty." I grabbed Benjamin by the throat when he made the mistake of taking another step. "She managed to inflict at least one bloody nose, and I imagine a few other injuries. So what makes you think I'm scared of a crew who can't even manage to wrangle a single girl?"

"We were...," Benjamin stuttered, and I squeezed harder, "having...fun."

"Game's over." I shoved him back and watched him gasp for air as he stumbled toward his group of friends before I sent them off with my final warning. "And if you do want to try me, remember that even if you win, I'll be counting on the boss's gun to your head afterward. I believe you all are supposed to be working tonight, yet you smell wasted, and you're down here causing trouble. Either find a productive way to use the rest of your day or I'll send you to the dregs."

I grabbed Gabe before he could head for the stairs. He needed a solid reminder of who was in charge. "You and I will have a long discussion later, Gabe."

He scowled and shook off my hand, leaving me alone— in the last place I wanted to be.

I tried to keep my eyes off of her as I ordered her to sit up. She shivered but obeyed, trying to keep me in full view. She couldn't have been much older than twenty-five, if that. She wore jeans, a now torn shirt with lettering across the front, and sneakers. She wasn't dressed up to go anywhere fancy—not even a night club from the looks of her, so I had to wonder where on earth Gabe had snagged her.

Her begging sent shards of ice through my veins, but it worked to my advantage in a way. The only way to resist her, the only smidgen of hope I had for keeping us both alive—was becoming the Ice-man, with no feelings or emotions. Yet, I couldn't even look her in the face as I condemned her to the worst fate. I couldn't tell her, couldn't say it.

Instead, I took the shoe that remained on her foot, as well as the one she'd lost in the struggle and threw them both in the trash.

Welcome to your new life.

She begged, her soft pleading eyes churned my stomach. Guilt, hatred, doubt, anger.

Anger. That I could use. Or so I hoped. I already stood on the knife's edge—anger made it possible to survive there, but it could just as easily shove me right off.

She continued to shake—whether from fear or cold—as I dragged her to her feet and up the stairs. I had to solidify what I was about to do. I had to drag the newest acquisition right through the middle of the complex and up to Ross's office if I wanted to stake my claim.

Did I want to?

If I looked back at her and asked myself that question again, I had no idea what I'd be capable of, but it'd probably get us both killed. So I kept my sights straight ahead, ignoring everyone and everything until I got to the elevator and shoved her in, punching the button for the tenth floor.

She pulled away and slumped against the wall, rubbing her head, but she looked like she was going to vomit. That'd be just my luck—and well deserved.

"Do you remember what happened?" I asked. It was a stupid, idiotic, insane idea. I wasn't supposed to care, but how the hell was I supposed to make sure she was okay?

She shook her head, grasping the railing as the elevator halted. I yanked her out of the elevator and into the hallway that led to Ross's office.

"What is this place?" she asked, apparently now ready

to talk. I already had a sinking feeling that she wasn't going to make anything easy. She still didn't get that this was the end. The only way I could give her a chance was to convince her that there was no chance.

No going back.

It was the only way for both of us to make it out alive; but holy Hell if I could have given up my life then to get her out with full assurances she wouldn't be harmed, I would have done it.

I flipped her around and pulled her up until she stood on her toes to face me.

"Not listening is a good way to get yourself killed here, which is exactly what would have happened if I hadn't come downstairs to see what trouble our resident dipshits had dragged in. You have yet to be ripped to pieces or to be removed of your ability to speak. If you want to keep it that way, I suggest that you learn to obey simple commands. Shut up."

Every word was true, but I felt like an asshole for delivering it—even if it was the only way to save her life.

I dragged her into Ross's office—our first test. As I suspected, he was kicked back in his seat, with Kat servicing him. They were the perfect couple—not that either of them were or would ever consider being exclusive. He had power and money, and she was a slave who desired just that. Both conniving, manipulative, and entirely self-serving—given that description, Gabe would fit quite nicely into their relationship as well, but he lacked their careful tact.

"Don't tell me you decided to keep their toy." He kicked Kat away, and she crawled to sit next to his desk.

I took a breath and shoved the girl toward him. *You're Kirk, not James.* It was the first time I had to remind myself of that in months. "Faulted though their tactics may be, she might be a nice addition."

Ross wasn't going to be an easy person to convince—especially not if I wanted to keep her to myself. But one of his complaints was that I didn't have a usual companion at business dinners—and he prided himself on making sure everyone had fun.

Fun as a tooth extraction.

Ross would be the kind of person who thought that watching such a procedure would be fun.

He moved toward us, looking her over. "Seems like the kind that's easier to break than bend, which makes her no use to us."

I watched her shake and recoil under his glare but then redirected my gaze to detach myself again. "We all need a challenge from time to time."

"So, is a challenge what you're interested in? I was beginning to think nothing could get you riled." He circled her, a rueful smile dancing on his face as he pressed his fingers and hands against her exposed skin.

At least she managed not to snap at him. I had a moment of relief until he stopped in front of her.

"Take off your clothes," he said.

Fuck. I may as well have jumped off a cliff with no idea how I was going to land.

The girl didn't budge.

I rooted my feet into the floor as Ross's hand shot out and took her by the throat. *Don't move. Don't intervene. He's not going to kill her yet.*

"She has skewed sense of self-preservation," Ross snarled, staring at her like a rabid dog preparing to take his prey. "Is your modesty worth death?"

She stumbled toward me as he released her, but she

wasn't stupid enough to take her eyes off of him. He held out his hand waiting for her compliance.

One final chance.

Finally, she tore off her shirt, but instead of handing it to him, she threw it at his feet. This woman had guts, and I hoped I wouldn't be watching them get spattered across the carpet. Once she'd shed all her clothing, she stood tall in front of him.

From the quiver I saw in her chest with each breath, I knew it was an act, but even that small act could get her killed.

Ross stared at her for a few minutes, making his verbal assessments—each laced with insult, before finally granting her to me to "train".

She was demoted from human to sex toy.

From young woman to piece of ass.

After taking her to Clarence, our on-call doctor, to begin her medical tests, I finally took her back to my apartment—the only place I had of momentary respite. Now I had no choice but to keep up the façade twenty-four-seven.

All I wanted was for something to ease the pounding in my head—and to make matters worse, I knew Trent would be on edge since I'd missed my last check in. But I couldn't make an escape anywhere to contact him just yet. Since Silver had nearly passed out at least once, first I had to make sure she had food, water, and rest.

Once she slept it off, though, she was back to her feisty self. So, I let her free into the hallway and invited Miles up for a little game of cats and mouse. The easiest way to get her to make her decision between fending for herself with anyone else in the building and me.

But even that only worked for a little while, and after she

begged me to take her back inside, what did I do? I shoved a butt plug up her ass and tied her to my bed.

Her mini-induction—but more importantly, my moment to get out and regroup my thoughts. She had to come face-to-face with what she'd been dragged into, and I, for the life of me, had to get away.

I also had to finish my report—which was going on more than eight hours late.

How the hell was I supposed to explain?

I took the phone and went up to the roof. The only place that was never bugged or monitored—even though a few of our crew sometimes liked to use it for hookups, as if there wasn't an entire compound of places to do it.

After checking the area, I sat against the wall near the edge and did what I didn't usually do—I called in.

"How's the weather?" Trent asked—he sounded alarmed, but didn't give anything away. We had a code— one that hadn't appeared in any code books except the ones we wrote as kids. It was simple enough but served our needs.

"Feels like rain. And that's not the least of my worries."

"Sounds like you could use a drink."

"It's a girl problem," I said somberly. "A major one."

"Aren't they always?" Trent was quiet for a moment, then came back on. "Lines look clear."

"They brought her in today. Picked her up off the street, I'd guess. Can you get her out?"

"Fuck." I heard a rustle of noise, but silence from Trent. "Only if we bring the whole thing down early. I can't even guarantee we can do that at the moment. I can call in. See if we can get everyone mobilized."

"Damn it, T—" I cut off before saying his name. "*She's in my bed*. It's either them or me."

"You can keep her with you, then? Without putting either of you at greater risk?" He made it sound like that was the obvious and easy solution.

"We're already at greater risk. The only way I can get away with it is to train her, and you know what that means."

"I'll take this up and we'll look for an extraction opportunity."

"One that won't get us killed, preferably." I knew I didn't have to remind him, but speaking it made me feel a smidge more confident.

"Don't blow your cover."

This was all more than I bargained for when I came in. She was an innocent girl—not that the others deserved any of it. They were the only reason I could justify the naïve hope that any of my work would make a difference in the long run.

"Remember how far off the books you are," Trent said. I was the first and only person to infiltrate this far, and it was only through doing things that were in no means legal or scrupulous.

"No price too high for one man's head. An unplanned raid doesn't increase either of our chances, so I'll play my part and keep her as safe as I can, but I can guarantee she isn't going to like it."

"I'll make damn sure she's taken care of when we find a way to extract her. Get me her name, and I'll keep the heat off as well."

"Appreciated. Is this what you'd do?" I had to ask, had to be sure I wasn't deluded and using some excuse made up by my warped subconscious to keep her.

"I'd keep her alive. There's no way to sneak her out?"

"Gabe isn't exactly discrete about anything. Everyone already knows—they knew before I got involved."

"Do what you have to."

"I don't think this is what they meant by 'any means necessary'."

"They sure as hell didn't mean it was going to be easy."

I disconnected the phone and took one final breath of fresh air before heading back down to my new twenty-four-seven torture chamber. I had hoped that she'd calmed down while I was gone—or that she was at least smart enough not to push, but I was wrong. Shortly after I opened the bedroom door, she snapped once again.

"I have to piss."

Did she not understand where the hell she was or what she was in for?

Back at square one again. Who the hell was I kidding, that would have been an improvement. My jaw spasmed because I was clenching my teeth so hard. Anger wasn't going to be so hard to come by—she was going to get us killed. "Try again."

She didn't open her mouth, though she looked like she was going to, and that was enough to give anyone away around Ross.

I turned away. I needed a shower before dinner, so I figured I might as well let her sit and stew, but I added a final warning before I left. "If you piss my bed, I'll take payment out of your ass when I get back."

"Please," she called.

That damn voice could get even me to waver.

"Please, let me go to the bathroom."

But I couldn't give in that easily. I turned back to look at her, leaning as casually as I could manage against the door frame.

I watched her struggle between her own needs and her will, before she whispered, "Master."

Her eyes closed as she uttered the only acceptable title she could use to address me, and my stomach twisted. I swallowed my own disgust and nodded, "I guess that'll do for now."

I freed her from her chained prison, but before she could step away, I had to solidify our understanding. "Crawl."

Of course, she didn't take that as well as I hoped either.

"Is this how you get your jollies?"

"You're going to become very familiar with how I get my jollies." As soon as I stepped toward her, she lowered to her knees. I tried to watch, just in case she looked back, but once she was out of sight, I plunged onto the bed.

I knew there was no way I could keep up with the exhausting charade—not as long as she remained as obstinate as a mountain. And I had to figure out a way to overcome that without breaking her completely. I picked up the chain, mindlessly swirling it and wrapping it around my fingers.

She came around the corner on hands and knees, and I saw her face visibly pale as soon as she saw the chain in my hands, but she approached anyway. Stubborn, belligerent, and brave.

Three traits that'd get her killed.

I dropped the chain to the floor next to the bed. "Come up here."

She paused, but finally climbed onto the bed and straddled my lap as I directed, and damned if I didn't feel like I was losing it. The bruises from her encounter with Gabe's buffoons were starting to set in, but she pulled back and shut herself off as I examined her.

Such a degrading way to make sure nothing was broken, but if she didn't believe my act, no one else would either. I realized the plug in her ass was probably growing even more uncomfortable with time, especially if she hadn't experimented with them before.

Not that I could ask since I wasn't supposed to care.

"Hate me all you want, Sugar," I said, hoping to get her to walk a fine line between trust and fear where she might listen. "I'm the only ally you have."

"Ally...?" she whispered. "You're going to hurt me." Her eyes filled again, but she blinked it away and held back just like she had in the basement, and I couldn't face her any longer.

"I am," I replied—it was as much honesty as I could muster. Then, I lifted her off of me, flipping her over. "Ass up."

Even though she kept up her protective walls, I saw her body visibly relax when I pulled the plug free and sat it on the side table. It was going to be hard enough for her to kneel through dinner. I hoped the threat of it might make her more compliant.

The mix of vulnerability countered with her impossible stubbornness had an aphrodisiac effect on me. I had been convinced this was the only way we'd survive, but for the first time, I truly considered the effect it was going to have on both of us.

Chapter Three

NO ESCAPE

THE NEXT DAY, my cousin Evan came to pick me up. I couldn't wait to get out of the hospital—a night's sleep that didn't involve being woken by nurses and a day that didn't include Dr. Combs clawing through my memories sounded like heaven. But between checkups, the three appointments a week Dr. Combs insisted on, and interviews and paperwork that I had to complete, I wasn't sure how the hell I was supposed to get any rest.

Dr. Combs was trying to fit in as many sessions as possible in the time I'd agreed to not contacting Rose, but I was convinced that it would be her questions that would push me over the edge.

Rose. I kept repeating her name over and over in my head, trying to rewrite my mental programming. I tried to picture her face as well, happy and smiling as I imagined it now. Free from the torment and stress of being with me at the Retreat. I needed a new positive image to shed the memories.

But with every attempt my mind snapped, reeling me

back with images of her face twisted in pain. Memories of other women kneeling at my feet or laying helpless across the dinner table as Ross forced them to endure sexual acts.

Once I was settled in at Evan's house, the only things I really cared about were the bed and the bathroom. While I got relatively comfortable, he and Trent went to pick up a trunk of my clothes from the storage container.

Step one to pretending everything is okay apparently included a touch of nostalgia.

"Do you need anything?" Katie asked quietly from the doorway. She'd been downstairs with their two-year-old son Jack when I'd come up to lay down.

"No," I mumbled into the pillow.

"You sure?"

"No," I repeated, lifting my head so that it was a little louder.

She came into the room anyway and leaned against the footboard of the bed. I'd known Katie for more than five years—since she and Evan had started dating. Evan was the closest member I still had of my family. His parents had moved to a warmer climate after retiring, and although he, Katie, and Jack visited them for a few weeks every year. I was thankful that they stuck around. We'd grown up within an hour of each other, but I started spending more time with them after my sister's death. It hit my parents hard, and they followed her a few years later.

"Evan has an electric razor tucked under the sink if you need to use it," she said.

"I look that bad?"

"Nah," she curled her lips, "not if you're going for the rugged hitchhiker look."

"And I take it no one trusts me with a blade?"

"I thought it would be easier, but I'll pick you up some razors tomorrow if you prefer."

I buried my head in the pillows. "Has someone put down some kind of order that I'm supposed to talk for a required amount of time each day?"

"No." She brushed her cropped blond hair back, digging her fingers through it a couple of times. She didn't continue speaking, but she didn't leave either.

"Say what you want to say, Kate. I'm sure it's not something I haven't heard or already told myself."

"I didn't particularly come to *say* anything."

I propped my forearm under my head, so I didn't have to strain my neck to look down at her.

"Even injured, you're not the kind to stay silently in bed all day. Is there anything I can do?"

"Sounds like you did have something to say. And, not really. Sleeping is my only escape at the moment." Even though it wasn't really effective once I started dreaming.

"I'll be downstairs if you need anything—company included. And, no questions—I hear they make you cranky."

I smiled. "Thanks, Kate."

"Offer never expires."

As she disappeared, I drowned in my own thoughts again. I wasn't going to admit it to anyone, but I wanted to see Rose so bad I felt like my chest was being sucked in on itself.

MY EYES SHOT OPEN. I was curled up in the bed like a five-year-old trying to hide from the boogie man. I could barely remember the dream, yet its fog twisted my brain into a tailspin of paranoia, fear, and anger.

I wiped my clammy hand over my face and threw the blankets to the side.

Dr. Combs was right. Fuck me, she was right and the realization made my hands quiver. I clambered to the bathroom and splashed a handful of cold water over my face. I looked like a mess. A screwed up, and—as Katie had pointed out, rugged—mess.

I fished the electric shaver from under the counter and frowned. I hated those things, but I figured it'd have to do, to at least get rid of the scraggle forming.

Once I was moderately presentable again, I considered curling back up in bed, but I forced my legs to bypass quiet respite and headed for the stairs.

Katie was on the couch—sitting sideways with a book on her lap while Jack slept on a little cot nearby. It was quite possible that the living room was a bad idea since the kid had obviously decided to booby trap it against my entry.

"Sorry," Katie said, jumping to her feet.

I waved her back and settled in the recliner near the entryway. "I'm good."

"I didn't think you'd actually be down."

"I need a dis—" *distraction*…. I couldn't say that word. For the last month, Silver had been my distraction—or Kirk's distraction. Separating myself from that identity and leaving him for dead was harder than I thought. "I need something else to think about."

"You can put on a movie. Evan just messaged me and they'll be back soon."

I reached for the nearby remote as Jack stirred across the room. He rolled over, and his eyes opened wide as soon as he saw me. After blinking a few times, he jumped from the cot and ran over to join his mother on the couch. Snuggling up between her and the back of the couch and watching me.

"Don't take offense, he's like this with most people," Katie said, stretching to grab some yellow toy off the floor and handing it to him. "Give him a day or two, and I'm sure he'll yack your ear off."

Truth be told, I could live without him yakking my ear off. Cute as he could be, I was just fine with him keeping his distance. I smiled because I didn't have any other response.

"I know I said I wouldn't," Katie whispered.

"You have a question." My voice was dry and emotionless. I knew it was unavoidable. I hated the questions, the prying, and most of all the awkward answers, but sometimes they felt like my only way of connecting with the real world. "Go for it."

"If they offered you witness protection would you take it?"

"No," I licked my lips. "I gave up a year. Like h—" I looked at Jack and his wide brown eyes and reminded myself to choose my words carefully. "I'm not giving up my entire life. Besides, it's mainly for witnesses who are in danger of getting knocked off before they testify. I'm not really in either boat right now. No one knew my real identity and most of them didn't even know for sure the mole was me. The ones who found out are dead." *Mostly*. In a way, I already had a new identity—one the people who might be after me wouldn't know. I had all the papers to fully assume Kirk's identity going into the operation, so my deal worked in reverse. Except I was still living in the same town.

"Trent mentioned a girl."

"He's keeping an eye on her. She could get called as a

witness, but I doubt the Feds will need her. I stashed away enough evidence before I 'died' to ensure they'd have everything they needed to make it stick. The teams recovered even more during the raid." We'd wiped one "retreat" off the map, any stragglers who might be left were likely scrambling to find a new opportunity or getting out of town and hooking up with one of the other facilities.

Milo had been the head of a network of sex retreats, and quite a few, I heard, which trafficked more than sex on a regular basis. Various law enforcement groups had been working for years to bring him down in hopes that it would land a blow to the network and weaken the system enough to dismantle the entire operation. The biggest hitch in that plan was Milo's tendency to stay hidden—only the upper management of each facility had contact with him, and even they were nearly impossible to catch. Beyond impossible to turn. Everyone in Milo's service would take a bullet over even hinting at something that would jeopardize the operation.

Apparently when you ply people with all the sex, money, and power they could ever want, they tend to be quite loyal.

They never expected a cop to work his way through their ranks. I'm not sure what it said about my character that I could play a criminal well enough to convince those bastards, but I'd done it. I'd spent nearly a year in their ranks, gathering everything we needed and waiting for Milo to finally show his face at an opportune time.

When he finally did, the SWAT team shot him on the roof trying to grab a ride on the private chopper he'd probably come in on. Ross got his justice, too, but apparently Miles was responsible for that bullet. I'd already been laid out unconscious from blood loss.

I fiddled with the remote against my leg, debating on

whether or not I even wanted the mindless noise it could provide. I wanted to enjoy the quiet—for the first time in months, I didn't have to worry about who was doing what, whether or not I'd make it through the day without being killed, or how long I had until my next check-in was due.

And most of all, I didn't have dozens of girls to worry about—even though I still worried about them. The effects of the raid—most of them had been in one retreat or another for so long, they probably didn't have much of a support system anywhere. If any at all. And I wasn't even sure how they'd all react to being out of the Retreat.

Alley was one of my biggest worries. She was a sweet girl, who'd won Miles's heart long ago. She was probably the most significant reason he cared so much about the other girls. Not that Miles didn't have a caring heart underneath all the muscles, scars, and tattoos.

I'd found it easy to work for him because of that—even though most of the things I had to do were still illegal and sometimes degrading and unspeakable. If not for Miles's redeeming side, I probably would have lost my mind long ago. He did what he had to in order to survive. Maybe he hadn't made the greatest choices along the way, but I still felt obligated to him, especially since he'd saved my life in the end.

Right after Silver had been brought to the Retreat, Miles helped me scare the shit out of her when I feigned releasing her into the building on her own. He stepped off the elevator just in time to send her scampering back toward my room. We hoped that it'd be enough to deter her from any hair-brained escape plan, but at least she'd been a little easier to deal with after that. He was the only one I'd trust around her, as much as he might love indulging in the slaves, he was about as committed as he could be to Alley.

And I knew he wouldn't hurt Silver—not nearly as much as anyone else would.

I even sent Silver to stay with them both while I had to work—meetings with Ross's contacts in the city to make sure we had supplies and the right people in our back pockets.

Silver and Alley became close, and Alley managed to convince her to cooperate in ways I couldn't.

And I had another set of eyes to help look out for her.

A hand clamped down on my shoulder and I nearly jumped out of the chair, to break free.

"Easy, man," Trent said, putting up his hands. "I was beginning to wonder if you were okay since we've been standing here talking and you've been off in your own little world."

"Just thinking."

"Obviously. You didn't rip a stitch, did you?"

I felt a twinge in my side, but nothing more severe than I typically felt. "Funny."

I was sitting in the middle of the room, and yet I was the outsider. Like watching a movie—distant, impersonal, and irrelevant.

Nothing took my mind off Rose long enough to make any sense of the rest of the world.

———

THE NEXT SEVERAL days weren't much unlike the days I'd spent in the hospital. I no longer had people prying or poking me every hour, but now I was surrounded by conversation and laughter that was just as difficult to connect with. Even though I refused the pain medicine, everything passed in a haze.

A self-induced haze to protect myself from my own thoughts. Thoughts and memories only brought on frustration, which in turn brought on anger bordering on rage. And I couldn't afford to be taken over by rage.

And yet my dreams took me there again, and again.

The only thing I knew for certain was that I had to get rid of the war waging in my head.

I craved Rose. Some nights I was convinced that merely the touch of her skin would turn the nightmares away—as if she wouldn't be enough to drive me to madness herself.

The churning emotions drew a thick chord of tension through my body—one that I wasn't sure I wanted to pluck without knowing what was waiting for either of us at the end of that coil of lust.

Part of me wanted her spread out and vulnerable for my taking. Part of me craved her obstinate resistance. And all of me wanted to strip her and have my way.

Whatever that meant.

I'd always thought my sexual desires fell somewhere in the average range. If a few years ago a girl had asked me to tie her up for sex, I probably would have. I wasn't against trying anything new.

However, if someone presented me with butt plugs and clamps and all manners of sexual torture, I might have hesitated. A vibrator was one thing—no problems coming up with some twisted uses for that. It was the toys that ran the gambit between pleasure and pain that once made me uneasy.

Pain and pleasure. The threshold that taunted me.

I had traipsed near the border before—had no problems navigating it with former girlfriends who enjoyed things like fisting. No problem using that skill to give Rose a brief respite from the horrors of the Retreat. Pushing her to trust me as I took her to the brink of pain and pushed her down in waves of pleasure.

But now it was different.

The fantasy wasn't about what Rose wanted—it was about my own sick desires that I wanted to inflict on her. I wanted it out of my system, every memory of that place purged. Even the most innocent visions turned into something dark and twisted.

I wanted to get rid of the fucking pain, not cause more. But that's where my mind always went.

Desire. Pain. Ecstasy. Anger. Rage.

It was a slippery slope.

And none of it led to release.

Just more pent up frustration until the cycle built up all over again.

I flopped onto my stomach, my erection pressing painfully into the mattress. Pain—the cycle continued.

Fucking hell.

I dragged myself up, and into the bathroom. Lifting my arm, I stared at the scar stretched across my left side. With the stitches finally removed, I was nearly free again—physically. The splintered bones and muscle damage were going to take a little longer, and the area still ached when I moved around too much.

I turned on the shower and let it run hot, then stripped off my boxers and tossed them in a basket under the sink. My attention-starved cock sprang free, still hyped up by whatever the fuck gave it its jollies of late.

"Is this how you get your jollies?" Silver had asked me when I told her to crawl.

"You're going to become very familiar with how I get my jollies."

My cock throbbed as I remembered watching her crawl

across the floor. I wrapped my fingers tight around its base, maybe I could just strangle it to death.

Or at least to the point it'd leave me alone and stop planting crazy ideas in my head.

As if I could blame it all on my dick.

I rested my forearm at eye level against the wall of the shower. I told myself to stop fantasizing about Rose—but that was technically easy since I didn't know who she was. Aside from a few moments of weakness, she'd kept her former life from me. All I knew is that she wore jeans, a T-shirt, and sneakers out to meet her friends, topped off with shiny silver nail polish.

I knew that she couldn't cook.

She'd had a big fall out with her sister.

And she lived less than fifteen minutes from where I was staying.

Much as I tried not to, with every thought that flashed in my head, I stroked my cock. One time. One release.

Who was I kidding? It wasn't going to fix anything.

My hips thrust, joining in an agonizing counterpart to the movement of my hand.

Silver. Before her, it was all a job.

Mindless. Torturous.

Fucking was fucking.

And once I was done. I could leave it all behind. Kirk would disappear.

I knew that was too easy. A false hope of salvation after everything I'd done and given up. It likely would have shattered to the floor once I got out anyway. The doubts and guilt were something I came to expect.

This was different. I wasn't struggling to leave it all behind. I was struggling to hold on to individual threads of a rope that couldn't be undone.

Threads that wound through my chest, up to my brain, and down my spine, right to my cock. They were mixed with shards and thorns that I'd come to grapple with every day as they shifted inside me creating new wounds and aggravating the old ones.

Silver was the worst thing that could have possibly happened to me while I was inside—all because she was also the best. She went from contingency to ally. Her will stronger than I could have imagined, and yet willing to bend —to bind her purpose to mine. All without ever giving in.

I stopped, moments from orgasm as my cock pulsed— tingling ripples waited at the base of my spine for their release, but instead I pressed my hand into the porcelain tile of the shower wall. Reminding myself that this wasn't my home, and a hole through the wall probably wouldn't be appreciated.

Especially at four in the morning, when the sound would undoubtedly wake everyone up.

At least there wouldn't be anyone waiting on hot water anytime soon.

I held her against the refrigerator, nothing under her long soft robe, except the angry stripes of skin left from the punishment I was forced to inflict. Yet she continued to goad me, to pull me deeper into the fantasy —to solidify my role as her Master.

For that, I guess I should have been thankful, but it tipped me over the edge. Every cell in my body seemed to spring free, coming to life as if they'd seen the sun for the very first time. I yanked open the robe, pressing my fingers against her smooth, hot skin, tasting her lips as my knee parted her legs.

At that moment—of all moments—she laughed, pulling me back to reality.

"I think I just figured part of you out," she said.

The feeling of freedom slammed to a halt, leaving a block of concrete where my heated blood ran cold. I saw fear cloud her features, but instead of backing down, she held my gaze and explained.

"The only time I really get a rise out of you is when I stand my ground."

A deadly mixture of bittersweet poison for both of us. "Standing your ground is dangerous."

"You're the only person here, and it seems like the only thing I'm in danger of at the moment is—"

I sealed my lips to hers before she could continue. No more chipping away at the façade. If she got much closer—God, I couldn't even think of what I would do. "Quiet, Silver."

For once, she did as she was told. Letting me guide her quietly away from the cold refrigerator backward toward the couch. The soft robe dropped away from her shoulders, leaving her bare skin and taut breasts mine for the taking.

She shuddered and pressed against me as my lips explored her neck, taking in her taste and smell. "You're strong," I whispered, pinching her tender flesh between my teeth. "Hold onto it, but be careful about who you let see it."

I shed my pants and followed her down onto the couch, taking her mouth and her breath until she gasped for air. The sound may as well have been her hand clenching around my cock, dragging me toward a prison I'd never escape.

But I wasn't quite convinced that it wasn't all an act until I slid my hand between her thighs, to meet her hot, wet pussy.

If she was faking, she was a better actor than me. No need for further warm up, I lifted her hips and slid inside her perfect depths. Stroking her clit, I thrust inside her, every cry, gasp and whimper inching me closer.

My body bucked and my teeth sunk into my forearm, muffling my groan as I milked the last bit of cum from my cock. I slumped against the wall, the hot, humid air filling my lungs with every heaved breath while the water washed away the evidence.

Although the strain in my muscles and the load on my mind felt significantly lessened, I knew it wouldn't last. It never would until I got what I wanted.

I was obsessed, but it didn't help matters that I didn't have much else to think about. I needed something to do. I was used to being active, being the doer and the problem solver. But my current condition and status put me on the outside of everything I once knew.

I couldn't return to my job until I was medically cleared —mentally and physically. I couldn't even go to the gym or participate in my old hobbies --since most of them weren't compatible with my injury—which barely agreed with me leaving the house on some days.

At first, my thoughts focused on just one thing—getting through the next four weeks—the appointments and the painful, awkward discussions, so I could finally check on Rose myself. As I neared the half-way point, I became more enveloped in the possibility that she'd moved on. I also considered that it might be for the best since I wasn't certain I'd be the best person for her anyway. I'd only serve as a reminder of her pain and torture.

Possibly worse than a reminder, the way my brain was currently functioning.

After I dried off, I crawled back into bed, not expecting to get any more sleep for the night, but somehow a merciful, dreamless sleep found me.

Chapter Four

FIGHTING TO MAKE PEACE

WITH FIFTEEN MINUTES before Trent was due to pick me up for my appointment, I sat down at the kitchen table to work a crossword. Although I felt better knowing he was looking in on Rose, he wasn't much help to my current mental status either—holding true to his oath not to play double agent for either of us.

My car was still at his house and there was always one excuse or another as to why I couldn't pick it up—I'd had my stitches out for nearly a week, and yet for some reason I still couldn't drive or get clearance to return to work—not that I had explicitly asked for the latter. The only thing worse than not being able to do much was everyone treating me like I couldn't do anything.

When Trent arrived, he didn't even bother to knock, knowing that I was the only one there.

"You're still not ready?" His boot squealed against the floor in protest. "Of course not, because you're now using the mindset of a stubborn five-year-old to prove your point."

I filled in the next word on the puzzle and dropped the pencil, lacing my fingers behind my head. "I thought you always appreciated a good non-violent protest."

"Uh huh."

Opting not to spend the rest of the morning staring him down, I shoved my chair backward and went up to my room to throw on a pair of jeans and a new shirt. I rubbed my hand over the new layer of scruff forming on my face.

I needed to find something to do before I lost motivation to even get out of bed—again.

Trent stayed silent during the drive to Dr. Combs' office —apparently well aware of my sour mood. I wanted a fight, but I saved it for the doctor rather than my best friend.

"You're late again," Dr. Combs said in her usual quiet, chastising voice once I closed the office door behind me.

I lifted my shoulders. "If people would let me have my own car, I might get around faster."

"You're ready for that?"

"Granted I have a healing wound that vacillates between itching like the canine host of a flea carnival and stabbing pain when I stretch, cough, or roll over on it. I'm fully capable—"

"You keep saying that. I don't think anyone is questioning your strength, independence, or capabilities."

"Just my character, then?" I dropped onto the couch, stretching out my legs and crossing my ankles in front of me.

"Of course not. You've expressed how much you're grappling with your emotions and decisions. Are you thoroughly convinced that you won't do something rash?"

"Yes." Had I admitted to that much? Most days I rode the sway of emotions from guilt to anger. I'd do what I had to in order to protect Rose—even if it meant staying away. "I want control over my own life back."

I closed my eyes remembering my promise to Rose. She had wanted the same thing.

I hoped she was enjoying it now.

"Tell me more about Silver."

Always Silver. That was practically the only issue she was concerned with.

The all-consuming topic.

"Or," she said. "You can tell me how you feel about going back to work."

That was the first time she'd broached that topic. I desperately wanted something to do—but I also associated work with my losses and current situation. "Indifferent."

"Then why are you here?"

To have someone to fight with. The honest answer was a jumbled mix of reasons. The forefront of which was that I wanted to move on, but I had no idea how to do that. Or how to admit my weakness. Instead, I fought everyone's attempts to help me and put on the façade of only coming in because it was a requisite of going back to work. That was the easy excuse. The one that protected what was left of my ego.

"You're struggling because you can't seem to reconcile everything within you. The more you keep denying yourself, the worse it will become."

"What do you want me to do?" I stood, needing to move, and glared out the window. "You want to hear more about the horrible things I had to do? How some of them got me off?" That was the topic I most tried to avoid. "How I reveled in seeing Silver at my feet? Watching her slowly place her trust in me, even though she didn't know a damn thing about me or what I intended to do to her."

I closed my eyes, seeing her stubborn face in my mind.

Her soft lips, green eyes, and smooth cheekbones that turned irresistibly pink every time she was embarrassed.

"You were protecting her."

"And fighting myself not to enjoy it."

"So after months of watching girls come and go—girls who had already been broken, who had mastered staying detached and feared the consequences of disobedience—a girl comes in who breaks all of those molds, and you find it odd to have been attracted to her?"

"Attracted to her? No. I didn't find that odd."

"More than physically attracted?"

"She was everything I wanted." *Still is.* "But that made it more dangerous for both of us. I lost control around her. Ross knew it, too. He pressed it at every opportunity. He had a special room beneath the main room where he conducted business meetings. There were glass tiles in the floor overlooking that lower room. Ross sent us down there, where there was nowhere to hide. He could even listen if he wanted—"

———

IMMEDIATELY UPON ENTERING THE OVERLOOK, we'd been directed toward the stairway, and I felt my insides rearrange in some anatomical game of Tetris. I'd just gone from predator to prey.

Ross wanted to watch—to see how I handled the situation. He got off on watching people squirm. I had played his games countless times before, but this was different. This time, I may as well have dropped a firecracker into my pants.

The night before, she'd thrown a fit in my apartment— she threw a cushion across the room, breaking a picture frame, and smacked me. Stupid me, let her get away with it. I shut down, stunned into silence by her reactions and my own guilt. That was the first night I'd taken her in front of everyone in the middle of "The Outlook" during one of Ross's dreaded "business dinners".

The Outlook was Ross's pride and joy, and I have little doubt that Ross loved it more than his own children. He certainly spent more time there than he did at home. The two floors were set up like the swankiest nightclub and lounge with little to decorate the glass-enclosed spaces except scantily clad women. Sex slaves who were subject to the whim of every man who entered the building.

Every business dinner included some kind of debauchery along the way. Ross enjoyed spreading the girls out in the middle of the table and forcing sexual acts upon them—or simply opening it up for a free-for-all for everyone involved.

On Rose's second night, that girl was her. She looked to me for help, and every glance just made Ross more furious and determined. I could claim her as my personal slave, I could give her some level of protection, but the Retreat operated under Ross's rules. Rule number one, the boss could take any woman whenever and wherever he wanted or even order her to serve someone else.

Rose was afraid, but not afraid enough, and the insolence continued the next morning as soon as she woke up. I threatened to kill her—to drown her in the bathtub—even though I thought part of her knew I wouldn't go through with it. Threats to turn her over to the others did far better, but even then, there was no guarantee.

With all of this in mind, I followed orders and took her down to the play room. It was more of a rat cage, where Ross could sit above, like a mad scientist watching his own warped social experiments. I strapped her to the table, but her mouth continued running. I had to wrap myself up in my role—nipple clamps, hooked up to a small electrical current, the remote control butt plug I'd inserted in the apartment, and a vibrator strapped to her clit would do the trick. I had the remotes to all three and knew they'd work from the room above.

I left her to be teased and brought to orgasm multiple times while I went upstairs to watch through a window.

She was in as much pain as pleasure—albeit forced pleasure. And so was I.

By her second climax, my damn cock bulged against my pants. Aching to be released, so I took one of the other girls —Kat.

She was trouble—played the part of slave so perfectly that she got nearly everything and every man she wanted.

The girls were excused away as playthings—powerless. Stripped of everything including their real names. Some of them, it shattered to pieces, some of them adapted and thrived, but Kat adapted and schemed for more. She found her own kind of power in it—and because of that, I knew she could give me exactly what I wanted in the least amount of time necessary.

I fisted her curly auburn hair. Pulling it tight with frustration and rage as I came in her mouth. Before that point, I'd only done what I had to do.

Sex was torture in its own way, but I could shut down the part of my brain that cared. I became Kirk, left behind James—his morals, doubts, ideologies.

It was the only way to survive. I thought if I purposefully left myself behind, fully taking on the new identity, I could do the reverse when it was all over.

But that was before I was faced with something I wanted to hang on to.

———

EVERY TIME I had to talk about Silver and my experiences in the Retreat, it brought those feelings to the surface again. If I was supposed to be letting her go, each appointment seemed to be pushing me in the opposite direction.

I tapped my thumb against my thigh. "Because of Silver, I started to shed that skin too soon. It became personal," I whispered. My muscles were itching for an escape again, and I glanced toward the clock. "Do you know what it's like to live every day with something you want to change? Things you could change with just a few words? The abuse, the corruption. Sometimes I refused to hold back, but every time I stepped in to right some wrong, I risked blowing my cover. Maybe I could stop one girl from being hit, but if I died in the process, the bigger situation continued. And wouldn't be stopped until someone else could find an 'in'."

My superiors had made the decision. I got a small in— the opportunity to take down some of the lackeys, but it wasn't enough. This wasn't an organization where any of the lackeys would turn on the leaders. If it was possible to get to the top, and take down the boss—take down the very man who organized all of the retreats—it was possible we might be able to make a difference. We had hoped that the imbalance created in the organization was worth it.

"So you think you did what needed to be done?"

"If taking out Milo did what we predicted, then yes." Unfortunately, I was taken out of the loop as long as I didn't have clearance to work. Yet another thing removed from my control. "I want my job back."

Dr. Combs raised her eyebrows and tilted her head. She had about three looks, and I could never tell what emotion each one indicated. She'd be a hell of a poker player.

"I don't like not knowing what's going on," I explained. "I did what I could—I did it to the best of my ability. I want to make sure it's finished."

"And then what?"

"And then I can move on," I said quietly. I wasn't a good planner and never had been. I worked best when I had to think on my feet. "I'll figure that out when I come to it."

"You really think you're ready to return to work?"

I jumped to my feet again. "I come in here and spill my guts because you said—"

I looked down at my clenched fists.

"You're getting there," she said. "Anger can be a useful tool, but only when it's controllable."

She closed my file and laid her pen across the folder, clasping her hands together and leaning forward. "I understand your need for control when you feel like everyone is taking it from you—"

"I'm tired of my own friends not trusting my judgment."

"Do you trust your judgment?"

I didn't have an answer.

The question rang in my head long after Trent picked me up. Rather than taking me home, he informed me that there was something he had to attend to at the station and that I was coming along.

I hadn't been there in over a year. The last time I'd set foot in the building, I would have never considered myself capable of the things I'd done. And it just meant I'd have more familiar faces to stare into, revealing their disdain or pity.

Trent already had most of the details. I fed the reports to him while I was on off-site assignments or errands. There weren't a whole lot of reasons to leave the compound. Unless you wanted a change of scenery and a new variety of food or company—I usually found myself wanting all three, and struggling not to give in to keep from looking too suspicious.

At the station, I trailed behind as Trent and I navigated the long corridors in back until we got to his desk. All of the walking was a pain, but I was grateful not to have to deal with all of the crowds at the front of the building. Most of the people around were wrapped up in their own cases and barely glanced in our direction. Trent grabbed a few things from his desk, then nodded toward one of the interview rooms.

"I figure you're more inclined to tolerate a quiet room and fewer interruptions."

"I'm inclined to know why we're here."

But he turned away and pushed open the door anyway, pulling the blinds as I sat down. If I didn't know Trent, I'd have a sneaking suspicion he was trying to pin something on me, but even knowing him didn't prevent the knot forming in my chest.

"You know we captured Milo on the roof of the building."

I nodded.

"He fired on the officers, and they fired back—he was dead before he hit the hospital."

"I know all of this—I was a little drugged out, but I know."

Trent's face was flat, with no hint at whatever he was leading up to. "They're claiming he wasn't Milo."

I straightened and reached for the folder his hand rested on. He pressed his hand down preventing me from taking it.

I grunted. "You wouldn't have brought me here and told me anything if you didn't want my help."

"You can't help. As far as they know, you're dead, too. Your communications on this case end with the notes I found hidden in your room."

The only other reason I could come up with for the meeting was Rose.

"Bull sh—No," I said, jumping out of my seat. "You want to bring in Rose. You know I'll disapprove, but I also know that nothing I say on the subject matters, so what do you want?"

"Not Rose," he said, calmly shaking his head. "There's no way she could prove he's Milo—even if he introduced himself to her. They're claiming that there are a number of people who are known as Milo for security's sake."

"They're saying not even Ross would have known? Because I assure you whoever that was—Ross wouldn't treat just anyone like that. I don't buy it."

"We need someone to cooperate who was inside longer than you—someone who might be able to verify whether or not this is a bluff."

I scoffed. "Then you want Miles. Have you tried—"

"He pretty much refuses to talk about anything, his girl…." Trent snapped his fingers as the Rolodex in his brain turned. "Alley. She's kept silent, too."

"What do you expect?" I shook my head. "And how the hell am I supposed to help?"

Trent tilted his head, leaving me to figure it out.

"He wanted out, but even if he didn't think I'm dead,

he believes I betrayed him." I closed my eyes and took a deep breath. "I trusted him with my life and Rose's life while we were in there."

But it was different now. He knew the truth, and I had the rest of my life to lose.

"Miles was my friend—if that's the term you want to use. I'm not even sure anymore—but I can't guarantee he'll be open to amicable terms with me and if he spills to the others," I trailed off not wanting to even imagine how bad it could get if everyone found out about the truth.

"Seeing your friend come back from the dead could be enough to shock him into talking. As I understand it, he killed Ross to save you and Rose—seems to me he's not going to throw himself to the wolves now. Word hasn't gotten out about what he did, so, if worse comes to worse—"

"Are you considering blackmailing him?"

"I'm just ensuring that everyone's best interests are addressed and contingencies are in place."

I scowled and jerked the folder away from him, reminding myself that on any other case, under any other circumstances, I would have fully supported the contingency plan. But I felt for Miles—I'd wanted to find a way out for him as well. He'd even spoken of getting out after I had to punish Rose for running. He had the potential of a good man—Alley in particular brought that out in him. I wanted to see something good for the both of them. "Fine, set it up."

"Done," he said, sitting back in his chair with a smug expression on his face.

That would have already taken some extensive planning —I wouldn't be able to go anywhere near the prison. It was too big of a risk for someone to see me and put it together.

Even with the best of planning, I wasn't confident that something wouldn't go wrong with so many inmates involved.

"He'll be brought in tomorrow," Trent said.

"The others will suspect he's talking."

His smug expression faded. "I didn't start yesterday. It's all covered. He'll be here tomorrow afternoon and no one will be the wiser."

I gave him a flat look. He was asking me to jeopardize my currently safe situation, yet he'd jumped to the conclusion that I'd be on board. "What if I hadn't agreed?"

"Plan B."

"You would have winged it."

Trent stretched out his hands, a grin tugging at his features as he laced his fingers behind his head and reclined back. Throwing me to the wolves, and yet he was just as calm as usual.

"Just like I'll be winging it tomorrow when I come back from the dead." I rubbed my hand over my chin, trying to relax my clenched jaw. I envied Trent's relaxed demeanor, but the prospect of not being on edge felt foreign and outside my realm of possibilities.

"It will be interesting."

Part of me wondered if some sadistic part of Trent just wanted to see the look on Miles's face. Flipping to the first page of the file, I saw Milo's pale white face on a slab in the morgue. I knew in the deepest portion of my consciousness that he was the man we'd been gunning for all along. Now we just had to prove it and force their hand.

They'd operated under the belief that they were invincible. I hoped that meant they didn't have a contingency plan. "What about the rest of the operation—what's going on with the other retreats and dealings?"

"It's all gone dead silent. If they're fighting internally, they're keeping it out of sight."

We knew they had the manpower, but we had taken down nearly their entire operation here—not accounting for a few stragglers. "Wouldn't surprise me. They're vicious but tight-lipped about getting what they want. They fight dirty —attack when no one is watching, but they're also all business about it. Reputation and apparent strength are everything."

"That's what I hope. I still find it odd they're not at least trying to retaliate."

"Bluff until we come back for more," I guessed. "They wouldn't want anyone to know, so they're playing it off like a minor stumble—after all, they're claiming the man we killed wasn't even in charge. So, why would they bother to make a fuss?"

"The other operations are out of state, so I don't have any insider information on any of those investigations—the only reason I've been able to maintain it here is you. Like hell I was passing off your handling to some guy who doesn't know how you work—I don't care how much experience he had."

"We pulled it off." I snorted.

"And luckily after a few months, the guy who was supervising got off my back and figured the constant babysitting was a waste of his time."

It was a damn good thing Trent had fought for his role in the investigation. He had the patience, the knowledge, and the time since he wasn't double handing the whole thing and trying to keep up with the other operations as well. The moment my handler decided that keeping tabs was a waste of time, I would have been up shit creek.

Closing the folder, I returned it to Trent—Milo's dead

body was all I was interested in confirming. "Anything else I should know?"

"Not at the moment. The ball is only staying in our court now because Miles isn't cooperating with the feds. You still have an in that no one else can match."

"Lucky me," I mumbled.

"You keep saying that lately."

"Trying to convince myself it's true. Any chance you're going to release my car from its prison in your garage now?"

Trent gathered the file and tapped his pen on the table. "Evan is picking you up. I need to stay and work."

I groaned but held back the full explosion. "Tomorrow then?"

"Tomorrow. Hope you didn't write down the mileage before you left."

"As long as she's tuned up with a full tank of gas." I'd left the car with Trent not only because I trusted him, but because I knew he'd drive it once in a while and keep it in good condition. I had no idea how long I'd be gone and I didn't want to return to a leaking car with a tank full of bad gas to deal with. Any extra miles added in the process were an easy concession.

"Three-quarters."

I shook my head and left him to his work, deciding to head out the back and wait for Evan. Although that didn't make avoiding the looks and questions easier since I still ran into people I knew, most of them at least kept it to a minimum.

Chapter Five

DROWNING IN MY PAST

IN THE MIDDLE of the night, I woke covered in sweat, panting for air, and shaking with a mix of nausea and anger.

I'd dreamed that the girls had followed me home and showed up in my damn bed. Right before I woke, I saw Kat lying next to me. I had rolled on top of her, pinning her to the bed, and kissing her so painfully hard I felt my anger at not having Silver rattle me to the pads of my feet.

I could still see the smirk on her face when I pulled away, realizing what I'd done.

Flipping out of bed, I tugged on a pair of jeans and T-shirt. My fingers dug into my palms as I crept down the steps, trying to contain myself long enough to at least get outside where I stood a much smaller chance of waking Jack—or anyone for that matter. I definitely couldn't handle a kid, but I wasn't sure I could handle adults at the moment either.

Unless it was someone who might give me a good

excuse—or a remotely acceptable one—to smash something. I was losing my mind and out of control.

All of the days that I wanted to knock Gabe's block off were nothing compared to now. That I could live with. His record and attitude gave me a daily reason and no one could tell me he didn't deserve it.

This was different—uncontrollable, boiling, to the point that I thought my flesh might combust.

I dropped to sit on the top stair of the porch, staring out into the cloudy dark sky that perfectly reflected my state of mind. Even in the cool night air, my blood wove a twisted torrent through my body until my nerves hummed and my muscles shook.

I heard the floor inside the house creak and closed my eyes, climbing to my feet and preparing to escape. A long walk to anywhere.

"What are you doing?" Evan asked in a hushed voice.

"I need out—need air."

"It's three in the morning, you can't just take off walking—especially not…."

"In my condition? I'm fine."

"And you'd say that even if you weren't. Don't forget, I've known you even longer than Trent has."

"I can't go back to bed. I just need… *out*," I repeated when I couldn't think of another way to phrase it. I did need out—out of my own body and mind before they both collapsed under the strain of one another.

"Let's go for a ride then. I'll drive you wherever you want."

Wherever I wanted. I stared at him for a few moments, considering the possibilities of where I wanted to be—only one place came to mind. "Just drive."

I wasn't giving away my destination too soon. I hoped

that by the slimmest of slim chances that although Trent might have told Evan who I wasn't supposed to see, he hadn't told him where she lived.

We climbed into his SUV and he headed for the highway—it'd likely be quiet at this time of night and it lacked the harsh assaulting lighting of town. I watched the exit signs as we drove farther out, and spotted what I wanted within ten minutes. "Take the next exit."

"I thought you told me to just drive."

"I want some scenery."

His indicator clicked on, even though there was no one else around and we followed the exit ramp to a more rural area of town. I'd looked up her address enough times to know exactly how to get there—no one could stop me from doing that. Not even my own conscience, which kept informing me that I was turning into a stalker.

We followed the main road a few minutes longer until Evan stopped at a stop sign.

"Turn right."

Hands tightening on the steering wheel until his knuckles whitened, Evan cocked his head and glared at me. "Leave it alone."

That fucker.

I raised my eyebrows and shook my head, feigning ignorance.

"He told me to keep you away from this area, I was giving you the benefit of the doubt, but we're not going to find her."

Rather than keep up with the pointless argument, I slid one hand to the seatbelt release and the other to the door handle. Releasing both at the same time and jumping out. I slammed the door behind me and headed up the street myself.

Seconds later, feet pounded against the pavement behind me. "James, stop. You know this isn't a good idea."

"She's only a few blocks away," I said without looking back.

Evan grabbed the collar of my shirt, pulling me to a stop.

"I'm not going to let her see me," I said, twisting to get away. "I'm not even going anywhere near the front door."

"You just want to play peeping Tom? Come on. I shouldn't have brought you this far."

"I won't mention it to anyone. Just let me go, damn it." I swung my arm back trying to dislodge his grasp, but my shirt stretched tighter around my neck.

Before we could continue our mini-confrontation, a police siren cut through the cricket-filled night and lights flashed behind us as the spotlight shined on Evan's SUV. Two officers climbed out, then directed flashlights toward us.

"Problem, gentlemen?" one asked.

"Minor disagreement," Evan said eying me as he headed the thirty feet back toward the SUV.

They approached cautiously, hands over their weapons while they aimed the flashlights high and into our faces. I put my hand up, angling my head away to avoid the blaring light.

"IDs please," the taller officer asked.

Evan went for his, but my pockets were empty. I still hadn't even bothered to go through my things to look for the damn thing anyway.

"Don't have it," I said. "James Carter—I'm a cop, just look it up."

"Think I just joined the force yesterday?" He asked, nudging me down the hill toward the vehicle.

"No, but I'd wager it was within the last twelve months," I said dryly.

"What's that supposed to mean?"

"It means I've been undercover." And I was seconds away from breaking again. Although he blinded me with the light, I caught a glimpse of his arm moving out and I stepped back to balance myself against the hood of the SUV.

"You just decided to leave your car in the middle of the road and take a walk?"

"No, I decided to take a walk. He—" I gestured toward Evan, "Decided to come after me on foot rather than run me over."

"We got the order to stand down," the other officer said. "He is a cop. But—" He turned off his flashlight and waved it at Evan. "That doesn't mean you should be parking your car in the road in the middle of the night."

Evan and I agreed—both probably with an excess of niceties out of desperation to get rid of them—and climbed back into the vehicle as the officers drove away.

"I should have fucking let you go," Evan said.

Rubbing my hand over my face, I laughed so hard my ribs ached. Like a couple of stupid high school students, we'd been on the verge of getting busted for sneaking out in the middle of the night to see a girl.

"Look, James—"

"I know," I patted the air with my hands for him to hold on to his lecture. "I got it. Universe telling me to stay away."

Evan squinted and put the car in drive. "Right. You go a little mystic in the past year?"

"Nah, but I figure this time maybe I should follow the hint before I get myself in more trouble."

"Good. Katie would have killed us both if you got us arrested."

"You're the one who left the car in the road." I stared at the intersection through the passenger mirror. I needed to stay away, but as the distance grew, I became more fidgety.

"Next time I will just run you over."

———

THE NEXT MORNING I woke to cooing and tiny beats against the mattress. Jack backed away when I opened my eyes, then held up his fist—shiny from his incessant need to shove it in his mouth. He'd become mostly accustomed to me in the last few weeks, but I still wasn't sure he trusted me entirely.

And I certainly wasn't complaining that he hadn't yet started yakking my ear off as Katie had promised.

"Tasty hand?" I asked.

He smiled, flashing his little white teeth, then held up his other hand, which held what looked like a tiny fish cracker. It was hard to tell since it too looked like it had been sucked on a few times.

"Nah, I'm good."

"Jack," Evan called in the hallway—keeping his voice quiet since he apparently thought I was still asleep.

"Your errant child is in here."

Evan rounded the corner in his bathrobe—his hair wet and face half covered with shaving cream. "Sorry, he wandered off while I was shaving. I put up the gate to the stairs but didn't think he'd be brave enough to wander in here."

"Surprise." I rubbed my hand over my face, trying to diminish the never-ending sleepy feeling. "Not really a big deal though. Despite my reluctance to spawn, I don't mind him."

"Reluctance—I think you took reluctance to a whole new level as soon as you got snipped."

"And you spent a month trying to talk me out of it—which *only* made me wish I hadn't told you."

"Still don't regret it?"

"Nope."

"You're just a carrier, it doesn't mean—"

"It means enough." I cut him off. His mother didn't have the gene like my father did, so he didn't have anything to worry about. It was much easier to dismiss it when you knew your kid wasn't going to suffer from a debilitating illness that could make even breathing nearly impossible.

I watched my sister struggle her entire life. There were times she was so weak she couldn't get out of bed. When she'd come up for a lung transplant, we hoped it'd give her some relief. But she still suffered, fighting off new infections that she eventually lost the battle against.

"Bad things happen, even when we think they're impossible. It's not just the cystic fibrosis that worries me. I've added at least a hundred more things to that list over the years, and nothing I saw while undercover helped. I don't want to debate the pros and cons or the selflessness and selfishness of it all."

"I wasn't going to go there," Evan said. He reached for his son who faked left then slid out of his father's reach.

"I'll watch him while you finish shaving—you look like a foamy Santa Claus."

Jack squealed and stomped his feet, it could have been an agreement or refusal for all I knew. I still didn't have a knack for two-year-old communication and I doubted I ever would. But it didn't much matter either way. Since the front door opened, announcing Katie's return.

"You're free today, right?" Evan asked, watching Jack run through the hallway to greet his mother.

I nodded and rolled to the edge of the bed. "Trent is picking me up. He has a scheme."

Evan made a sound in his throat—he too was familiar with the possible ramifications of a Trent scheme since he'd been both the victim and accomplice on many occasions.

———

LESS THAN TWO HOURS LATER, I found myself staring through the one-way mirror at a man who'd been my comrade for the duration of my undercover assignment. He hadn't known until the night I was shot that I was the person who'd ratted out the operation, but he still only knew me as Kirk—the man who turned narc because he wanted out.

Despite my betrayal, he'd put a bullet in Ross's head to save both me and Rose. Which I only knew from retellings of Rose's account.

I took a final swig of water to quench my dry throat, but it didn't help for more than a second.

"Sure you're ready for this?" Trent relaxed against the frame of the window, dividing his attention between me and the man on the other side of the glass.

"Going to be the shock of his life."

"I'm not so sure of that. "

I snorted, stretching out my muscles and rotating my neck to get rid of the tension as I pulled down the sleeves on my shirt and buttoned the cuffs. With my head lowered, I stepped into the room, keeping my back to Miles as I closed the door.

"What the fuck do you all want? I've already told you, I'm not giving you anything."

As soon as I turned and he saw my face, I could almost sense his blood turn cold. His mouth dropped open, moving as if he was talking, but no sound came out. He stood, his eyes traveling up and down my body until he finally found words. "Must've been a hell of a deal you got."

"I didn't get any deal." I gestured toward the chair for him to sit, and I took a seat across from him. "My name is James. I was undercover the whole time."

His knuckles paled as he clenched them against the table. "And you're a damn fool for telling me that."

"You going to go back and rat me out?"

"I should." He growled, but I watched the indecision dance across his features.

I jumped straight to it since pleasantries seemed oddly inappropriate. "I need your help."

His head moved in something that resembled a cross between a nod and a shake. "This about your girl?"

My spine tingled, and I fought to keep the sting out of my expression while I continued single-mindedly toward the task at hand. "No, it's about Milo."

His mouth twitched and spread into a thin line. "Don't know anything about him."

"He's dead," I said simply.

Miles frowned and shrugged, staring past me into the mirror. "News to me. Where'd you find him?"

"You're a terrible liar." So I put the ball in his court. "What do you want?"

He leaned across the table. "What do you *think* I want?"

"To survive. To be with Alley. You can't do that in prison or if you're dead."

"And you think there's any alternative you can offer me? You don't have the authority to give me anything."

"I'll make sure you get it. We'll transfer you to a secure facility—"

"So I can serve the rest of my sentence in maximum security?" he scoffed, leaning back and shaking his head. He barely resembled the man I know.

"Somewhere no one can get you. Give us what we need, we'll push for a reduced sentence."

"I want to see Alley."

"Fine," I said. I didn't blame him. He'd had her by his side long before I came along and tore them apart. "I'm sorry I betrayed you."

"Are. You. Really?" He drew each word out, but it didn't sound like a question—it was a challenge.

"Yes, I wanted things to be different. I hoped I could get you out as well—"

"Is that what you were trying to pull on me? I didn't need saving."

"No, you were quite capable of protecting yourself—and you talked about it. You mentioned wanting out, but it got too dirty too fast and I had to concentrate on protecting Silver."

"I won't give you anything until I can talk to Alley and I have an official offer. You want to make up for it, you better make sure they don't screw me over." His twisted expression reminded me of the conniving man I'd met when I started the undercover assignment.

I nodded. "I will."

I started to rise, but Miles reached across the table, stopping me. "You should have asked why I mentioned your girl."

I squinted, my heart struggling to push the sludge through my veins. "Why?"

"They suspect you're still alive." His smirk was as unnerving as the news. "They've been watching her, waiting for you."

If I had shown up at her house the night before, it all could have been over. For all of us. "Who? How am I—?"

He put up his hands and leaned back. "You haven't earned anything yet. I happen to like Rose."

His use of her real name an explicit reminder that he'd been the one to give me her license that they'd found in her belongings.

"Did you tell anyone where she lives?" I asked.

"You don't think they weren't smart enough to figure that out for themselves?"

"I know they are, I just—" I shoved my hands in my pockets to subdue my nerves.

"Have you seen Alley?" he asked.

"Only you," I said moving slowly to my feet. I didn't have any information to give him. Even if I had, I couldn't escape the swirling mess he'd set off in my brain long enough to put anything else into words. "Thank you," I muttered as I made my escape.

The bombardment of voices as soon as I entered the connecting office almost knocked me on my ass. I could barely sift through my own thoughts, adding theirs to the mix was complete chaos. I sat against the desk trying to make sense of all the questions and statements.

Trent put up his hands, and everyone in the room stopped talking. For a young guy, he had the makings of a leader for the department—if only he was inclined to get involved with internal politics.

"We have a watch on Rose," Trent said.

I'd figured that much, and it didn't make me feel any better about the revelation. "You knew they were watching her?"

"We had our suspicions and decided to play it safe. We've eyed three men keeping an eye on her in shifts."

I lurched forward. "And you don't think they have their suspicions about whoever you have watching her?"

"We're doing it from the house across the street," Trent explained, pushing me toward an armchair in the corner. As much as I wanted to fight, I was so off balance he didn't even have to work for it. "We're staying as out of sight as possible."

"Except you."

"They'd expect that though, don't you think?"

I shook my head and pressed my hands to my temples. He was probably right, but that didn't make it any better.

"I'm a little more concerned with Miles's terms," he said, sitting next to me.

"You said you could get him moved and there's a good chance he can get a reduced sentence—," I said, jerking to my feet. "I told him exactly what you all wanted."

"That's not the problem," he said, his hands emphasizing his words. "It's Alley."

The spring inside my gut contracted and released again, sending my insides against my lungs.

"She refused our help—," he said.

I tried to interject, but he silenced me.

"She went off the grid, and we haven't been able to track her down."

"Well, you better do that." But I knew the chances. It

wasn't so easy to track down someone who had no ties. Nothing to lose.

I charged out of the office, ignoring all of the voices and glances as I passed by the lines of desks, detectives, and officers. Up the back flight of stairs and into the employee lounge where a heavy punching bag was installed, hanging from the ceiling.

I didn't bother with wraps or gloves. The pain and risk of injury didn't matter. And the shock to my hands and wrists was nothing compared to the searing it opened up in my chest and back.

"James," Trent yelled, coming at me.

I put up my hands and slammed my fists into the punching bag again.

"You're going to fuck up your side."

"I'm going to fuck up something else." My voice quivered, my entire body felt like it was only operating in starts and fits like a car with water in the gas supply.

The room spun, and I blinked, looking down in amazement that I was still standing under my own volition.

Trent grabbed my shoulder, steadying me. "Guess it's time for a follow-up appointment."

I put my hand out pressing my palm against the wall as the wave of anger continued to ebb. It didn't help shit that my body felt so fragile. "Take me to get my car."

"Not in your condition."

I stepped toward him, scowl on my face. "My condition?"

"Doctor first. If he gives you the go ahead, I'll take you to pick up your car."

"I'm sick of negotiation," I yelled, taking a step toward him. "This isn't a fucking chess game. It's my life and I'm sick and tired of making concessions just because someone else thinks it's the best thing to do. After what Miles said, I'm sure as hell not stupid enough to go see Rose so there shouldn't be a problem."

Trent crossed his arms over his chest, appraising my argument, but ultimately gave in and drove me to his place.

He lived alone in a small house about ten minutes from the station. He'd been lucky to get a place with a decent sized yard in the city, but of course, he decided to build a three-car garage in the back since his favorite hobby was rebuilding and tinkering with automobiles of all sorts. His current project took up the far part of the structure. The frame of a hot rod that he'd started building long before I went undercover—it didn't look like he'd made much progress.

"Your freedom, Sir," Trent said, waving at the car with a sardonic smirk. Then, he pointed over the roof at me. "Remember the bargain."

"I will… at least for the next week—and until we know for sure my presence won't endanger Rose again."

"Guess I better convince everyone to crack down on the goons watching her then."

"And find Alley," I reminded him while I stared at the keys in my hand. My first step toward getting my life back. "You should tell Miles about Alley. He might know where to find her."

"You didn't even take the news that well. I imagine his reaction will be worse. I'll mention bringing it up, but he's still involved in the fed case, so I have to get their clearance, especially since it might make him pull away again."

"I want back on the case," I said.

Trent's eyes widened. "You need to get back on the roster first."

"I can handle desk duty and consult. I need something to do."

"You're already consulting."

"I'm not a victim you have to protect," I spat. I was tired of being spoon fed. "You're keeping information from me. Information that pertains to Rose." I wanted to recall that last part as soon as I saw Trent's eyes glint. It told him I was doing this for all the wrong reasons. Even though it felt right, my reasons were volatile and most likely to end up in someone getting hurt.

"You know why I didn't tell you. I needed you to do the opposite of what your instinct would be telling you to do."

Today's revelation meant that no matter how counseling went, at the end of my four weeks I'd still be faced with the danger I could put her in by showing up. I didn't want to admit it, but it was almost a relief.

I climbed into the car. "Yes, I remember that I have an appointment in the morning—I won't need a ride."

Chapter Six

SHATTERED

WORST DAY AT THE RETREAT.

My sessions with Dr. Combs just kept getting worse. She sure as hell spared no expense when it came to my sanity. I reckoned she'd never lived in a nightmare where day after day, you lived the worst day you could imagine.

My jaw pulsed until I thought my teeth would shatter. "You really want me to qualify how depraved days could get there?"

"Give me something. Your biggest regret."

What pissed me off more than her questions was her ever calm and even tone.

"Not. Getting. Her. Out." I grated the words out.

"Did you ever have to hurt her? Personally, I mean."

"Fuck," I threw my hands up, then dropped them to the top of my head. Reliving it with a shrink was worse than being there in the first place—far worse because then it required me to analyze every detail that I had skimmed over to survive. "Of course, I fucking hurt her. Can't you just read the damned report?"

She went back into her "you need to talk about it" spiel, but I was lost before she got out the first sentence.

———

ANGER HAD BEEN the only reliable thing I could maintain around Silver. If I couldn't be angry, I'd be the one to fold first, but that also meant that when she pushed my buttons, my anger tended to get out of hand.

I threatened to drown her, I smacked her, I dragged her through the apartment, and I even tied her up and tortured her with sex toys for an evening. All to get the point across that she was mine and couldn't go back.

She wasn't easy to bend, and although I thought she'd be far quicker to break, I wondered if even that was possible after the first couple of days.

Just when I thought things had settled down and she might give me a chance to do what I had to do, she tried to fucking run.

It wasn't that I didn't think we'd catch her. That was a given, and that knowledge gave me time to slow myself down and think about what was going to happen.

Ross had undoubtedly been notified, which meant he'd be waiting for us so that he could dictate the terms of her punishment—that is unless he'd already left. His wife had been demanding family time, but all she really wanted was to get him away from the slaves, even if for a little while. Most of the time, I thought the kids were just pawns in their game. And I had my own suspicions that her demands to get away would result in another pregnancy. They already had two innocent pawns who had no clue what their father did, or why their mother mined his money and time. At least I hoped they didn't know.

If all worked out, hopefully, Ross was already off dealing with that himself, and Silver's punishment would be left up to me and Miles. I couldn't get away with letting her off too easy, but it'd be nothing compared to what Ross might order.

Rose was in the stairwell, so Miles came up from the bottom while I closed in on her from the top, and we pinned her somewhere between the second and third floors. Her face was ashy white when she saw me. She already knew there was no hope and dropped to the stairs.

I told Miles to meet us in the basement, and with one final look, he disappeared down the stairs, and I pulled Silver up to her feet.

With the first words from her mouth, she begged me not to kill her. I couldn't understand why the fuck she decided to run—I'd already shown her that there was no way out. And now I had to cement that thought into her brain.

"I saw Gabe. I panicked." Her pleading voice ripped at my heart.

I considered the possibility, but even if she did, there was no getting out. It didn't matter why one of the girls decided to run—the only thing that mattered was when they did, they were punished.

I took her to the basement. It was usually free for punishments, and Ross liked that it was especially degrading.

To my chagrin, he hadn't yet left the building.

Silver tried to explain, but Ross didn't look remotely swayed—not that I expected him to be. Guilt or innocence, he wanted this moment from the minute she'd appeared. "You really think she's worth the trouble?"

I grunted. All I needed to do was keep her alive. "She will be worth it."

Then, he turned toward her, already kneeling on the floor and helpless. He liked that—relished in pushing people as far past helpless as he possibly could. "You've yet to show any evidence of that." He grabbed her hair and yanked her head back. "Are you worth it?"

I put my hands behind my back, resisting the urge to go after him—there wasn't a way out.

"No," Silver whispered, "but I want to be."

"Prove it. Show your Master you can do something productive with your mouth. Keep your hands laced behind your back, and stay on your knees." He released her, shoving her in my direction.

A blow job. He wasn't letting her off easy—it was a test, like nearly every other situation. He wanted to see us both squirm.

Me, because he wanted to know if I actually had any attraction to her. Even though, I figured I'd proven that time and time again. He liked to make it as difficult as possible.

She, on the other hand, had to prove she could obey and perform. I still wasn't convinced of either.

She undid my pants with her teeth, and I blocked out the room, blocked out Ross and Miles, as I stared down at her, trying to find some way to get lost in her even though her eyes were full of trepidation.

And Lord help me, I wanted her.

Her vulnerability did something to me. I hated watching her in pain, but some part of me had gotten so whacked out of common sense after spending months at the Retreat that some twisted part of me actually enjoyed it.

That was the only thing that kept me alive—allowed me to blend in.

She nuzzled away the remaining bits of fabric and took

my hardening cock into her mouth. Blow jobs were usually the easiest because I didn't have to do a damn thing.

She sucked and licked, and I closed my eyes. In my head, I was running for the door, searching desperately for an escape, even though I wasn't entirely sure what I was running from.

I felt her thrust forward, taking me deep, and my eyes shot open. Ross was holding her there, holding her to the point that she gagged and struggled around me. The motions and sensations arousing while the look of terror in her eyes threatened to rip me away.

He backed off and she breathed, relaxing and returning to her own pace. I just had to get there and get it the fuck over with. The throb built in my balls, wrestling up my spine and into my brain. I jerked, tightening my legs, keeping them planted as the spasm ran through me, and drained into her mouth.

She licked and sucked until she'd cleaned away the remnants of my cum, then I pulled myself away, zipping up my pants and hoping that Ross would settle for that bit of the spectacle and leave.

"That's quite a show from someone who nearly refused to strip a few days ago. But she still has to pay for running. Twenty lashes, then throw her in lock-up until you're sure she's learned her lesson. I'd love to stay and watch the rest, but I have a plane to catch." He headed up the stairs like he'd just asked us to clear his paperwork, or clean the windows.

I pulled Silver to her feet, then spun her around so that she was facing the stairway and her back was to me. "Take off your shirt and shorts."

Kirk, I repeated over and over as I watched her strip. Then I jerked her forward so that she was bent over and her back was flat. "Hold the pole." I'd seen the look she'd gotten when I pulled her into the room. Going anywhere near the table would be too much, but she'd need some kind of support to get through this.

Miles took off his belt and folded it over, placing it in her mouth for her to bite down on.

Twenty lashes. Fucking hell. I was reasonably sure that he wanted to see her broken just to prove his own damn point. He wanted to be right at any cost.

My stomach threatened to dump its contents as Miles picked up the whip from its cradle in the corner and handed it to me. I fought to keep my hands from shaking. I was about to give myself away—to give everything away.

Failing at the mission had to be better than this.

Miles brushed all of the hair off her back, her crisp white back. It was about to be marred and burning.

I raised the whip over my head and nearly collapsed when it came down with the first sickening crack. I sent my own mind away into hiding while my body doled out the first round of her punishment. I thought I heard her muffled screams under the crashing noise in my head, but my mind refused to return. I counted the beats and nothing else until she was on her knees bawling.

I stared down at her, snapping back to reality. I'd only made it to eight. Holy fucking hell, I wasn't even halfway done.

Miles pulled her back to her feet, bracing her for a second before I laid two more stripes across her back.

This wasn't what I'd signed up for. This went so far beyond "any means necessary" that my mind reeled past screaming.

She choked and gasped, her chest shaking with the effort to simply breathe, and her knees quivered with the threat to dump her again. I had to force myself away again. Ten fucking more. I was gone. Done. Certain I'd murdered myself and already gone to hell.

I added five more strikes before her cries shattered my subconscious. A dull thud echoed through the space as her knees landed against the concrete again. I didn't even raise the whip again, but she screamed out.

Miles lifted her head, putting the belt back in place as she wordlessly argued with him.

"Silver." I moved beside her. "Stand up."

She heaved with the effort to take each breath, saliva and tears ran down her face and pooled on the floor under her.

It was the most horrific gut-wrenching scene I had experienced. And it was all by my hand.

I thought my teeth would shatter from the pressure.

Miles and I lifted her back to her feet, but her legs shook so bad she couldn't stand. While Miles held her weight, my hand moved through her hair, caressing the back of her neck. I felt her tense under my touch, but I leaned closer.

"Don't break, Sugar. Push it away. Focus on something else."

She took a deep breath, and her knees locked.

I wanted to pick her up and run. Fuck every guard between her and town—I'd kill them all.

But I knew that wasn't possible.

I let the last five strokes slam down on her back. This was the deed I'd never walk away from. The final nail in my coffin.

Miles and I each took one of her arms, as soon as we pulled her upright her hair brushed over the fresh welts and she cried out. Holding her shaking body steady, I pulled the loose strands over her shoulder where they wouldn't add to the misery.

I would have done anything to take it back. To take it away. If I would have had to take ten times as many welts, I would have. The problem was if I disobeyed the punishment would be in bullets, not strikes.

Her eyes were glassy, glazed over with exhaustion as I pulled her back to sit against the table. I saw her chest expand, and imagined the pain that even that small effort would cause—if she could even tell the difference by this point. She didn't even seem to register anymore until she saw another member of the security team leading Alley into the basement.

"Please, Master," Silver whispered, looking back and forth between me and Miles. "It wasn't her fault. She didn't have anything to do with it. Please, don't punish her too. *Please*."

We had told Alley that she was responsible for any trouble that Silver got into—promising the same punishment, but as soon as Silver saw the blonde girl on the stairs—despite the pain she must have been in—her only concern was for Alley.

I couldn't fucking take it. She may as well have taken everything I had left, shattered it to pieces, and forced me to eat the shards. I was supposed to leave her in lock up, so Miles and I took her upstairs and left her on the small cot in one of the tiny rooms. There wasn't a damn thing I could say to her.

What could I have said? Sorry? Don't worry? I couldn't promise that everything would be okay or that I'd take care of her.

As soon as I left her, I went down to the security room, leaving Miles to deal with his own slave—I knew between

Silver's punishment and subsequent begging, Alley would get off easy enough, so I didn't concern myself with it. Instead, I needed answers. I needed to know why she'd run.

Alan was sitting at the monitors when I threw open the security office door. "I need to see the slave's general quarters."

His eyes widened, but he spun around in his chair and brought up the image on the larger of the screens.

"Rewind. What was going on thirty minutes ago?"

"Clothing delivery, nothing significant." But he cued up the footage.

Calling clothing delivery "nothing significant" around these girls was like calling an African elephant a teacup pet. I squinted at the monitor, trying to make out faces, but as soon as I saw Gabe step off the elevator, I had my answer. "Why was he there?"

Alan shrugged. "Helping with the delivery I'd guess since he is carrying in a ton of clothes."

"That wasn't my fucking point."

"You stole his prey," Alan said, spinning toward me. "I've seen her and don't blame you, but that doesn't mean anyone else is going to go out of their way to keep him away from her."

I glared down at him, debating over whether I should give him some shit assignment for not keeping his observation to himself, but I went back to my rooms. The first place I wanted to be was releasing Silver from her room, but once I'd done that I didn't intend on immediately disappearing, and I needed to send a message off first.

Need fucking drink. NOW.

Then I erased it, knowing it'd send Trent into an unnecessary panic. But maybe that's exactly what needed to happen. I'd just beaten the shit out of the girl I was supposed to be protecting.

We should make plans for a drink. Need to get a girl off my mind.

He'd know it wasn't insanely urgent—as in sending in the SWAT team and helicopters, but it might light a fire under his ass to get Silver out. After I stashed the phone again, I headed back up to lockup. Silver didn't seem to have moved.

She barely seemed to be breathing. "What do you want, Silver?" As much as I wanted to pick her up, and hide her in the safety of my room, if we were going to survive, she had to make a decision.

"To live. To not hurt this badly. I'm scared....I panicked."

"I know. We watched the surveillance video." I lifted her from the cot. I had to force her to walk since there was no way I could carry her without hurting her more. "Let's go upstairs."

Once in my living room, I cradled her over my lap, giving her as much comfort as I could afford—pain medicine, ointment, and time. I had to hold on to the shattered illusion. I still had to be her Master, and she had to be my obedient and currently broken slave. She relaxed once the pain salve and pain medicine kicked in, but I could still feel her struggling against me.

I rested a hand on her thigh and wove my other fingers through the hair behind her ear. "Bend, don't break, Silver."

Slowly losing her battle for consciousness, she fell into a fitful sleep that lasted until Miles brought up pizza for dinner. I could barely look at her while she leaned against the back of the couch, slowly feeding herself bite after bite of pizza.

By that point, food had no taste. It didn't even matter. I was just eating out of habit, a natural response to having food plopped down in front of me. There were no more words, actions, thoughts, feelings, it all faded away into nothingness and confusion.

I had no comprehension what the hell I'd gotten myself into or how I was going to get out of it.

I wanted to rip off the mask, tear apart the entire apartment, and break down and tell her.

Tell her how much of a sadistic bastard I was for getting off on it, but I shoved another bite of pizza in my mouth and held it in until she settled back over my lap again. And just when I thought I couldn't fall any farther she thanked me.

My nerves shattered worse than the picture frame when she'd thrown the cushion at it. My hand moved against the back of her thigh and she whimpered—not in pain—it was breathless and needy.

I'm already fucked. "You want a distraction?"

"No more pain."

Pain wasn't what I intended—endorphins were. "I'll be gentle."

After a pause, she agreed, and I pushed down the blanket, running my fingers along the inside of her thigh. Still white, smooth, and perfect in contrast to her welted red back.

"Remember the kiss you gave me yesterday?" I asked.

"Yes." She paused a moment, her tense muscles indicating her mental battle, but then her legs parted as I moved my hand up between her thighs. I stroked her gently until I found her clit and circled it with my index finger. She moaned and moved against me, spurring me to press harder as her back arched.

She was already wet with need, and I slid my fingers inside, pressing toward her g-spot as I stretched her open and she rocked against me.

I readjusted, pulling her forward and sliding myself underneath her until my knee rested between her legs. I was giving her the opening—the sliver of control.

Her moans melted my insides, and it all poured down to my stiffening cock—which was, fortunately, tucked under a pillow where she wouldn't feel it. I stroked her hair with one hand while my other moved inside her.

She inched up my leg until she groaned and shook with the building orgasm. I slowed my motion and she fisted her hands against the pillow under her head. I rubbed my hand over her once more, gathering her fluids and pressing my thumb against her ass. She moaned and tightened, but as soon as I slid a finger back in her pussy, she rocked back and allowed my entry. My thumb pressed deeper inside her while my fingers still filled her pussy.

Her toes curled pressing into the arm of the couch and she ground her clit against me. With a final shudder, she tightened around my fingers and gave in as the spasm took control of her muscles, leaving her writhing in my lap.

"How's the pain?" I asked.

I heard a faint sound, and then she spoke quietly, "I'm good."

It was all that I could give her. Of all the stupid things that might give her some relief, I was the sick bastard who jumped to sex.

But then, I knew firsthand how much it could erase when necessary—and the bitter taste it could leave afterward. I was going to get her out of that place. Find a way to put all of the pieces I'd ripped apart back together, and make sure she made it back to her life.

Chapter Seven

FRIENDS IN DISPARATE PLACES

WHEN I ESCAPED the memory hell of Dr. Combs's office, I listened to a voice message from Trent. Miles had been moved to a new facility to ensure his safety while he cooperated, but he couldn't convince Agent Michaels that it'd be helpful to ask him if he might know something about Alley's whereabouts.

There were so many pieces of so many lives that I felt obligated to put back together.

Since I wasn't yet back to work, no one could say I was ignoring the plan or their orders. Trent hadn't mentioned exactly where they'd moved Miles, but it wasn't hard to figure it out. They'd moved him away from other members of Milo's organization, but I still thought the facility was more oppressing than he deserved. I hoped for something better for him—that one day he might be able to put his life together—but there weren't a lot of programs here to help that.

It took ten minutes to pass through security and get

signed in, but the wait for them to get him into a secure room took longer.

It was a good thing I wasn't in a hurry.

Miles's bright jumpsuit was a harsh contrast against the concrete walls, as he sat across the steel table from the door. "I expected it to take you a little longer."

"I'm not here officially."

"Came to shoot the breeze then—just like old times." He kicked back in his chair and gave me a sardonic glare.

I wasn't sure how to take cynical Miles, and I wasn't ready to jump to the bad news without getting a feel for him first. "I need to figure out how to keep Ros—"

"I already know her name, may as well say it."

His knowledge wasn't the problem—it felt strange, like every part of my life colliding in an astronomical disaster where timelines cross and worlds explode or vanish into nothingness. "I need to know how to keep Rose safe."

Miles barely moved, keeping his arms crossed and eyes dead set on me as he spoke. "You're not even officially back on the force.... What about my request?"

"I came about that, too."

His lip twitched. "Yet you're amazingly alone."

May as well take the leap, I thought. "Alley went off the grid—I didn't know anything about it until after I spoke to you."

"Then you have a problem." He tilted his head, but that was his only reaction. He was holding back, tucking everything away so I—his current enemy—wouldn't have a thing on him.

"Yeah, I do. I was hoping you might know something."

"I've been incommunicado," he said simply, "in case you haven't noticed."

"Is there anyone that she has a connection to? Anywhere she might go?"

Miles sighed and shook his head, slouching in his seat as if he'd given up on the façade and let his guard down. "You know her story. There isn't anyone I'd know of from her past that she'd go to. Anything else?"

"Look Miles. I never wanted to let you go down." I hoped that by coming clean he'd loosen his own lips. "I know you care about Alley—I want to find her, not just for you. I want to make sure she's okay."

"Have you talked to Rose? How much does she know?"

He wanted more than for me to come clean—an equal exchange of information. I shook my head. "We haven't spoken since the day I was shot. I didn't want to put her in danger."

"You're going to find Alley." His voice nearly tipped up into a question, but he held it steady.

"I said I would."

Miles swallowed and he scanned the room. "I assume your plan was built on the assumption that taking out Milo would cause an internal struggle."

"Yeah," that wasn't where I expected the conversation to go, and it took me a moment to get my bearings, "But apparently everything has gone dead—aside from claims that Milo was a decoy nobody."

Miles smiled. "You did a little more than cause an internal struggle over command—you worked your way to the top, and whether they think you were a cop, or that you simply betrayed Ross, no one knows who to believe."

I pressed my palms against my eyes. "It worked?"

"They'll probably give up on Rose soon enough. They don't really have a lot of options left—or even a reason to stay here."

"How do you know all of this?"

The edge of his mouth tipped up, his expression stuck halfway between a smirk and a scowl. "Half of the men blame me for not figuring out we had a breech—the other half believe I got shafted more than anyone. I hear talk, even behind bars. Who the hell do you think our lawyers work for?"

All we had to do was keep going, and it was possible the entire organization would fall. "So I just need to convince everyone to clean up what's left of the mess. But I assume you're going to deny this whole conversation until I find Alley?"

Miles grinned and reared back in his seat. "I assume since you're not supposed to be here, that would be quite a task to explain anyway."

He had me there and I nodded. "Then why'd you tell me anything?"

"Like I said—" his expression relaxed into something I was more familiar with. "I'm a fan of your girl."

At least we were in agreement about something. He finally reminded me of the man I hadn't minded scheming with.

He leaned across the table folding his hands together. "Why are you so intent on helping me? I'm sure if you tried you could find some other kind of leverage to get me to cooperate."

"Like threatening to leak who killed Ross?"

He flinched. "Something like that."

"Because I think you're better than that. And," I smirked, "I happen to be a fan of your girl."

Miles scoffed and sat back in his chair. "At least we're playing from equal grounds."

Even though I knew he'd be safer in the current facility,

it was painful seeing him there—and even more difficult leaving him there. The strange circumstances surrounding our relationship aside, I couldn't deny a certain level of respect for him.

On the way to the parking lot, my phone rang with another message from Trent. I had a feeling that I was going to have to come up with an explanation for visiting Miles whether I wanted to or not.

"Yeah," I hoped he was just being a douche and calling to see if I'd gone to my appointment.

"You really think you'd go in there and no one would let me know?"

"No, but it was worth a shot."

The phone crackled as he exhaled across the mic. "Did you find out anything?"

I explained briefly what Miles had told me as I climbed in my car.

"He gave you all of this without Alley?"

"He knows I'll find her. He didn't outright admit it, but he's not going to back me up on the info until I do."

"So I'm supposed to take an unsubstantiated story and do what? Hand it over to the feds and argue for Miles to get what he wants even though he claims the info didn't even come from him."

"Something like that." I really wanted to say that it wasn't my problem, but as much as I wanted to, I couldn't protect Rose alone.

Trent went silent but didn't end the phone call.

"There's something you're keeping from me," I said.

"Not keeping," he paused again. "I could use you at the station."

I wasn't sure if his cryptic request was a request for help

or bait to get me there so he could give me a chewing out in person.

I went in through the front door of the station this time, nodding to Officer Hudson as he buzzed me through. Out of the corner of my eye, I also saw the two officers who'd stopped Evan and me. They didn't acknowledge me, so I kept walking without a second glance, choosing to avoid confrontation.

Once I reached Trent's desk, I twisted the chair around and straddled it to face the desk—keeping my back to the wall so I could see the whole office. My still-empty desk still sat across from us.

"You seem different," he said, giving me an appraising glance before he revealed his motives.

"Maybe because for once, I have something productive to do."

"Something you're supposed to be staying out of," he said pointedly. It was a fair warning, which I chose to ignore.

"Then, you wouldn't have asked me here." Unless he really did just want to call me in for a lecture.

His gaze traveled over the room—it was quiet for the moment. Experience said it wouldn't last.

Trent's hand went to the top drawer and he pulled the folder from the bottom of the stack of cases he kept there. "A few of the other girls have gone off the grid."

"Not surprising. Unless you think there's something more behind it."

"The feds were handling their relocations—setting them up with living accommodations, therapy, and job training or placement organizations. Some went quietly along with it—a few reconnected with families and others were quite vocal about their disdain for the upheaval. Alley was one of the quiet ones—but seemed more depressed than anything. She wasn't the first to go off the grid. We've tracked down two of them, they'd both simply seemed to want to go about things on their own. Moved in together got jobs. Didn't raise any flags—"

But it could lay the foundation for others to do the same.

There were thirty-seven girls living at the Retreat at all times. Some guests brought their own, but they weren't on site during the raid. Ross had wanted nothing he couldn't control while Milo was visiting—but he got far more than he bargained for despite his caution.

It was a damn shame since I would have relished bringing a number of the clients down as well. The investigators should have recovered all of the Retreat logs and videos—tapes were reviewed and regularly erased, but Ross kept his own collection for "insurance." The big news of the raid probably sent most of those people into hiding though, so any attempt to bring them all in wouldn't be easy, and the Feds had more pressing matters to deal with.

"How many of the girls are missing?" I asked.

"That we haven't managed to track down—four."

That didn't seem like an exorbitant number considering the circumstances, distrust of the system, and shame. Life back in the real world wasn't so kind when you were looking over your shoulder waiting for someone to see your bad deeds through the pearly façade.

"That doesn't include the ten who refused help that we did manage to track down, including one picked up for prostitution last night."

"I'd expect that number to climb—it hasn't even been a month."

"At least two girls are working for an escort company,

but we haven't been able to prove there's any wrongdoing or connect it with the other cases. But if they believe they've found someone to take care of them, odds are they're not going to roll."

A few of the girls knew how to play the system and if they found the right situation they were probably making a killing themselves. Either way, former sex slaves in an escort business seemed far from innocent.

They were doing what they knew how to do. What they'd been trained for—in some cases most of their lives. Whether anything illegal was going on or not it was not a healing situation. If they weren't the ones taking advantage, they were putting themselves in a position to be manipulated.

"Which girls?" I asked, gesturing toward the file and hoping for a peek.

Trent flipped it open. "Chelsea Sea—"

"I don't know their real names."

Trent raised a brow and nodded. He took two sheets from the file and slid them toward me.

"Trick and Babs."

"Were all of the names that bad?"

"Kat, Gabby, Raini.... Ross didn't like anything too vulgar, but every name had a reason."

Even Silver. Although I didn't devise that one as much as fate did. I'd done the unthinkable and let her choose her own name, and she chose the color of her nail polish, but it was ironically fitting in every way.

She was strong enough to take everything we threw at her and malleable enough to survive and retain her strength.

I heard Trent scoff and lifted my gaze.

"I can tell who you're thinking about," he said.

I stuck to the business at hand before he could say or ask more. "Trick was one of the more dominant girls. She and Babs worked in tandem a lot, but Babs was a follower."

Before I could explain further Captain Richards came out of the corner office and headed straight for us. He was wearing his usual brown tweed suit, but his greying hair was even sparser than I remembered. Since he was nearing retirement, he was extra cautious about anything getting in his way—namely me and this case.

"What are you doing here, James?"

"I needed more info on a couple of girls," Trent said.

Richards' face twisted until he looked like his head was deflating. He pursed his lips and stared at me.

"Just helping out," I said.

"You're no longer cleared to be flying under the radar. Time for both of you to start playing by the rules. Let the Feds handle the rest of the case, and move on."

"I'm working the prostitution case I brought to you this morning," Trent said. "Not the Fed case, but James knows the girls who might be involved, which makes him just like any other witness."

I winced at the words, but it was an apt argument.

Richards placed his palms on the desk and leaned toward us, lowering his voice. "Witnesses don't interview suspects."

I wasn't sure which occasion he was referring to, so I kept my mouth shut.

The captain pointed to me. "I'm not just talking about yesterday."

So much for acting independently. "Then put me back on the case."

"First, I don't have clearance from any of your doctors. Second, I'd be daft to put you on a case where the suspects believe you're dead. The shooting was unfortunate, but it gave you a clean out, and you should keep it that way. As long as your buddy, Miles, hasn't already outed you."

"Miles saved my life," I said dryly. I may have been apprehensive at first, but our conversations told me that I could at least trust him as far as this situation was concerned. "He's not talking. And I can work the case without anyone figuring it out."

"Until you're called to testify. Right now the Feds have a lid on it, so don't push it."

"I'd be surprised if the whole death thing would hold up either way. Their lawyers are smart enough to pull the right strings."

"What about the missing girls," Trent asked. "It's an unrelated case that won't put his name back in the official records for the federal trafficking cases."

"Right," Richards threw up his hands. "We'll have him track down girls who think he's dead."

This argument was going to keep going back to the same place. "I know them better than anyone here—I can help track them down without revealing myself."

"I'm sure you do know them," he grimaced, but I tried not to take offense. This whole case had gone against his better judgment and taste and I didn't entirely blame him. "I still have no paperwork to reinstate you."

"Then, I'll get it."

"How well can that side of yours be healed after only three weeks?"

Nearly four. "Well enough to push papers and do interviews."

"Until someone gets miffed."

Trent sat back in his chair, threading his hands behind

his head, with a smug expression on his face. "That's why he has a kick-ass partner."

I could have rolled my eyes, but Richards' scoff was enough to hold me over. The sound of his shoes squeaking against the old tile floor as he headed back to his office was his only response. I'd be lucky to ever leave a desk again. But even that was better than sitting at home.

Trent immediately returned to the case at hand as if the interruption had never occurred. "Anything else I should know about the girls?"

"Trick." I pushed her photo toward him. "She knows how to get along just fine."

She was a lot like Kat in that respect, but far less pushy and bitchy about it.

She was more subtle. Conniving. But she was well-liked by visitors. Especially those looking for two women, since Trick and Babs were nearly inseparable. "Trick and Babs were something of an item."

Trent's jaw went slack although I could tell he was trying to hide his reaction. "Item as in—"

"Hard to tell in those circumstances, but I'd say yes. Babs has more of a submissive personality, but she can still be a handful."

"And the chances their current arrangement is non-sexual?"

I snorted. "It's suspicious, but is it related to any of the other girls?"

"Haven't uncovered anything." Trent tucked the papers back into the file and returned it to his drawer. "The girl who was picked up last night had a number for the same escort service but denies that she took their offer. How about you get your clearance so you can help me figure it out?"

"Working on it."

Chapter Eight

BECOMING KIRK

GETTING MEDICALLY CLEARED for work was much simpler than my psychological clearance.

Four weeks.

My four weeks was up, but we talked about my going back to work, dealing with the memories in a different setting, plans for reestablishing myself.

What I looked forward to wasn't dealing with the memories, it was an opportunity to heal while doing some good and bringing the rest of the case to a close.

There wasn't a peep about Rose—or Silver—during the entire conversation. Dr. Combs was probably waiting for me to broach the topic, but as time passed, it seemed like there was more in the way of ever seeing her again. Whoever was watching her—to be specific. And then there was my lingering uncertainty about whether or not it was a good idea for either of us regardless of the danger.

Paperwork finally in hand, I prepared to return to the station, but I stopped along the way to check my messages.

T: steer clear of station house—busted R's spies.

Well, that was one obstacle out of the way.

I laid my head against the steering wheel, the pistons in my head pumping out more ideas than I could process.

How long had it been since anything felt relatively normal?

I'd been on the path to this moment most of my life.

———

TRENT and I had made our plans long before we graduated high school—taking advantage of a local program that allowed us to take college classes in high school, we both had justice studies associates by the time we graduated. Then, we went straight to the police academy, flying just as smoothly through those courses. We worked our way up to detectives as fast as possible—our coursework and high marks made us nearly impossible to stop.

As did our youth, energy, and commitment to getting the job done.

We had social lives, but they weren't the center of our life.

Back then, it seemed like we had it all figured out. Moved in and up through the station house, while many of the older officers were retiring or moving to less physically demanding jobs.

One night, we happened to pick up a case regarding a lead on a crime ring. Little did we know it was bigger than that.

"You have no idea what you're dealing with," the suspect hissed as I hauled him to his feet. I handed him off to the officers as a phone rang. I traced the sound to the area where I'd tackled him and found the phone under the table.

Trent shrugged, so I took a chance and answered.

"Kirk?" The voice on the other end was a calm, smooth baritone.

"Yeah." I kept my answer short in case he recognized the difference.

"You haven't run into a problem, have you?"

"Nothing I can't take care of."

The man on the line grunted. "Look, I'm sure you were good in your old ring, but we don't deal with slip-ups or potential problems. Maybe we should find someone else."

He hadn't pegged me as being someone else, yet, so I pressed again. "I'm the one you want."

I had no idea what the hell he was talking about, but the only way to find out was to keep him going.

"Fine. We'll meet up tomorrow—I'll call with the time and location. You have until then to get the medical supplies we need."

Fuck.

"You'll receive the list tonight."

That was promising, but I wondered *where* he was sending it, but without further instructions, the line went dead.

"Well?" Trent asked. He hadn't moved or made a sound since I answered the phone.

"Looking for medical supplies—said he'd send a list," I explained.

"Narcs?"

I shrugged, "We could ask our new guest."

Back at the station, however, "Kirk" refused to tell us a damn thing, until I mentioned giving a call to his new boss and explaining that he'd been so kind to talk.

"You have no idea—" he began again.

"That's what they all say. How about you give me one?"

I reclined in my seat wearing a thick veneer of ease to cover the whirlwind in my brain while Trent hung back waiting for an opportune time to jump in. This could be a huge case —an enormous bust if we could get closer to the man on the other end of the phone call.

"They're bigger than one little police station. Connections you wouldn't believe."

Trent scoffed. "Then, why do they need a crummy street criminal like you? What'll happen if you screw up this delivery tomorrow? We could release you right after the scheduled drop. Or...," he pointed one finger at the suspect. "Better yet, we'll give you everything you need and set up nice and pretty at the drop."

His eyes widened and he tensed. He was definitely more scared of them than us—

I slid a piece of paper across the table. "Give us the list or it'll be big news that you got busted and screwed up."

"They've never seen me."

I smirked, but he snorted in response, sitting forward in his chair. "All you're going to do is get us all killed."

"I'm sure they'll have no problem finding *you*," I said.

"And if I give you what you want?"

"You remain an anonymous criminal," I said tapping the piece of the paper.

"Phone has access to an email account." He scribbled something down on the paper and slid it back to me—a crudely drawn hand flipping the bird.

Trent opened the door and flagged in two officers. "Send him to lock up and tell them to hold him until we get word from his friend on the meeting. Then stick a tail on him and tell his anonymous friends where to find him."

"You wouldn't," Kirk started to stand, but I shoved him back into the chair. "It's unethical or whatever."

Trent smiled. "Crashing your little ring is entirely ethical. We may as well get some enjoyment while doing it."

Kirk shifted his gaze to me.

I shrugged. "All I want is a password. I doubt you got this far by being a complete idiot, but when I spoke to your *friend* earlier he did mention not tolerating screw ups, and you have already been caught. I doubt they made it to the status you claim they have by being forgiving. We'll figure it out either way, but you have about sixty seconds to determine your own fate."

His eyes narrowed and nose flared. "Password EN1F37R6."

I pulled up the account and typed in the information. Miraculously, our not-so-smart thug had some sense. I squinted as I scrolled through the list.

"Narcs?" Trent asked again.

"Hardly." I continued reading—Aspirin, bandages, rubber gloves, condoms.... "It looks like they're building an enormous first-aid kit. Depo-Provera?"

"Birth control?" Trent asked, looking over my shoulder. "What kind of operation is this?"

Kirk smirked. "An undercover clinic devoted to fighting evil. What the hell do you think it is?"

"Sex trafficking?" I growled, feeling my blood heat, coiling my muscles to dangerous extremes.

The scumbag crossed his arms and leaned back.

I planted my fists against the table, getting into his face. "You look smug for the idiot who just got busted and ratted them out."

"Maybe so, but you'll be the ones to end up dead. See, I, too revel in the little things."

Trent pulled me back. "Give us a name."

He raised his chin, then frowned and shook his head. "Doesn't have one."

I rubbed the back of my neck, turning on my heels to get out of the room.

Trent met me in the hallway as the unis hauled off Kirk. "What's the possibility there's a sex trafficking scheme of this caliber operating here?"

"We could find out." I held up the phone and wiggled it. "He said they haven't seen him—they don't know what he looks like."

"He seemed to be goading you in that direction. He looked quite amused with the turn of conversation. What if these guys know more than we think?"

"Then we bust whoever shows up and figure out a plan C before I get shot."

We went forward with the plan, and surprisingly even Captain Richards backed the idea, probably betting on a huge break before his retirement.

The next evening, the message came in: *6:15 under 12th Street viaduct.*

"*Shit,*" I glanced at the clock. "We have less than twenty minutes."

We loaded everything into an old car that we'd requisitioned from a drug bust, and Trent mobilized officers to act as backup while I headed in alone.

I parked under the viaduct and got out of the car. My gaze traveled around the area while I leaned against the trunk. With my sleeves rolled up, the snake on my forearm was on full display—at least it helped me look the part.

I crossed my ankles in front of me to look confident— nonplussed by the situation while I surveyed every movement around me.

Fifteen minutes later, a large red pickup appeared with two men in the cab.

The man in the passenger seat rolled down the window. He had scraggly black hair and bright green eyes, while the driver had long blond hair pulled back in a ponytail and dark eyes like a weasel.

"Load it up," the passenger said.

"I'm not a mule," I scowled

They both glared back at me.

I stepped aside gesturing to the car. "Don't you even want to check the merchandise—verify it's all there? I wouldn't want any misunderstandings later."

"If you don't sound like a fucking college prick," the passenger said, flipping the door open so it narrowly missed hitting me. "Not how Miles described you."

"First impressions and phone conversations can be misleading."

The hairs on my arms stood as a second pickup appeared, this one black, but slightly smaller. I hoped that Trent and his men were close but that they'd stay out of sight.

Two trucks were overkill for the haul, but a tall, broad-shouldered man with rich dark skin stepped out of the second truck. He was dressed markedly better than the other two, so I assumed he was the leader of the operation.

"Didn't expect a party," I said, opening the trunk. Maybe it was best to get things moving. "Your order."

"Gabe," the new man said, "Check it out—discretely, then load it up."

The green-eyed man grunted and scowled at me as he passed to rip open the first box. He sifted through the contents before following suit on each of the following boxes while the rest of us quietly waited.

My heart pounding a steady supply of anxiety through my stream. Gabe nodded then waved to the blond driver, who stepped around, taking the first box, and together they loaded up the truck.

I stood by and waited for another order—I wasn't doing anything unless told.

"How'd you manage to get it all so fast?" Miles asked.

I smirked, "Connections. I called in a few favors and finagled from there. I want more work."

He turned away. "I'll call you if I need something."

"I'm better than a gopher," I said quickly. "And I'm betting you know that since you came out here to see for yourself, Miles." I hoped my assumption was right.

Miles glared back at me with a mix of disbelief and derision, but it was nothing compared to Gabe's soured expression. "Gabe, Alan—head back and check in."

"You've got—" Gabe began, but Miles silenced him with a flick of his wrist, without ever taking his eyes off of me. "I won't remind you where you stand after last week, Gabe."

The tires of the red truck spun against the loose and cracking pavement as Alan gunned it out of the empty lot.

"You are just a gopher—replaceable. I'm here to make sure you're not a liability."

I didn't stand down, even as he moved closer, slamming the car's trunk closed.

"If you're not interested," I shrugged, starting to turn.

"Confident," he said. "*Stupid*, but confident. Did you leave a trail?"

I knew what he meant, but I opted for a smart-assed comment to keep in character. "I can find my way home just fine." I opened the driver's door, catching his glare out of the corner of my eye. "It's all clear. No one will be tracing it or following me. Can you offer me steady work or not?"

I needed something more. I needed to know his role, something about the organization.

"I'll talk to my boss and *maybe* I'll be in touch."

I waited in the car until everything was clear, then drove around town a few times—making sure I wasn't being followed before meeting up with Trent at the station.

A crowd filled one of the briefing rooms and Trent stepped outside to meet me before I could get close.

"They're waiting on *you*," he said.

I squinted, not recognizing most of the men in suits who flanked the long table.

"Apparently this trafficking ring is big. FBI big."

My blood turned to ice as we walked into the room and not even the hot stuffy atmosphere could melt it. They took turns bombarding me with questions for the next hour— even though everything I knew could be summed up in about ten minutes. Their knowledge, however, went far beyond that. They brought in boxes full of information on locations in multiple countries linked to the one in our own backyard.

"If you know this much, why not take them down?" I asked.

One of the women in the group spoke up. "It's bigger and deeper, we need more information."

"We want their leader," the agent nearest me said. He'd identified himself as Agent Michaels and seemed to be in charge of the investigation. "He has a dozen or more similar organizations—ties around the world. We've been trying to get someone inside for a year—almost managed it a few months ago."

The phone in my pocket buzzed.

Zini's Bar 12:30am.

I exhaled slowly—it looked like they had that someone on the inside. "He wants to meet again at a bar after midnight."

"A public place is good," Trent said, but Agent Michaels eyed him before returning attention to me.

"You'll go," Michaels said.

"Wait a minute," I said, standing. "This is my life I'm putting on the line. What happened to the last guy—the one who almost managed to get in?"

The agent's steely glare said all I needed to know, but he answered anyway. "He was found out. Killed."

I rubbed my hand over my dry lips feeling a wave of nausea come over me. This was bigger than anything I'd ever imagined getting into. Not an international organization. I'd done small undercover jobs—this was mind-blowing.

Captain Richards approached me. "I offered them our full cooperation, but you don't have to go in if you don't feel comfortable."

"They've seen me. If we change it, up they'll know, and the opportunity will be gone. But if I am going in, and risking my life, I want to know how deep I'll be going."

"We're not sure how deep it goes, or the best way to get to the leader. We've brought in lower level associates before, but none of them will turn, and we've been hitting brick walls at every turn. If you go in, you'll be flying off the radar."

"Off the radar? It's a *sex retreat*." I rubbed my eyes. Were they really asking me to do this?

"We can have one of our counselors help you prepare if you decide to go in."

"If there's enough time for that," I said. Miles didn't seem the type to leave time for anything.

I was going in over my head. I was about to be sucked into the world of extortion and sex trafficking—more so than any cop would ever imagine. Sex, alcohol, drugs, violence. I'd have to seep into their world. Become the vile man of nightmares or die.

But it wasn't the fear of death that kept me going. If that was the case, I would have never gone in. It was the women. Girls ripped from their families, friends, and lives. With them as my reminder, I descended into the darkness, let it cover my soul, conceal my true intentions, and immerse me into my new role as Kirk.

Chapter Nine

FATED THORN

RICHARDS APPROVED my return to work the day after I turned in my paperwork, and despite the exhaustion that set in early, I didn't stop running the case once I started. I was supposed to stay behind the scenes, but by the end of my first week back, I'd realized that even long hours of paperwork and leaning over a desk was more than I had bargained for.

Friday night, I crashed on the couch, barely wanting to lift my head after pulling a ten-hour shift. Trent and I thought we had a lead on the missing girls, but it ended up a bust.

Jack was asleep on the couch next to me after a long day at the park with his dad. After which, I was left to babysit while Evan and Katie had a quiet dinner.

It was the least I could do since they'd put up with me and my unpredictable moods.

My phone rang and I moved carefully to answer it, not wanting to wake Jack. I slid off the couch and ducked into the kitchen. When Trent's name flashed on the display, I figured he'd caught another lead.

"What's up?"

"First off—she's fine so don't freak."

My pulse spiked. That's the last thing you should tell someone if you don't want them to freak. "Right—that works. What the hell?"

"Rose is at the hospital. I rode over with her and didn't want to panic you until I had all the details. She was shot—right shoulder—"

I didn't wait for the rest, hanging up the phone as soon as I heard the front door open. I said a silent thank you to perfect timing, which was for once working in my favor.

"How—" Katie began until she saw my face. "What happened?"

"Jack's asleep. I have to run."

I drove straight to the hospital and sprinted toward the information desk, but Trent caught me before I could make it.

"She's fine."

"Then, I want to see her."

"She's in surgery." His hands tightened on my shirt—sure not to let me slip away.

"That's *not* fine." I ground my teeth together.

"Went through the muscle. It looked clean so I don't think it hit any bone. They're debriding the wound and closing her up. She was a little shocky, but probably more from pain and the situation than anything else."

I didn't want to hear that. Shock. Pain. All more than she ever deserved. I ran my hand through my hair, pushing and pulling it in every direction. "Who? Why wasn't anyone protecting her?"

"You know we couldn't justify it after we brought in the

trio who had been watching her." He paused, longer than humanly necessary to compose a sentence—even though it was probably only a fraction of a second. "She said it was Alley."

That was impossible. All of the oxygen drained from my system. I couldn't imagine Alley wielding a gun—let alone shooting Rose. How did she even find Rose? It raised a million more questions that I didn't have time to think about.

I collapsed against the wall just as a doctor came around the corner.

"Detective Davis?"

I snapped back to attention as the doctor looked between us, confused for a second.

"Officer Carter," Trent said, pointing in my direction.

The doctor nodded. "She's doing well. She's awake now and in recovery, but it'll be a while before you can question her since she's still feeling the effects of the anesthesia. She was lucky—there was minimal tissue and muscle damage. She should be fine to go home day after tomorrow, but she's going to be uncomfortable for a while, and she'll need therapy as the muscle begins to heal."

Lucky. That was becoming the story of my life. I was going to have to get it engraved on my tombstone.

But it wasn't lucky. I'd already let her get hurt—so many times had I let her get hurt when all I wanted to do was protect her. Just like the day I'd left the compound for a meeting—my only opening at getting her out before the raid.

I had the meeting all set up and plans to pin her disappearance on Gabe—it would have been fucking perfect to watch him go down for it.

But then I got the call from Miles.

A single attempt at making everything right turned everything into an even worse shit storm. I was only a few minutes away from the compound, but by the time I got back and we tracked her down, they'd already stolen her body, drugged her mind, and polluted her soul with a darkness I could never erase. In an instant, we pulled Gabe off of her, and Miles dragged the bastard into the corner of the room.

In one afternoon, I thought my smart ass fighter had become a broken mess. I lifted her naked form off the bed—tucking her against my chest was the only comfort I could offer at the moment.

I was lost inside my own regret, details blurred with the train wreck of thoughts exploding in my head. Before I knew what she was doing, she reached for my gun. I realized that without thinking, I had left it on the bed. I shouted and reached to stop her, but it was too late. Even in her drugged and dazed condition, the bullet made a beeline for Gabe's head.

Perfect shot.

I pulled the gun from her hands, but her expression was vacant. What other secrets did my girl have to hide?

Miles met my gaze—his eyes as wide with shock as I imagined my own were. She had taken a life because I couldn't get her out. The darkness could drive people to do crazy things.

"Why'd Alley do it?" I asked.

"Rose wasn't exactly… talkative. But I wouldn't worry about her too much, her stubborn attitude puts you to shame."

I rubbed my hands over my face, trying to escape the all-consuming white noise.

Rose was asleep again by the time the doctor let us in to see her. At the sight of her laying in the bed, my heart lodged in my throat, leaving me lightheaded and off balance. Trent stayed for a few minutes before slipping out to do the detective thing. This time, I had no problem taking advantage of some time off. My desire to find out why and how this happened decimated by my refusal to leave.

Hours passed as she faded in and out of consciousness, mostly from the pain medicine and the lingering effects of the anesthesia. She'd always been a lightweight when it came to pain medicine—nearly the only thing I ever saw that kept her down for long. But her experiences with it were far from restful—I'd also seen it send her into delusions and condemn her to hellish nightmares.

I leaned against the side of the bed, yearning to touch her. But no matter the strength of the magnetic force she had over me, I resisted. Even with a small brush of skin, I felt like I'd be taking advantage of her unconscious body.

"Am I high?" her quiet voice rose from the bed.

"Probably." I remembered the last time I'd watched her suffer through both pain and the effects of morphine after Gabe had attacked her. I wanted to bleach the memory out of my mind and out of her life.

"Good," she whispered. "Getting shot sucks."

That was one thing she didn't have to tell me. I was only glad that she was awake, and the wound—although painful, probably wouldn't have the same recovery time as mine. Even though hers might be more rehab intensive since the damaged muscle would need to regain a wider range of motion.

"Are you real?" she asked flexing her hand.

Her fingers were cold as I laced mine around her and squeezed her hand. "Do I feel real?"

"As soon as my arm is healed I'm going to punch you, then decide."

I deserved it—in fact, I almost looked forward to it. I missed the stubborn belligerent girl whom I'd struggled to best on more than a few occasions.

She slipped back into a quiet sleep, but woke every so often through the night and into the next morning, until her eyes popped open like we'd never stopped talking, and she uttered the question I dreaded answering.

"Where have you been?"

"Around. I wanted to—" I had no idea how to explain. How to put into words how much I wanted to see her, but how much more I feared that desire would only serve to screw her up more. "My psychologist and my supervisor warned me to stay away from you. They said you'd heal better if I kept my distance. I wanted to see you, but I wanted them to be right. I wanted… I wanted you to be able to go back to normal."

"There is no normal."

Normal was the very thing I'd spent the last few weeks chasing. Maybe our normal wasn't like everyone else's, but I was convinced it existed somewhere. I had to hope for it—for something that at least felt *right*, because, at that moment, everything in my life seemed sideways and mismatched.

After another long nap, she finally seemed to be opening up, and my heart thudded a tune of hope when she asked me to hold her hand. But then, I made the lethal mistake of nearly calling her Silver.

Her eyes flashed and she straightened beneath the sheets. "You should have talked to me. Given me a choice. Said goodbye. Something. I deserved something."

I couldn't argue. Everything I'd done was a useless attempt at protecting her—the last an attempt at protecting her from myself. And I wasn't sure that she didn't still need that protection. "I'm sorry. I didn't even trust myself to make the right decision."

"But you still decided to make a decision without me. I

didn't expect to come back and have everything be fine, but suddenly, I was just on my own."

I dropped my gaze. The touch of her smooth skin against my fingers was almost enough to make me feel alive again—almost. I couldn't take the back and forth. The push and pull of acceptance and outright rejection.

I begged for one little thing—a minuscule clue that something I had done over the past two months had been the right thing. But if I couldn't even convince myself of that, I didn't see the point in arguing with her.

Watching her sleep and being near her was the only respite I had, so I stayed through the fits and starts. I refused to move, knowing the moment she woke up she might be the one to kick me out.

I could at least give her that privilege if she wanted it.

Trent came in and sat with me Saturday morning, giving me a brief update on the investigation. He also brought food and coffee, but I left most of it untouched, and he eventually left me to my silence as he sipped a cup of coffee and scrolled through messages and reports on his phone.

Around mid-morning, she woke in a panic. Yelling and batting her arms at some invisible enemy. Nurses rushed in, but the more people tried to help, the harder she fought.

"Stop touching me," she yelled.

"You're bleeding," Trent said as she finally settled.

One nurse shoved her way through—a persnickety expression on her face as if Rose was purposefully being a difficult patient. "You probably pulled a stitch with all of that—"

I growled in warning, and the nurse's eyes darted to me, and her mouth snapped shut.

It didn't stop her from running her mouth while she

checked under the bandage though. Uttering assurances that Rose had been lucky that she hadn't ripped the stitches out.

Rose took it all with a straight expression until the nurse mentioned pain meds.

"Can I get something else?" she asked. When the nurse objected, Rose continued to explain. "I don't like feeling so foggy when I'm awake."

The nurse promised to check on the prescription but gave us all a scowl as she left. At least Rose was fighting with someone other than me.

I needed to do something, but I felt fated to continue watching from the stands. A spectator who wasn't supposed to have any say in her life. I hated the way she looked at Trent, trusting in him while being pissed at me.

I was all over the place, but the moment that Trent stepped out, and I tried to make amends. I slipped up again. "Silver…." I began before I could recall the word.

Her eyes shot open. "You're going to have to break that *habit*. Kirk and Silver are gone—"

"They have been for a long time, Sugar." I had no idea why I called her that again either. It had begun as a taunt. A wedge to force some measure of distance between us, but her face softened when I said it.

"You—you're the one that requested this stupid protective detail, aren't you? Does that mean you're planning on leaving me alone?"

I focused on only the first part since it was the most straightforward to answer. "She found you and came into your house to attack you, but it was Trent who ordered it."

"You avoided the second question. Maybe the doctors were right." Her eyes glazed over. "You're the only person I feel connected to. I held on to that for the last four weeks. I couldn't move on, but even with you here. I—"

It was like listening to a tape recorder of my own thoughts.

"I don't think I can do this either."

I stood. I'd been expecting it, but I didn't expect it to feel like my lungs were collapsing. I wished my damn mind and body would decide what they wanted. And maybe, possibly, act in unison, just once.

"This time, I get to make the call," she continued. "James and Rose don't even know each other."

I heard footsteps in the hallway and breathed a silent thank you when I saw that it was Trent coming through the door. "Make sure she's safe."

———

WITH NOTHING LEFT at the hospital, I went for a drive. I needed to escape. To shut down the memories and thoughts. I hit the gym and took out my aggression on a punching bag and a long run around the track until my body couldn't take it anymore. Then, I went home taking every small detour to waste as much time as possible and stall my arrival. When I finally pulled up the drive, the SUV was gone. The house was locked, too, with a note inside the door that said they were with Katie's parents. I threw together a sandwich and took a shower, pulling on a fresh pair of clothes and headed back out again—desperate to keep moving.

My final stop for the evening was a bar downtown. I flattened my hair before climbing out of the car. The last thing I needed was someone recognizing me and calling

Trent—my ever ready guard dog—before I had a full opportunity to get shit faced.

Inside, I spotted an opening near the end of the bar and went straight up to sit down, ordering the tallest beer possible as soon as the bartender was in earshot.

I gulped down the entire thirty-two ounces, then ordered a string of double bourbons until I could barely recognize the text on my phone. I opened the messenger and slid off my barstool, leaving a pile of bills.

"Hey buddy," the bartender said. "You're not driving."

"No kidding." I waved the phone, grabbing the back of a nearby booth for support as the room swayed.

"Maybe you should wait in here for your ride."

And now I was being controlled by some stranger in a bar. I shrugged and dropped into an empty booth. I didn't really feel like making the effort to walk anyway. I typed in a message that I thought was slightly legible and sent it to Evan.

Then I rechecked, hoping I had really sent it to Evan.

I propped my legs up on the bench and laid my head against the wall, closing my eyes to the music and chatter.

Someone shoved my foot off the bench and I jumped, prepared for a fight. But I saw a slender blonde standing at the edge of the table.

Not the brunette I preferred, but at least Katie could get me home in one piece.

"What're you doin' here?" I asked.

"Picking you up apparently. Evan was up late last night, so he and Jack are at home asleep. I stayed up to wait on you."

I fought my way out of the booth and she propped my arm over her shoulder keeping me on track as we headed for the door and through the parking lot to her SUV.

I hauled myself into the passenger seat and fastened the belt as everything around me began a new blurry dance.

Katie slid behind the wheel and sighed, twisting her hair tucking it behind her ear before she fastened her own belt.

"You're pissed?" I asked.

"Not pissed. Just concerned. But Trent warned you'd be a little difficult."

"Was this a new warning?" I spoke as clearly as possible and assumed that it was halfway understandable.

"Not really, but he said it'd probably be worse."

A warm hand touched my forearm, and I opened my eyes—I hadn't even remembered closing them, but we were now sitting outside of her house. "That was fast."

"How much did you drink?"

"No clue."

She squeezed my arm. "Give her time."

"Trent told you the details." I wanted to be surprised—at least pissed—that everyone continued discussing my life, but I'd finally hit numb.

"He told me enough. She was shot, hun. She's pissed and in pain and she doesn't know who she hates right now."

"She was right to send me away."

"Why is that?"

"I'll break her. The darkness won't leave us alone, especially if we're together."

"You're drunk and melodramatic. Let's get you to bed."

"It's true, Kate. I hurt her. I'll do it again. I *want* to do it again, to drag her inside with me so I'm not alone anymore."

The light was blinding when she opened the door and I covered my eyes. Her door closed and seconds later mine opened.

So much for a temporary respite.

"Come on, hun." She pulled me out and helped me balance when my shaky legs hit pavement. "I can tell you this. You're not alone, and you shouldn't underestimate her."

I crashed into a table as we came through the front door and an upstairs light came on. A few seconds later Evan peeked over the banister and jogged quietly down the stairs. "How much have you drunk?"

I was too busy grasping the railing and holding myself up to answer.

"He doesn't remember," Katie said.

Evan grabbed my arm and I swayed toward him.

"You remember that time—" I started

"No, James. No drunken reminiscing in front of my wife."

Katie groaned and flicked the back of his head. "As if I haven't heard it all. I'm going up to bed. Don't kill each other getting up the stairs."

Evan may as well have been pulling me up a mountain, my feet were barely coordinated enough to hit the stairs— not that I could really tell where they were or judge distance.

He unceremoniously dumped me into bed and closed the door, leaving me to the darkness again.

Chapter Ten

REUNION

IF I THOUGHT the first week being home had been hard, it was nothing compared to the next day.

The worst thing about being drunk—aside from being stuck in your own head until you pass out and then tossing and turning all night, is that when it comes to an end, your entire body reminds you that it was a bad idea. ·

I downed two glasses of water before I even felt like I could hold my head up.

"How long has it been since you've drunk that much?" Katie's whispered voice pounded through my head like the bass at a heavy metal concert.

I didn't answer, just buried my face in my hands. I didn't care about feigning macho toughness and pretending my head wasn't about to explode and implode at the same time.

She laid a couple of Aspirin on the table in front of me and refilled my glass of water, then quietly took the seat in front of me while I forced myself to swallow the pills and lift the glass to my lips again. Even after all the fluids my tongue still felt fuzzy. I knew I wasn't twenty-one anymore, but even then, aside from celebrating after a big test, I'd never been a big drinker.

There had been a few wild days and nights—one in particular where Trent, Evan, and I managed all kinds of trouble we couldn't quite remember by morning. The mess had taken days to clean up, and the following week, the blonde who Evan had been seeing decided to return his missing boxers—not that he ever noticed they were gone.

Probably twenty minutes went by before either I or Katie spoke again.

"I have to get to work," Katie said. "Evan dropped Jack off with the babysitter on his way to make sure you could get some sleep."

"I don't mean to put you two out." Any more guilt and I was certain the scar on my side would collapse from the weight on my chest and let everything spill out. Even my hands tingled with the uneasy feeling that something was about to escape.

Two parts of myself waged a war within my skin—the problem was, I wasn't sure if the two parts were even distinct. No longer able to separate needs, desires, guilt, truth, or facades, I didn't know which side I wanted to win.

Or if they both actually existed.

What if I didn't really exist anymore?

Just the leftover shadow conscious, still trying to control a body that no longer belonged to me.

Katie stood, squeezing my shoulder as she passed. My already tense muscles reacted in sharp protest against the intrusion, but she paused, then moved behind me to squeeze both shoulders.

My head rolled forward, as she pressed the muscles beneath her small fingers. "She'll come around," she promised again.

"You said that last night. I'm still not sure if I take comfort in that possibility." I jerked as she hit a particularly sore muscle.

"I've known you for years, hun. I was there for the pranks, when you stood up as Evan's best man at our wedding, when you and Trent made detective, when you were making rush preparations to go under cover. And I know the story behind that damn snake."

My eyes flickered to the tattoo. The black ink stretched around my arm, a coil of tribal markings. As kids, my sister and I spent a lot of time at our grandpa's house—for me that usually consisted of hiking through the woods. He had a fond appreciation for his slithering neighbors and taught us how to identify them—especially how to tell if one was poisonous. We found a few snake skins over the years, and he explained how a snake shed off its outer layer when it grew too big to fit inside. He also told us that if a snake couldn't shed for some reason, it'd be suffocated by its own dead skin.

I never really wanted to see if it was true. After losing my sister and then my parents, I got the tattoo as a reminder to keep going forward. That if I didn't let change happen, I too would suffocate in my own skin.

At the moment, that's exactly how I felt—itchy, irritable, and too big for my own skin.

Katie found another sore muscle and I grunted. My body was just as unhappy with the violent workout I'd imposed as it was with the alcohol.

"And if I thought you were capable of ever hurting her, I sure as hell wouldn't let you around my son."

"You don't know what I did, Kate."

She leaned around to see my face. "I don't need to. I do

know everything I need to know—and deep down, so do you."

With a pat to the back of my head, I heard her footsteps heading toward the front of the house. "Your phone is on the charger—you left it in the car last night—and your car is in the drive. Make sure you eat something."

"Thanks, mom."

My headache significantly lessened, I thought about checking out the classifieds for my own place, though I hesitated to admit, I wasn't sure what I'd do with myself in an empty apartment.

I'd been around so many people for so long, I thought I'd relish quiet solitude when I had it again, but it only made me stir-crazy—just like everything else.

I fixed a peanut butter and jelly sandwich—the only thing I had the patience for—before settling down in the living room and turning on the television.

By afternoon I had dozed off, sleeping off the remaining grog of the hangover. When the doorbell rang, I jumped off the couch, nearly crashing into the coffee table before I caught my balance.

"Fuck," I muttered. My fingers rubbed against my stubble-covered chin. It was no wonder Rose had kicked me out —though my unkempt appearance was probably the least of her worries.

Pushing aside the crème colored curtains that lined the window next to the door, I saw Trent standing on the porch, in full detective attire.

"Did I miss something?" I asked glancing at my quiet phone laying on the charging station.

"I figured this news I had better give in person."

My stomach twisted so hard I grabbed the doorframe.

Trent put his steadying hands on my shoulders. "Rose

really is absolutely fine. She went home this morning. We found Alley."

I reached for my phone and keys. She couldn't be in great shape after everything that happened with Rose, but I was determined to find out what on earth she'd been thinking.

"Easy, James. Captain Richards wants you to stand down for a few days."

"Stand down? Why? I'm perfectly capable—"

"And you need to let me finish. She was found this morning after she overdosed on heroin."

Heroin. The world slowed to an agonizingly slow pace again, creeping around me and stealing my thoughts like burglars in the middle of the night. "What—she didn't make it?"

"No, dead on arrival. They don't think there was ever a chance of resuscitating her."

Oh God, I leaned against the stair railing, searching for any smidgen of equilibrium. "I need to tell Miles."

"The feds will flip if he backs out of everything."

That was the least of my worries. "We can't just lie to him, Trent. I won't. I don't think he'll back out."

"If you're wrong—"

"Then you plead ignorance and I'll take the blame. Does Rose know yet?"

"No, I'm going over there to tell her next."

I turned to the door, just to keep from facing him. I didn't know what I was capable of—or even thinking at the moment. I wanted nothing more than to be there for her, but it was the last thing she wanted, obviously. "I'm going to talk to Miles."

Giving Trent no choice, I stepped out and waited for him to follow so I could lock up the house.

———

I SAT in the parking lot for nearly thirty minutes before I had the guts to even climb out and head up to the facility where Miles was being held. In between every two steps I considered turning back. Wished I had better news. Pleaded for an alternative or a mistake.

But I knew there wasn't a mistake. Rose was probably getting the news right now. My fingers pressed into my palms until even my short nails dug into skin. I had to wait another twenty minutes while I got checked in and they moved Miles to a room where we could talk.

Pacing through the hallway did nothing to calm my nerves—and it probably didn't ease the concerns of any of the guards or staff either, so I finally dropped into one of the plastic chairs.

"Detective Carter," a guard stepped around the corner and waved for me to follow. He opened the large door at the end of the hall, and I stepped inside.

"I was beginning to wonder if you'd forgotten," Miles said.

"No. I'm back to work, so we've been working on it all day, every day for the last week." I slid into the chair across from him, flattening my palms against the table. I couldn't even make eye contact—it was the first time I'd ever been in one of these rooms and not been able to face the person sitting across from me.

"You found her," Miles said. His voice was thick with the realization of what I was about to say.

"Friday night, she broke into Rose's house—"

Miles grunted and twisted in his seat, the sound of the metal legs against the concrete floor rang through the room.

"She shot Rose, through the shoulder—" I motioned to

my own arm since I didn't have the words to adequately describe anything. "Rose is going to be okay, but Alley was found this morning. She'd overdosed on heroin."

I finally lifted my eyes off the table to examine Miles expression since he wasn't talking and seemed to have frozen into a statue in his seat.

"Why?" He finally said after minutes of silence. "Why would she come after Rose?"

"Rose said she was upset... about losing you. She blamed me, took it out on Rose. I'd assume that Alley was already using, probably high when she—"

"Stop," Miles said, jerking back in his seat.

"I'm sorry."

He shook his head, picking at his fingernails, the chain around his wrist, and then pieces of his clothing before looking up again. "It's not your damn fault."

"I wanted to be the one to find her. I wanted her—"

"I know, *James*."

My own name sounded foreign coming out of his mouth and the way his name twisted after saying it told me he felt the same.

"You're a damn good actor," he said. "But not that good. I always knew you weren't like everyone else. I pulled you to the top, not because I wanted to see the place fall, but because I wanted more control over what the place became. And I knew you could make it happen. I was sick of seeing scum like Gabe get everything they wanted."

"Why work at a sex retreat at all?"

"Never told you that one, did I?" He eyed me for a moment, then looked away, turning so he sat sideways facing the brick wall beside us. "I was recruited by Milo— when I was eight and he killed my mom."

Eight. Miles was older than me by a few years, but that meant that he'd been with Milo for nearly thirty years.

"My mom was one of his first," Miles continued. "I saw this shit for as long as I can remember, but he never fully trusted me—and for good reason, I reckon. I was usually left with the slaves. There weren't exactly many people my age around. I was fourteen when he invited me to my first 'business dinner'."

He stared down at the shackle on his arm. "Always knew eventually I'd end up here. Figured this would be a fitting end—although it's slightly poetic that I'm sitting here talking to the enemy."

"I don't like being your enemy."

"Nah." He sat back, straightening his legs. "I don't much like it either, but at the moment, it is what it is. I'm a felon, you're a cop."

With his hand clasped over his mouth, he stared off—his eyes distant and glassy. "Didn't think I was genuinely capable of caring for someone until Alley. Considering everything I continued to put her through, I'm still not sure."

My chest buzzed as if I'd inhaled a swarm of bees.

Miles turned back to me. "When you see your girl, take her some chocolate," he said, with a glint in his eye. He'd been the one to bring her chocolate cake after Gabe attacked her. He said that Alley informed him that it fixed everything—but it didn't and it certainly couldn't fix this.

"She told me to stay away."

"I'm sure she did." He shook his head, twisting to face me again. "Do you love her?"

"We don't even know each other."

"That's not true—you know each other better than anyone can. Most people see the good, the façade people want them to see. But you've seen each other at your worst. Stripped of ego, in a place where nearly anything goes." He leaned over the table, clasping his hands together. "When did she find out who you really are?"

"Gabe," I whispered, "Gabe figured it out—told her when they attacked her."

Miles stiffened, searching my eyes until his own widened in understanding. "She killed for you."

The realization I didn't want to hear aloud from someone else's mouth. I picked at a fraying patch on the leg of my jeans. "She killed for us. She did what I couldn't."

"Promise to buy her some chocolate, and our deal is still on. It's still for Alley," he clarified after a moment. "I'll testify that it was Milo, give you all of the informa- tion you want—although, now that I'm locked up here, I don't have much on current affairs. Not that I'm complaining—the food here is a smidge better," he winked.

"Guess I can keep my job, then."

Miles snorted. "Once again they don't know you're here. Do you ever do anything you're told?"

I scratched the back of my head. "Often as I stay in trouble, I'd say no."

From my car, I reported the conversation back to Trent —who also informed me that Richards was serious about me taking time off and if I showed my face at the station before my three days were up, he'd suspend me rather than forcing me to take even more time off with pay.

———

I LAID IN BED, unable to sleep. After ruling out another night of heavy drinking—I did have a couple of beers with

Evan, but long after everyone went to sleep, I was still trying to work everything out.

I wanted a solid answer—why Alley had gone after Rose, how she'd known where to find her, and who the hell was supplying her with heroin.

Ticking off each question and possible turn in the investigation, I kept myself up well past midnight, until my phone jerked me out of my mental prison and into tense reality.

It wasn't a number I had programmed into my phone.

"Hello." I may have been awake, but it was the middle of the night and my body felt like sludge.

A strangled sob came through the phone and I bolted upright. "Hello? Are you okay?"

"No." The voice was female, quivering, light, and stripped raw. I would have known it anywhere, and I wasn't sure if it was a positive sign that I'd immediately know her voice in its worst state.

My chest pulsed until the twinging sensation filled my body, pushing out all of the rational and methodical thought I'd held onto earlier. "Rose?"

"I'm sorry." I heard her choke back her cries.

I turned on the bedside light and stared at it until the burn in my eyes faded. "What can I do for you?" I didn't know what to say. What she wanted. What the hell the middle of the night call was supposed to mean. And I was afraid to read too much into it.

"Talk…. Say anything… Just… She's dead."

Rustled sounds filled the phone as I leaned forward against my knees. "I know," I whispered. "Take a breath, Rose."

Her audible gasps slowed, but only slightly. "I'm sorry for what I said to you."

"I get it. You needed to speak your mind. I'm glad you did and I'm glad you called."

Aside from her sniffles and muffled sobs, the phone went quiet. My chest ached with how bad I wanted to be with her. The need to erase the tears, take away the bad emotions. I'd arranged for her meeting with Alley.

Alley could win nearly anyone over, and I figured if anyone could help Rose find a way to make it through, Alley could do it. She wasn't like the other girls—not conniving, she was obedient to Miles, but not broken either. Miles had seen to that.

Whether we wanted it or not, those days were permanently etched within us. The heartbreak continued long after we saw our last days within the walls of the Retreat. Dr. Combs was right—healing wasn't so much about cutting it off and letting it die. We could do that, but the phantom of it would always be there.

We had another option—more difficult and possibly more haunting—to rectify the jumbled messes inside of us. To work with what we had, and try to find a way to build something positive out of it.

"Are you okay?" I asked. I knew her answer, but it was the only thing I could think of to say to get her talking again.

"No," she said without pause or explanation.

"Will you be okay long enough for me to get dressed and drive there?" It was a long shot, but I threw it all out there, giving her the opportunity to shoot me down and tell me where to shove my need for her. I waited for it.

"I—"

My chest seized. Seconds drew out until I felt like I couldn't breathe.

"I can be."

The vice grip around my chest loosened and I nearly fell back on the bed in relief.

Within fifteen minutes, her house was in sight. I took a breath, steadying myself, my nerves were far worse than they'd ever been on any first date—or even a stakeout. I considered sitting in my car to give myself a moment to catch the thoughts weaving in an endless race through my mind.

I noticed movement in the dark house, and by the time I climbed out of the car and made it to the porch, she had the front door open. Her eyes were puffy, bloodshot and circled in pink—like a miscolored raccoon costume gone terribly wrong. She hugged her right arm against herself, her eyes jumped, darting past me, and taking in the dark street.

"Easy, honey," I whispered, pressing my palms against her cheeks. Her gaze fell on me, and in a single breath, she went from a tiny frightened animal back to the green-eyed wonder woman I'd stared down so many times. I kissed her forehead and we moved inside, locking ourselves away from the world.

I glanced around the small house and pressed her toward the living room couch. Innocuous enough, but still plenty of room for us both to get comfortable—and to demand our own space if necessary. I took a seat and she sat against me, her back to my chest, head tucked under my chin, and my arms locked around her waist.

Over time, her muscles relaxed and her breathing slowed. I thought for a moment that she'd fallen asleep until she wiggled her fingers and readjusted her injured arm.

"I do have a question," I whispered. "How'd you get my number?"

"Um…" Her hand tightened into a fist then she splayed her fingers against my arm.

"Trent?" I asked.

She nodded. "When he came to tell me about—"

A series of thuds sounded from the hall, and I prepared to jump up until I saw a grey tabby cat stretching in the foyer before continuing on down the hallway.

A cat, I thought, mentally laughing at the irony.

"There's my little hobo," Rose mumbled. "I've been—I wanted to pretend that none of that was me. It was all Silver, and she's gone now."

She broke my grasp and turned to face me. "I was pissed at you for disappearing, but if I cut off Silver and let her die, then nothing exists between you and me."

I pushed back her hair, letting my fingers glide through the soft strands. Her hair smelled so much different now— *she* smelled different. And hell if it wasn't even more intoxicating than the alcohol I'd downed at the bar.

Listening to the words come out of her mouth, I knew it was the same problem I'd been bashing my head against every day. It had begun long before the bullet tore through my side. I knew one day I'd have to face letting her walk away if Silver and Kirk were no longer meant to be. "It's impossible to make it so black and white. You survived. We survived together. And as much as I'd like to erase some things. It'll always be part of us. We both have a lot of work to do. We can't exactly pick up where we left off and we can't just forget what happened."

"What happened to shedding it all away or smothering?" she asked. I'd explained the snake to her as well, the day we'd spent on the grounds, near the lake, away from everyone else.

Maybe the problem was that we were trying to shed too

much—trying to shed the wrong things. It was impossible—seemed impossible to think that any good could have come out of that situation.

I didn't want to be thankful that she'd landed in that situation. "It takes time." I tucked her back against my chest —not wanting to ever let her go again. "And work. And maybe something to work toward."

"Together?" Her question a quiet, whispered breath that brushed against my chest.

"You sure you want to try that?" I asked, praying for a yes.

"Yes. But I don't want you to do it for me."

"Good." Together... we agreed, but what had I gotten myself into? She was going to turn me into a ruined man—even if it were for the best. And even if I enjoyed every moment of it. "But, maybe we should work on becoming friends first."

She grunted and wriggled to look up at me. "I assume that means no sex," she sighed, the traces of a pout drawing down her features. "Anything else?"

Anything else? Didn't she know she was already fucking me in every other way possible? I couldn't look at her eyes, so I drew my gaze away from her face, drawing my fingers through her hair again. "We stop apologizing about anything that happened and trying to act like it didn't happen."

"Easier said than done. You might have to remind me a time or two, but I can handle that."

I laughed, and the vibrations moved through my chest, reorganizing every nerve and muscle until they fell back into place—finally right where they were supposed to be. Even my mind finally stopped racing. "If I only have to remind you a time or two, I'll be worried."

She twisted around, returning my smile for several long seconds, and I drank in every moment of it. "Does no sex include sleeping in the same bed?"

"If you want me to stay, I'll sleep down here. We're both tired, and even I can only resist so much." I kissed her neck, inhaling her scent.

"Yeah, do that again, and I'll make it much harder."

"Go to bed, Rose. You're exhausted and so am I. We'll talk more—" I had no idea what time it was, but I glanced toward the window already lightened by the breaking dawn. It was a good thing I was forbidden from coming into work. "We'll talk more this afternoon."

Chapter Eleven

FIGHTING STUBBORN WITH STUBBORN

"STOP," Rose choked out, as her face reddened. The *result of my hand locked around her throat holding her down in the bed.*

I wanted to stop, begged my body for control, but all I could do was stare down into her green eyes as she gasped and clawed at my arm.

A knock jerked me out of the nightmare and it took me a moment to recognize the room. I was getting tired of being woken up in such a manner, but I'd take it any day over waking up at the Retreat again. That happened enough in my dreams.

I peeked through the living room window, overlooking the porch, and the family resemblance of the girl standing outside the door was unmistakable. She held a baby carrier in her right hand and had a slightly more curvy build than Rose—which made sense given the young child. She also had the same facial structure and similar, but shorter hair.

Rose's hurried footsteps moved down the stairs as the knock sounded again. When I heard the front door open, I stepped into the opening that led from the living room to the foyer and received a long and assessing stare from Rose's sister.

"Is that your protective detail?" she asked.

Rose's cheeks were pink when she turned to look at me. "Chey, this is K—"

At least I wasn't the only one screwing that up.

"—James. James, my sister Chey and her daughter Laney."

"Nice to meet you," I said, as the girls descended into what was unmistakably a quiet sibling teasing session. I leaned against the wall as they chided each other with hushed voices. Apparently, all had worked out between them, just as I'd predicted.

Watching them together reminded me of my own sister —even when she was sick we could have rivalries that would shake the walls. We pestered each other into fights for the hell of it. Time never made that loss easier.

I left the girls to their chatter so I could slip on my T-shirt and shoes. Rose and I had plenty to discuss, but I was sure she also wanted family time. And at the moment, the two didn't mix.

"You don't have to leave," Rose said, catching me in the doorway while her sister settled on the couch with the baby.

"You should spend time with your family, we can talk anytime," I leaned in for a kiss but she pressed her lips into a line and drew back.

"At least stay for lunch."

Lunch, I laughed, imagining that could only consist of delivery or burned frozen pizzas. "You cooking?"

She crossed her arms and smirked. "I've gotten damn good at spaghetti."

"Uh huh. Without burning it?"

Chey gasped. "So, this totally wasn't a one-night stand!" she said with a giddy smile.

Rose's face, on the other hand, went slack and bright red as she tried to cover it with her hand. "You've got to be kidding me."

"Come on," her sister laughed. "Just kidding. I'll be good."

She might be good, but I wasn't going for it. I still enjoyed that shocked expression and the red tints of blush that touched Rose's forehead and cheeks. And I intended to get as much out of it as possible while I had the opportunity.

I grabbed her hips, pulling her against me before she could object. Her eyes widened even more as her hand dropped to my shoulder, and our lips met.

I may have sworn off having sex with her, but I wasn't a total masochist. "How about I go pick up something to eat. You two can do the sister thing, and then we'll all have lunch."

She nodded, but her lips scrunched, in what I assumed to be feigned disapproval since she hadn't seemed to mind the kiss. Not waiting for a response, I headed for the front door, with Rose following behind. As soon as we were out of Chey's sight, she smacked me in the arm.

"You're violent today," I whispered. "Are you sure you want me here? Or is there a reason—"

"I want to spend time with you. We're supposed to be moving on, right? I just...." Her eyes flickered as she lost her way in the sea of thoughts.

I reached for her jawline, pulling her back to me and tracing my thumb gently over her lips. "I'll be back."

On the way out to the car, I checked my phone and was shocked that I didn't have half a dozen missed messages since I'd snuck out of Evan's house in the middle of the night. Guess I skipped that natural step in growing up as a teenager, so why not tackle it now?

I hadn't stuck around long enough to ask what anyone wanted so I headed over to the dairy bar that Katie managed to pick up some basics—hamburgers, fries, and shakes sounded like a damn good decision to me.

Katie's gaze fell on me as soon as I stepped out of my car, and she waved me over to the side window. "I was hoping you'd turn up."

"I had an emergency." I leaned against the tiny counter that jutted out from the window. "You *might* have been right."

She smirked and wiggled her eyebrows.

"You don't need to give me that look."

"Um, yes. Yes, I totally need to give you that look." Her taunting face turned into a gentle and hesitant smile. "Is she okay?"

I nodded, not really committed to the answer. "We're working on it."

"That's a start," she plopped an order pad on the counter. "What can I get you?"

Sometimes, I imagined what my sister would have been like now, and usually that image ended up a lot like Katie—minus the blonde hair. The two of them probably would have gotten along pretty well, and made a team at torturing me.

"A trio of burgers, fries, and shakes?" I said.

"There something I don't know about your girlfriend?"

I leaned toward the window as if I had a secret and whispered, "Her sister is with her."

But my little trick didn't diminish her enthusiasm at all. "Oooh, meeting the family."

I groaned and scraped the bottom of my shoe against the brick wall under the window. "Can I just get the food, please?"

"What flavor would you like the shakes?"

I thought of Miles. "Chocolate."

Chocolate fixes everything.

"Of course. Give me ten."

I took a seat at one of the picnic tables and watched the group of kids playing putt-putt while I waited. One of the mothers—probably barely older than me—glared at my uncovered tattoos, but when I smiled and tipped my head, she promptly spun around.

"Come on, trouble," Katie called, sitting the bag of food and drink carrier on the counter. "Food for your lucky girl."

I flipped a twenty and a ten on the counter and grabbed my order. "Thanks, Kate."

———

WE ALL SAT around Rose's small kitchen table to eat, with Laney taking up most of the table space, cooing and waving while we chowed down.

As we were clearing up, Chey excused herself to the bathroom—much to Rose's shock and dismay at being left alone with the baby.

And I thought I was bad.

The worry wasn't entirely unwarranted, however, because as soon as Mommy was out of sight, baby started to fuss.

"Know anything about babies?" Rose asked, looking at the kid like she'd just turned magenta and sprouted a second head.

I grunted, trying to hold back a laugh. "They like being held."

"I'll get right on that." She pointed to her shoulder.

I had to give her that one, even though it that put an end to my fun. I shook my head and lifted Laney out of the carrier, snuggling the little bundle of unpredictability against my shoulder. She whined a bit, and I suspected wiped her nose on my shirt, but I managed to fish the pacifier out of the carrier and popped it into her mouth.

We once again had a quiet baby.

"Show off," Rose said, with an attractive growl to her voice. Flustered was also a good look for her.

When Chey popped back in, she laughed and rescued the poor kid from my grasp. "You really did pass her off to him."

"Bullet hole in the arm, people. What the heck am I going to do?"

"Excuses." With a roll of her eyes, Chey loaded Laney back into the carrier and strapped her in, giving her sides a tickle before she put up the handle. "I better get going. Don't forget you promised to go dress shopping with me."

I zoned out, clearing the rest of the table as the sisters said their goodbyes and waiting for the moment when Chey and the baby were out of sight. I drew Rose against me, finally indulging in the touch I'd been craving all morning. She latched her uninjured arm around my neck, staring up at me with her wide green eyes.

"I told you everything would be fine with you two," I said, but the moment clouded and nearly disappeared just as quickly, as I glanced toward the door as the nightmare crept back into my conscience. "I should get going too."

My fingers brushed through her hair, but all I could see was the image from the dream of holding her down, my hands wrapped around her neck. I wasn't sure where the exact images came from—but it made my fear of hurting her even more of a harsh reality. Maybe it hadn't actually happened, but I still felt in my gut like it had.

"How are you?" she asked.

"I'm here. And I'm alive, thanks to you, but...." My insides had shifted until I didn't feel like my skin fit again. "Are you really sure you want me around, after everything I did to you?"

"Yes, James. I already forgave you."

"How?" I squinted at her. I'd taken everything—her dignity, trust, hatred, fear, hope.... "Every time I get close...."

She pressed against me, laying her cheek against my chest. "It wasn't so hard actually. You told me that my only choice was to give up control or die, but it applied to you, too. And unless you played your part, we both died. Once I started seeing the real you, the emotion and regret you tried to hide, I didn't have it in me to hate you for something you obviously hated, too."

"You're a strong woman, Sugar."

Her lips curled up when I used the name again. I didn't completely understand it—my own desire to continue using it, or her encouraging reaction every time.

"Stronger than I was a few months ago. It still hurts, every day it still hurts, and after the last two days... I just want something good to hold onto."

I stretched my hands against her back, wanting contact with as much of her as possible. "It's going to take a lot of work."

"We've already escaped hell, I don't think 'work' is going to stop us," she said, reaching up to kiss me.

I wanted to get lost in that moment. To believe in those

words, and forgive myself, but no matter what she said, I didn't believe that task could be so easy.

When she backed away, I smiled—forced and unnatural, it was the only thing I had. "What was this 'dress shopping' you and your sister were talking about."

Her shoulders drooped. There was no way to hide that I was pushing the subject away from me—away from anything she wanted to talk about.

"She and Peter are getting married in four months. She asked me to be in the wedding."

Peter—I remembered from one of our awkward, pain-induced chats that Peter was somehow the epicenter of Rose's fight with her sister. "And you're okay with that?"

She squinted, pulling her injured arm tighter against her chest and rubbing the muscle beneath the injury. "I'm not fond of glamming up in fancy dresses, but I guess this'll be an exception. Hopefully, I don't have to wear a sleeveless though."

"You'll be all healed up by then." I couldn't tell if she, too was playing the avoidance game, so the next time I didn't give her an out. "Wasn't Peter the reason you two were fighting?"

"Sort of—it's a bit more complicated than that—not just that I had a crush...," she grimaced again, closing her eyes. "I had a crush and yet she was the one to get him, and sometimes she treated him like crap. Like she didn't want to settle down, didn't want to grow up."

I watched her wince, pain written on every movement, even though she tried to pass it off. "You have pain medicine?"

"Been taking Tylenol, but I swear it's getting worse." She dropped into a chair, looking like she was about to do more than double over.

"The swelling should be going down, and you'll regain sensitivity. They didn't give you anything stronger than Tylenol—something that would help with the swelling, too."

She peeked up at me without raising her head. "I didn't get the prescription. I don't like—"

"I know, sweetie." I beyond knew, I understood exactly how she felt, but I couldn't sit around and watch her in pain. "I can go pick up your prescription."

She shot to her feet, wincing again. "No."

"Then, where do you keep the Tylenol?" I sighed. I was helpless to argue, and it had to be better than nothing.

"Left it upstairs." She choked, stumbling back toward the counter, still cradling her arm.

"Sweetie," I lifted her face. Seeing her cry, even if not by my doing, was devastating to the slice of sanity I'd managed to preserve through the night. "I think you're going to need something a little stronger while it's healing."

"I can manage—it's usually just a dull roar." Her voice held the edge of a growl as pain and anger clashed within her.

"Until you move. Your body is trying to heal, and it's going to be rough for a while." I was amazed she lasted the last two days without anything stronger—but not entirely surprised given all that I'd seen her survive. I had refused meds when I got home, too, but I'd still had them for a week in the hospital.

"I know." She sighed, lacing her fingers through mine. "I don't want you to leave, yet. I just got you back."

I kissed her forehead, in misery because I couldn't draw away the pain—emotional as well as physical.

Some of it, I'd caused myself. I feared I'd never escape the onslaught of "what ifs" that dragged me backward, never letting me free, like a pool of quicksand. Every step, took me deeper, with new worries that neither of us could ever recover.

What if I'd gotten her out sooner?

What if I'd told her the truth earlier?

What if I hadn't left her alone for the past five weeks?

"I'll call Trent and have him pick it up. Where's your script?"

"Trent made me drop it off. I just never went back to pick it up."

She wasn't so different from the girl I'd gotten to know through all of the insults and debauchery. "Stubborn as ever."

"Look who's talking. You could just take my mind off—" she dropped her head and turned away.

Sex.

Had I done that to her?

"Rose, I—"

"No, you don't have to. I don't need you to explain. I get the whole no sex thing. We used it as a distraction and it's probably not a brilliant way to…. What are we trying to do, exactly?"

"Let James and Rose get to know each other." *And ourselves.* I still needed to figure out myself.

"If I agree to take the meds and go insane, do you promise not to leave me? Even if I don't go insane, I don't like the groggy feeling it gives me," her voice started to shake as tears filled her eyes.

"Of course." I caressed her cheek lightly with my thumb and she leaned into my touch, closing her eyes. Simply watching her was enough to rile my body down to every nerve ending. I brushed my lips against hers, inhaling the sweet minty smell of her hair.

She nodded. "Deal."

"Go try to get comfortable, I'll have him pick it up." I made the call to Trent and settled with Rose in the living room. She laid across the couch, with her head in my lap staring up at me. I rubbed her forehead, although I was hesitant to believe it, it seemed like my touch at least soothed her superficial discomfort.

"Have you talked to Miles?" she asked.

"Yesterday afternoon, right after Trent came to see me."

"Is he okay?"

"About as okay as he can be, I guess. He's being held in a separate facility, usually under strict watch, but it's the only way to keep him away from anyone who might find out he's cooperating. It's not the greatest solution, but he says the food is better. Once we confirm everything and make sure the Retreat is truly out of business, he's going to get a reduced sentence." I closed my eyes and leaned my head back. "I'd like to get him put in a different facility, where he can get more help rather than being locked in a room alone all day, but hopefully that'll come with his deal. I was supposed to find Alley. She's been missing for weeks."

"Trent never said anything," she whispered, squeezing my wrist so I'd resume rubbing her forehead. "I—I should have—"

"Don't, Sugar," I understood as much as anyone what the "should haves" could do. How they could drive someone insane in their relentless pursuit to cause agony. "You did what you had to do."

"I should have been there for her. She was—she was...."

I wiped away the tears as they burst past her eyelids, and she took a deep breath and stilled.

"Has Trent been the only one looking in on you?" I figured her family and friends might have been in as well until I saw her reaction to her sister.

"Um—pretty much. I, uh, have psychiatric appointments twice a week, but I usually keep to myself. Charlene is back in Oklahoma staying with her folks. Yesterday was the first time I've had a prolonged conversation with my sister. They tried to check on me, but I never know what to tell them."

She moaned, and I felt her body tense, becoming almost as rigid as a steel frame.

"He'll be here soon." Or so I hoped. He said it'd take only a few minutes, but he lived at least that far away—not counting the stop at the pharmacy along the way.

Rose closed her eyes, so I didn't push her with any more questions. I trailed my fingers through her soft dark hair and traced the skin along her jawline and neck.

With another moan—a very different kind of moan, she opened her eyes again. They glittered with need—hard desire softened by her slack muscles. I considered giving her that distraction. Giving in to the tight line of attraction drawn between us.

But, thankfully, a knock on the door sent those desires back into hiding.

Rose groaned and grabbed ahold of the back of the couch to pull herself up, so I could answer it.

When I opened the door, Trent held up the bag. Something between a smirk and an inquisitive expression drew his features taut. "You two were made for each other. Could either of you be more stubborn?"

The cat sped down the stairs, trying to sneak by us and out the door, but Trent caught her first.

"Hey," Rose said, peeking around the corner. She pressed her cheek against the wall frame. "She's probably hungry. I'll open her some food."

"Take your meds," Trent said before I had a chance.

Then, he patted my shoulder, "Take care of her, and I'll feed Trapper."

I raised my brow. He even knew where the cat food was. I didn't know that—not that I'd even been around for twenty-four hours, but it still pissed me off. It had been a long time since I'd wanted to punch my best friend— even though I admitted that it was far from called for simply because he had done as I asked and kept an eye on Rose.

However, it also reminded me that the last time I wanted to hit him was also about a girl.

Trent released the cat, and as Rose returned to the couch, he whispered, "I'm not the enemy."

"Wha—"

"Saw the look you were giving me." He flagged me toward the living room. "Go tend to your girlfriend."

I opened the pill bottle and fished out one of the white oblong tablets.

"Can I just have half?" Rose asked when I held it out.

"Does your shoulder only half hurt?" I handed her a full pill. I weighed knowing how much she didn't like pain medicine with her reaction to the pain over the last twenty minutes and making sure she wasn't grimacing in pain every few minutes, the full dose won out.

"Is Trent staying, too?"

I shrugged. "Want him to?"

"Didn't know if you'd want company after I passed out and started drooling on you."

I returned to my seat, rubbing her shoulders and back before she curled up, using my lap for a pillow again. Trent took a seat in the armchair across from us.

"Stopped by the dairy bar for lunch, and Katie mentioned you left in the middle of the night."

I scowled at him, feeling Rose jerk and her gaze burn through me.

"She's my cousin's wife," I said to her, giving Trent a blatant glower, but he only shook his head. "I've been staying with them. Though I guess it's about damn time I find an apartment before everyone blabs to half the town my every move."

Trapper jumped up on Rose's chest and I tossed her back to the floor, but she only turned around and tried for a second attempt. I blocked her jump and she sat at my feet for a moment, flicking her tail at me. Her cranky expression reminds me of Rose the first night at the Outlook. Even though she knelt quietly at my feet and managed not to anger Ross too much, she never lost the glare in her eye.

Perturbed by the situation, Trapper finally turned away and opted for Trent's lap instead.

"I thought your post-retreat plans included becoming a cat person," Rose whispered.

I scowled—in truth, cats were worse than kids. I'd only brought it up to lighten the situation. "Still not fond of fur."

Rose laced her fingers through mine. She was obviously fighting to keep her eyes open and within the next ten minutes, she'd succumbed to quiet sleep.

"I need to head to the station in an hour," Trent said. It seemed he was waiting until Rose fell asleep to talk. "Alley's family is coming into town tonight. I'd like to be there and make sure everything's under control."

"I'd assume I'm still banned from the station?"

"You," Trent waved toward Rose's sleeping form, "have enough to take care of right now. How the hell has she made it this long without her prescription?"

"Obstinance and Tylenol." I'd come to appreciate just how much she could accomplish with sheer will alone. I was living proof of it. Having seen her in action, part of me wondered what I was so worried about. Rose wouldn't take shit, not even from me. She'd be first in line to set me straight if, under some crazy circumstances, my nightmares became reality.

Except I didn't believe it would require crazy circumstances for it to happen. Too much of my subconscious still longed for the pain and clung to the darkness. I wanted her, but not just her body. I wanted everything—needed to see her on her knees. The control, the power, the look in her eyes as she reluctantly gives me what I want and I reward her for her generosity tenfold.

Reward.

What kind of sick twisted reward involved forcing the girl I cared about on her knees—holding her down and making her purposefully uncomfortable to suit my own twisted fantasies.

Trent snapped his fingers. "You've left earth again. Maybe I should leave."

I shook my head.

"Didn't you practically spend the night here? And you still don't trust yourself with her?"

"Why would you think that?"

"Because I was on the other end of the line during every report. I know all the things you had to do. I've seen you nearly every day for the last month, when you've longed after her and teetered on the brink, barely able to stay away from her. And, I've known you for years." He dropped Trapper onto the floor and dusted the fur from his pants. "She's in good hands, and I do need to get going anyway. I should go home and change."

He was dressed down, not his usual getup—even for a day off. And since he wanted to give me a hard time about everything, it was only fair to return the favor. "Should I ask where you were when I called?"

He grinned and scratched the back of his head. "No. But it wouldn't be news."

I'd figured as much considering the voice I'd heard in the background when I called and his prompt arrival despite living on the opposite side of town. "Didn't mean to interrupt."

"You didn't. Just put a new air filter on her car."

"That what you're calling it now?"

He snorted. "No. Unfortunately, that's really what I was doing."

"Why don't you two just make it official, you've been on and off for years?"

"The key to that is the 'and off' portion. And it's all past tense now, she's seeing someone." He picked another piece of fur off his pants and dropped it to the floor. "We've been off for months—nearly since you went under."

"My head feels funny," Rose murmured. She didn't open her eyes but squeezed my hand.

At the sound of her voice, I immediately forgot about razzing Trent. "Funny how?"

"Drunky funny."

"Sleep, sweetie," I whispered, brushing her hair away from her face until it laid out in a shiny layer across my leg. I kept my eyes on her as Trent stood, still utterly amazed to have her back.

"Be good," he whispered as he passed and let himself out.

"Did his girlfriend dump him?" she asked after the door closed.

"You've been eavesdropping again." But for the time

being, she was safe—and I hoped, no longer in so much pain.

"Not sure." She yawned, arching her back as she stretched. "It's kinda hard to tell if I'm awake or asleep."

"She wasn't really his girlfriend, more like...." I wasn't sure how to put it nicely.

"Fuck buddy?"

I nearly choked trying to keep myself from laughing. "Something like that."

"He needs a girlfriend. He's a nice guy."

"Don't tell him that." *And don't get any ideas.* I didn't need any fodder to add to my unwarranted suspicions.

"Why?" Her eyes drifted closed again, even though she was clearly fighting it.

"I—" My throat closed. I didn't want to have that conversation. "He doesn't take it well. Had a girl he loved once and it didn't...."

"She break his heart?"

"She broke a lot of people's hearts." Mine. Trent's. My entire family's.

Rose's eyes popped open and she shot upright, all traces of sleep suddenly gone. "He dated your sister? But—"

I pulled her back, lifting her so she sat in my lap, her head tucked against my shoulder. I wasn't sure how she figured it out so easily or if it was just a fluke of a guess. "They started dating in junior high school—even though I wasn't allowed to date in junior high, she managed to get her way fairly often. Even I tended to give her what she wanted—when we weren't too involved in sibling rivalries. She grew up fast anyway. When she was in seventh grade, he took her to the junior high school dance, and they continued dating for the next two years. He was with us every time she was admitted to the hospital."

He was with her until she died....

"You were friends back then?"

"Been friends since Kindergarten. He had a single mom, so my parents told her to drop him off any time she had to work. We were all close, but it was a surprise when he asked her out," I shrugged. I'd wrestled with their relationship a few dozen times. Trent had nearly a year and a half on my sister, and their relationship also meant that she usually ended up crashing our weekend plans, but I generally acted more upset than I really was, just to give her a hard time.

Usually being the operative word. There were also the times I wanted to blacken his eye over it.

Couldn't make everything too easy for her, and she'd have done the same to me.

"Is that why you don't want kids?" Her eyes widened. "You can totally tell me to shut up at any moment. I think I get verbal diarrhea when I have no brain power to stop it."

"You definitely do, Sugar." I kissed the top of her head, nestling her into my arms until I was content that she was secure from going anywhere. "There are a lot of reasons, but that's a big one."

I considered telling her the rest, but that was suited for a conversation when she was coherent and not fighting a losing battle against her exhausted body.

Chapter Twelve

A RAINI END

I CARRIED Rose upstairs to her bedroom, tucked her into bed, and stretched out next to her. It was still early in the evening and daylight outside, but she had light-blocking curtains over the bedroom windows. Either she was having trouble sleeping or worried about people seeing in—a mix of both was my guess.

With every slow breath, her face remained calm—not twisted by nightmares and memories. Quite the blessing after the strain of the last two months. I trailed my fingers through her hair, taking full advantage of the quiet peace.

My momentary respite from everything.

The unease remained on a slow boil, but it had tucked itself into a back corner of my mind. From the moment she'd shown up at the Retreat, she'd tested everything about me—my commitment to the job, sanity, strength, will....

There were times I hated her for it. Times I couldn't see straight because of what she'd done to me—because of the reality she'd forced me to confront.

But, she also gave me something to fight for after I'd

begun to go numb. She made me feel again, reconnect with everything that was happening to the girls in the Retreat. She made me reconnect with my own horrors that I'd faced every day for months until the façade became a twisted mix of reality, fantasy, and nightmare.

I lost control around her and I sometimes fucking enjoyed it.

I picked up her hand and intertwined my fingers with hers, vowing to take care of her this time around.

A call from Trent shattered the silence. Rose moaned and curled on her side toward me, fisting my shirt so I couldn't move away to answer.

"Hello," I whispered.

"How's Rose?" he asked with an even tone. If he'd called about something else, he wasn't in a hurry to get to it.

"Trying to sleep. You're not helping."

Rose opened her eyes and shook her head in a silent admonishment.

"Alley's parents IDed the body," Trent said. "They're making funeral arrangements."

"That's—," I'd heard similar reports dozens of times, but they weren't in reference to someone I knew. "Okay."

"Not the news you wanted tonight, I know, but I thought you should know. We also have another girl in here from the Retreat."

"What was she picked up for?" I twisted Rose's hair around my fingers, trying to concentrate on the conversation while staying as far from it as possible.

"She wasn't. She was asked to come in because she knows another girl who was recently recruited for the escort company—the girl has been missing for forty-eight hours. I can't believe we haven't made a list of all the aliases yet—

makes it a little difficult when we each know them by different names."

"What's she look like?" I didn't want to remember or picture their faces as I tried to place an identity.

"Dark brown eyes, about five foot three, long curly black hair. Can't weigh more than my right leg."

"Sounds like Raini."

Rose opened her eyes again and squirmed to sit up, but I kept my arm across her middle, earning a steely glare from a girl much too tired to fight. As far as I knew, she'd only encountered Raini in passing—if that.

"Can you come in?" Trent asked. "It's a nuthouse here right now, and I could use some help."

"Richards told me to steer clear or get fired, and let's be honest, I'm enjoying my night off."

"Unofficially then, I won't take up much of your time, but I need to pick your brain."

I leaned my head back and groaned, wincing when a finger dug into my side.

"Go," Rose whispered. "If you need to, I'll be fine."

"Give me about fifteen," I said and hung up the phone. "Are you sure?" I asked.

"Yeah, I'm in my happy place." Her smile was faint, softened by exhaustion. She didn't look like she'd manage to stay awake much longer, but I didn't like leaving her to the mercy of sleep. Unavoidable as it was, sleep made for a fickle and sometimes sadistic bedfellow.

"I promised not to leave you alone."

"Make it up by bringing dinner. And tell Trent if he keeps you too long, I'm coming for him."

"I'm sure he'll be shaking in his dress shoes." I kissed her forehead, drawing her toward me for one final moment before I had to tear myself away.

THE BACK of the station was a madhouse of cops and cruisers, so to avoid whatever drama was going on, I parked in front and took the long way around to our offices. Even the inside was an insane rush of people. Captain Richards was busy with a couple of uniforms and Trent was nowhere in sight. I watched the movement in the room, quite literally organized chaos—nothing seemed out of hand, but voices were raised, and there were far too many people cramped into the space and moving between our offices and the adjoining hallway.

"Kirk?" I heard a woman's voice beside me. She'd snuck up while I was watching a pair of officers lead a man into one of the rooms.

Fuck.

I steeled my features before I turned my head. I drew my gaze from the top of her head where her long black hair was twisted up in a messy bun except for the long bangs that fell over her face, and down to her sneaker-clad feet. She was dressed in casual street clothes—nothing like I'd ever seen her in before—loose fitting jeans and a black tank top, that hung from her small frame. I lifted my eyes back to her face before speaking. "Raini."

"I—no one has—" her bangs fell, shielding her face from my view.

I glanced around the room, searching for Trent.

Raini kept her head lowered just enough to avoid my direct gaze. "So, the rumors were true—about you being the narc."

"What makes you say that?" I asked, praying that no one walked over and identified me as a cop. Or maybe that would have been better since I hated putting on the façade again, but I had no idea who she was in contact with.

Although it obviously wasn't the group who thought I was dead.

"Nothing," she backed away, head down, but still looking in my direction. "Sorry, Sir."

Sir. I felt like someone had kicked me in the balls. She'd been free from the control of Ross and the Retreat for over a month. I wasn't sure if it was simply that they were still too broken to heal in that time, or if it was merely my presence that sent her reeling.

"What are you doing here?" I asked.

"Got dragged in. I um—I...."

"Kirk," Trent said the name so loudly, I almost plowed through the wall. "I told you to wait—" he grabbed my arm and jerked me into one of the empty interview rooms slamming the door behind him.

"She snuck up on me," I whispered.

Trent threw the file on the table and loosened his tie. "She said someone from the escort service approached her, but the friend she was having lunch with was interested and took the job a week ago, then disappeared two nights ago."

It sounded like he had it all under control. "What do you need me for?"

"You're my partner. You know—the guy who gives me information and bounces ideas with me."

"Didn't know you missed me so much." I peeked through a break in the blinds toward the room where I'd run into Raini.

About three months after I'd gone under, Milo had transferred her to our retreat. She was little more than skin and bone, but her frail condition didn't stop Ross from putting her through the ringer. I didn't think she'd make it through the first week so Miles and I conspired to get her away from Ross for a few days, and he finally lost interest.

The man was like a squirrel, collecting so many nuts he eventually forgot where most of them were buried. His idyllic life of riches and excess ended up squandered more often than he realized.

Trent stepped up beside me. "This whole thing is already turning into a shit storm. There's talk going around about none of the girls that we freed being taken care of. They say they're being forced back into the same way of life because they don't have options. Today, Richards decided to crack down on all of the known prostitutes and pimps in response to everything—I didn't get pulled in until Raini came in."

"Politics," I mumbled. Sex slaves or not, they were used to being provided with food, clothing, and all living arrangements. Now they were being expected to provide all such amenities for themselves. They had options now and they had made their choices—opting for what they knew, rather than working dead end jobs and barely making ends meet.

This was a world they knew little about, except how to use their bodies to get what they wanted.

"It's not like I can get too involved, she still believes I'm Kirk."

"And we're keeping it that way for the time being."

I shook my head and dropped into the chair. "So, Raini's friend, she wasn't connected to the Retreat?"

"Elizabeth Watkins." He slid a photo across the table—a skinny blonde girl smiled up from it, looking straight at the camera. The picture had been taken near a wooden lodge. I didn't recognize the girl, but the lodge did look familiar. "Wait, was she in A.A.?"

The cabin was frequently used by the local group who

liked to arrange meetings and small retreats in hopes that giving the participants something to do would help them in recovery.

"Her parents didn't mention it." Trent took the photograph back and squinted at the background. "You must've gone up there more than me."

Not entirely by choice. I'd gone with my ex-girlfriend to some of her meetings. When she was sober, she was one of the nicest people you could meet, but after a few drinks, she may as well have sprouted talons. As the drinking increased, I told her if she didn't stop we were done, and she had put in an effort for about a month. Until a wild bachelorette party for one of her friends and her subsequent arrest for drunk and disorderly and resisting arrest. That's when she started A.A. and I agreed to go with her—not because I thought we could work it out, but because I was afraid that without some kind of support system she'd end up killing someone.

That wasn't how she took it, and the next time I shut down her flirting, she ended up in trouble with the law again. I walked away after that one, and we didn't speak again.

"Think your ex still goes to the meetings?" Trent asked.

"I wouldn't count on it, and anyone else in the group is going to be tight-lipped about any of the members."

From the hallway, another detective tapped on the glass and motioned toward Trent.

Trent stood and gathered the files. "Won't hurt to try though. Raini's going to be talking to a sketch artist, so I'm coordinating with Detective Winsor to talk with her. You should lay low in here for a few."

My heel tapped against the floor in a steady rhythm. It was happening again. We'd taken down part of one large organization and only left the vacuum to be filled by another.

I sat back in the chair, fiddling with my phone to distract myself.

As I sent a quick message to Rose, asking what she'd want for dinner, the door flung open. "I—oh," the officer said squinting in recognition. "You're the guy who was wondering the sidewalks in the middle of the night over on the west side a while back."

"One and only. If you need this room—" I wasn't sure where else to go, but I'd gladly give up my cell.

"No, it's just chaos out here and Richards sent me around to check everyone who's waiting. Why are you in here alone?"

"Because Trent's questioning a girl who only knows me as a leader in an underground sex trafficking ring." Most people in the office knew enough about where I'd been, and as long as they kept quiet about it, I'd made it a point not to bring it up myself, but I wasn't in a mood to hide my blunt annoyance.

His eyes widened. "You're *that* guy."

My lips twisted together at the sour taste that putrefied in my mouth. And then I regretted the bluntness.

"I didn't mean anything bad by it."

"There isn't really anything good to it—especially considering the current circumstances."

The officer put up his hands, and I squinted at his name badge, Ryan Corell. He hadn't been in the department when I left, but he didn't entirely strike me as a recent rookie either. He was wide chested and had his light hair trimmed close to his head. "Captain sent us on a major campaign late this afternoon. No one is going to like us tomorrow."

"I heard. Fortunately for me, there's no use calling in the guy who can't be seen on the street by the people you're looking for."

"But you know more about those we're looking for than anyone here."

In so many more ways than I wanted to talk about.

"I've got to get back to it," Corell said. "Want me to bring you a coffee or something, since you're stuck in here."

I didn't want to be catered to, but I did need caffeine. "I'd appreciate it. Black."

Corell reappeared about five minutes later with a foam cup filled with coffee. "I can't guarantee it's not lethal."

"I came to terms with that risk years ago," I said dryly, staring down at the pitch black drink.

Corell nodded and reached for the door. "Sorry we hassled you that night."

"You were doing your job—and the intervention was probably a good thing since I was heading somewhere I had no business going at the time."

Giving me a crooked stare, he opened the door and once again left me to my thoughts.

What the hell am I doing here? Hiding out in an interview room wasn't police work, it was a ridiculous waste of time. Everyone involved in the ring who might have been a danger to me was slowly being migrated to maximum security prisons upstate, but if they found out I was alive, nothing would stop them from putting a hit on me and hiring a professional to do it.

I couldn't hide out forever though. And, as I told Katie when I came home from the hospital, I didn't intend on giving up my life.

Aside from the men in prison, the remaining active participants were either scattered or dealing with their own internal crises as they all vied for control over a crumbling organization. They had bigger worries than me, but that also meant there were about to be far more girls with nowhere to turn.

I was stuck somewhere in the middle—the cause of the fall. And now my hands were tied as far as doing any more for a large group of girls who thought of me as—what?

The guy who took advantage of the situation and then narced on everything? I wasn't even sure if that made me friend or foe to them.

I sipped the thick black coffee and pinched the bridge of my nose. A vibration sent my phone fluttering across the metal table.

ROSE: Chicken wings—something spicy.

It was already going on seven o'clock—mostly thanks to the fact that we'd slept until after noon. I'd really been looking forward to not spending the evening here, it never crossed my mind that I'd end up here anyway, just sitting in a room and staring at the walls.

The door opened again. Trent and Richards stepped in followed by two other older detectives, Hudson and Winsor.

"Raini just got done with a sketch artist," Trent said, throwing the paper on the table.

I squinted at the image and shrugged. My brain was only half in the game, but I'd seen hundreds upon hundreds of douchebags over the last year alone. "Looks like a dozen people I've seen or picked up in my life."

"Really?" Trent asked. "Blue eyes, sandy brown hair."

Kirk. I took another long look at the sketch. It was the real Kirk, the man whose life I had stolen to get inside. I hadn't even considered the possibility since I was sure he'd still be locked up on the drug trafficking charges for his last offense. "When did he get out?"

"A couple of weeks before the raid," Hudson said. "I just pulled up his record before we came in. Fiona says he called himself Bentley and that he and another guy who called himself Drisco approached her and Watkins as they were leaving a career workshop."

"Fiona?" I shook my head, knowing that he meant Raini. Aliases were a funny thing—they allowed us to detach, and yet they could also tell us much more about a person than a birth name. I hadn't bargained for learning any of the girls' real names, even though there was probably a time when it wouldn't have bothered me. Now, it just felt like the last year was taunting me—seeping into my real life in a not-so-subtle attempt to prove that it was real and much closer to home than I had ever bargained for.

"What kind of history do we have on Elizabeth?" I asked.

"None, really," Winsor said. "She's twenty-three, was picked up a few months ago on a drunk and disorderly, but that's her only run-in with the law. According to her parents, she dropped out of college, so they got her into the career workshop hoping she'd be able to make some connections."

"I noticed the picture her parents provided had been taken out at the A.A. lodge," I said. "I'm assuming her parents weren't particularly thrilled with the connection she did make. Were they aware of what she was doing?"

"Doesn't seem so. We had no idea until we found Fiona. She said they were supposed to be working together as accountability partners throughout the course of the workshop—setting career goals and such. They met for lunch at a small restaurant a block away from the workshop, and that's where Bentley and Drisco approached her. Fiona specifically, but Elizabeth overheard it, and contacted them the following week."

"So far, we haven't been able to match the second alias with anyone," Trent said, "but looks like we have a good excuse to call in your doppelganger and see what he's been up to."

That was going to be interesting. I stared down at the pictures strewn across the table. "I'm assuming I'm supposed to stay hands-off?"

"Why?" Richards asked. "This guy already knows who you are and his friend doesn't really matter. I can't keep you stowed away for good, and you have more intelligence than anyone on the folks involved."

I scoffed, returning my attention to my phone. I wanted this case more than almost anything but damned if I didn't want to get back to Rose first.

"I don't know a whole lot about Raini—or Fiona, I guess." I took a running start at the icy road anyway, preparing to skid off into memories I didn't care to explore again. "She never talked much, just did as she was told. It's just a hunch, but I don't imagine her turning them down if they confronted her over it. She was one of the worst off when she was transferred over—she'd endured a lot of abuse, so she'll stick with whoever's protecting her. We should make sure that's us if at all possible."

"And you also know about the man who tried to recruit her?" Hudson asked, pointing to the sketch.

"Kirk," I said. "I took his place when I went undercover. Honestly, I didn't expect him to be causing havoc on the streets so soon. That would have been brilliant to know since I'm sure he has a vendetta against me."

"I wouldn't actually count on the vendetta," Trent said with a muffled snort. "If he's scooping up all the girls from the Retreat, it sounds like he has something going for him—not in a good way, but he probably thinks so."

Richards' phone beeped and he leaned sideways to check the message. "I have the guys on the street watching for him. We might be in this one for the long haul if we want to get to the bottom of the situation—if these folks are as hooked up as suspected, we should keep things quiet until we have something solid. He's dealt with us before, and no doubt will do what's necessary to avoid it. Trent, you've been at it for a while, and James, I know you have someone waiting on you—not that you're supposed to be here anyway. Hudson and Winsor will run with the case for now, and if anything turns up, we'll call you in. Otherwise, you're both dismissed for the night. I suggest getting some rest."

Chapter Thirteen

DANGEROUS GAME

I PICKED up some chicken wings and a couple of small salads, and when I climbed back into the car, a message was waiting on me.

ROSE: I'm in the bath.

Fuck.

There's a key in the gnome by the stairs 2351.

Anger slammed me for a moment. The fact that she had a spare key right outside her door with everything going on didn't sit well, but I wasn't quite sure what the code was for until I got to her house and picked up said gnome. It was heavier than a standard lawn ornament and when I flipped it over, I realized why. The entire base was made of metal with a combination lock. I scrolled each number to match the code she'd sent, and the bottom of the gnome fell open, releasing a spare key.

Cute, I thought sardonically, shaking my head and bouncing the key in my palm.

I opened the door and was immediately greeted by a

speeding Trapper as she rounded the bottom of the stairs and charged through the living room and kitchen before heading back up the stairs at the same frenzied pace.

When I assumed cats were quiet, relaxing creatures, I had it very wrong.

I dusted my hand off against my jeans and dropped my keys and the bag of food on the table, reminding myself just how colossal this bad idea was.

Stairs. Hallway. Bedroom.

As I stood outside the bathroom door, I realized just how quiet the house had gone until I got to the bathroom door, and heard a gentle swish of water. I tapped the door. "You're probably going to turn into a prune."

The door handle wiggled and it opened a few inches, causing my stomach to flip. Weeks of fantasizing about a woman I wasn't supposed to have and then suddenly having her naked in a bathtub less than two feet away was momentarily debilitating. My eyes threatened to jump out of my head, I was torn between covering them, running away, and taking in the view.

But all I could really see was her face and neck.

Get a grip.

"Don't feel like yelling through the door," she said quietly. "I have a headache and Trapper isn't helping."

"Sorry," I rested my hand on the door handle not letting it open any further.

She studied me through the narrow opening and smiled. Not the typical shy smile I'd expect from her in the current situation. "You act like you've never seen me naked."

"In a way...." I trailed off, caught up in the overwhelming temptation. My cock twitched, demanding attention, and I felt the rolling boil of desire sweeping through my veins. "Maybe I should wait downstairs."

Rose's eyes fell closed, then she sat up and disappeared from my view as water sloshed in the tub.

Unable to restrain myself, I inched the door open. Little by little until I saw her back. She was still sitting in the water, but she had her head resting on her knees, her arms around her legs, tucking them against her chest.

I heard her take a long breath, and I did the same to steady myself, as I pushed the door open. I felt another twinge in my pants, but I ordered myself to behave.

Rose looked over her shoulder and gave me the softest most heartbreaking smile I'd ever seen.

"What's wrong, Sugar?"

"Nothing. And you don't have to come in."

"I'm not stupid. Nothing always means something."

"Really, James. I'm just tired."

You're not the only one, I thought, my body feeling heavier with each passing second as I strained against the urges. At least all of the most alluring parts were covered, I thought to myself, even though it wasn't totally accurate. I wanted her. All of her. The silky curve of her back, her hands that curled deliciously around her legs.

But the most damning sight was the side of her breast peeking not-so-innocently out.

She definitely wasn't covered enough. I knelt next to the tub, more to hide the evidence of my growing erection than anything. My jeans cut in, and I hoped that'd be enough of a deterrent to keep the fucking traitor from growing out of control.

"Didn't mean to make you uncomfortable," she said. "I didn't think. I just… don't want to get out of the tub and I wanted you here—selfish, I know."

"I'm fine."

She huffed a laugh. "Yeah, we're both just fine."

The urge became too great to resist so I traced the path of a drop of water down her back, and she shuddered, goosebumps rising along her skin.

Her brow twitched as she laid her head sideways to watch me. "If you want to step out, I can get dressed."

But the look in her eye said that was the last thing she wanted to do.

I brushed my fingers across her cheekbone. "Enjoy your bath. How's your head?"

"A little better. Tension headache. Last time I went to the doctor they gave me muscle relaxers for it, but a bath is more enjoyable."

"I agree."

With a giggle, she hid her face. "We're supposed to be *not* doing the sex thing. Me naked in a tub is not exactly—I mean I can't imagine it's making anything easy."

Easy. No. I brushed the tip of my nose against her shoulder and kissed her cooling skin. But it was enjoyable "I think I can bask in your beauty without losing all of my control."

It wasn't a guarantee though.

Her slight smile seemed to chase away a bit of the pain on her face. "You never let me see your scar."

I drew back. I'd lost the ability to swallow, let alone speak. I hadn't intentionally shown it to anyone. My fingers moved to her knees, but she brushed them away and tugged her legs closer. "I haven't shaved in a few days."

"You want to see my scar and you're embarrassed by stubbly legs?"

"You go first." The color in her cheeks deepened, the touches of red spreading down her neck and across her chest.

"What kind of game are we playing?"

She smirked. "One that isn't going to be ending in sex."

I doubted that. Despite my every intention to follow through with my own rule, I doubted that I had enough resolve to pull me through this time.

I lifted my shirt, only high enough for her to see the scar. She released her knees, placing her damp fingers on the raised and marred skin. The end of our old life permanently etched across my skin. The bullet's journey was effortless, but it missed its intended mark by inches.

"I didn't think you'd make it," she whispered. "Why did you tell him? Did you want to die?"

As soon as the raid on the Retreat began, Ross had turned his gun on her, believing Silver to be the breach in security. There had been at least ten feet and a table separating us, and I knew I couldn't cross the distance in time to do anything to stop him.

I choked, the tightness in my jeans no longer my biggest concern. "I wanted to save you."

"Saving me and leaving me to watch you die wasn't exactly my idealized end to it all."

I tried to put on a carefree smile, even as I watched the tears pool in her eyes. "Didn't happen though, did it? We're both here."

Her head drooped forward again, her eyes heavy and distant, and her hand fell to the side of the tub. I squeezed the back of her neck and her eyes closed, a soft moan escaped her lips like a siren calling me toward the rocks.

"I couldn't get to Ross before he killed you," I whispered. "There was no other way to buy time." And maybe I did for an instant want to die. That would have been my only chance of permanently escaping the horrors I'd seen and committed. I pressed and rubbed her neck and shoulders, slowly loosening her muscles.

Do you love her? Miles's question repeated in my head. He knew the answer to the question as soon as I'd taken a bullet for her.

"How about you head back to bed, Sugar. You look drained."

And I was going to be exhausted from holding back.

"Stay with me," she whispered with a shaking voice.

How could I say no to that? My chest ached like an earthquake brewing beneath the surface of my skin. Pressure building at every joint. I could do one night. I owed her one night.

But as I closed my eyes, I saw the image from my dreams. My memories. The whip. Tying her to the table in the play room. Watching her kneel at my feet and nibble at the food from my fingers. My body didn't know which way to go, aching in pain, regret, and need all at once. "I'll stay. The food you requested is downstairs though, if you're up to dinner."

She squinted, her eyebrows pinching over her nose as she lifted her head. "Everything okay with Raini?"

The shift in conversation brought me back down. "Yeah. I'm not supposed to be telling you anything, you know?"

"Yep, but I'm good at keeping your secrets."

I took a long breath, she was dead on about that, but regulations weren't the main reason I didn't want to discuss it. "Alley wasn't the only girl to drop off the grid. We're investigating a connection with an escort company—and the real Kirk."

Her mouth dropped open. "There's a *real* Kirk?"

"He was in negotiations with Miles, but I stepped in before they ever met, so I was able to take his place with all of the groundwork already laid."

"Smooth."

"Right, smooth." I stared down at the beige tiles of the floor. I wouldn't consider any part of the last few months smooth. "More like riddled with potholes and the possibility for a million things to go wrong."

Her hand wrapped around the tattoo on my forearm. "So far, so good."

"Thanks to a lot of luck."

She scoffed, her eyes gleaming. "And the help of a very remarkable girl."

"Oh," I chuckled. "You're developing quite the ego."

Suddenly her pleased face faded and tears erupted, sliding down her face.

I leaned over the side of the tub, rubbing my hand over her damp back. "Anything but tears, Rose."

I may have taken some pleasure in her submission to me —the look in her eye that told me that she was putting her trust in me even though she truly didn't want to. But I took no pleasure in watching her cry.

She sobbed. "I need tears. I'm tired—and I don't just mean I need sleep. I'm tired of being pent up, trapped, scared. I can't escape my own body. The memories—"

Her voice cut out and her chest fluttered as the tears continued. "I want to be emotional. I want to fall apart. Because at least then I feel like I might be able to put every-thing back together."

"You seemed to be doing good."

"I—it's harder at night. During the day, I can find some way to escape. And I don't want to push, but tonight is even worse. No matter what I do, when I close my eyes, I still see Gabe. I still haven't been able to admit to anyone what I did. Trent stayed up with me all night one night because I couldn't stop crying."

My fingers dug into the hard surface of the tub. I tried to compose myself, but the shattering in my heart was inescapable. "I knew he'd take care of you."

"He wasn't you, James. He wasn't the man I shared that crazy hell with and trusted to protect me."

Protect her. I'd stood by during her assaults. Left when she needed me most—when Gabe took her and dragged her through the building to rape her.

Left her to kill him, and him to haunt her nightmares as a result.

"But he was the only one *I* trusted." I climbed to my feet as she wrapped herself tighter into a ball. I pulled a large yellow towel from the rack. "Out of the water, Sugar."

She looked at me, eyes filled with something I couldn't read. Then, without a word, she obeyed. The very action nearly leveled me. Beads of water ran down her smooth skin. My temptation and salvation all rolled into one.

Before my cock could get me into trouble, I draped the towel over her shoulders, keeping my gaze trained on her eyes, then, I lifted her from the tub and to the bath mat.

"I want to take you," I said, pulling the elastic from her hair and watching the brown strands tumble around her shoulders. "I want to make you forget it all, but I don't know if that's the best thing right now."

"I'm good with that." She relaxed into my grasp, her weight pressing against my chest as her hair, curled from being twisted against her head in the damp bathroom, tickled my arm. "I just want you. I don't need sex. I don't even need words unless you want to tell me it's going to be okay."

"It is, Sugar." Heat radiated through my chest. "One day, I'll make it better than okay."

As soon as I got my head on straight and stopped dreaming about strangling people in my bed.

About strangling *her* in my bed.

I guided her toward the sink, pulling the bandage off that she'd taped and sealed to her arm to prevent the stitches from getting wet.

"Now I keep seeing Alley, too. Has anyone figured out what happened to her? Any idea why she did...." She trailed off.

"No," I gently patted the stitched wounds with a dry cloth to make sure there was no moisture and covered the area with a thinner bandage to protect it while she slept. "But we'll figure it out. If the information is out there, Trent and I will find it."

She gave me a wry grin and patted the towel she held around herself. "How about you step out and let me put on my pajamas?"

I nodded and left her to wait in the bedroom, staring at the full-length mirror on the back of the door until Rose came out in a pair of shorts and a tank top.

It was quite possibly worse than seeing her naked, especially when her lips turned up in a smile and she leaned against the doorway. The mixture of apprehension and confidence was doing in my control.

"Food is downstairs if you're hungry," I said, taking her by the waist and pulling her closer.

"Probably should." Her eyes were dull, and she leaned against my chest. "I missed you."

I couldn't imagine what she missed. Our entire relationship was like some code written in a foreign dialect with no clues to figuring out the key. Which parts were false leads due to insufficient or fabricated information and unsubstantiated beliefs?

And which parts were real?

Was it possible to miss someone you didn't really know? Miles said that we already knew each other as well as anyone could because we'd seen into the darkest regions of each other. We each understood how far the other was willing to go. How much pain we could endure. And how much we could dish out when the situation warranted it.

Her gaze was locked on me when I looked down. I tried to smile, but I wasn't sure that could hide my inner struggle.

"I missed *you*," she repeated, and for an instant I thought she wanted me to say something in return, but she continued. "Not the things we went through, not even most of the things you did, just you. I know you're more than what we went through, and I have a lot to learn about you, but during the quiet, after I found out your secret, there were times you just held me—we were simply there, no words, or facades, or expectations."

Her words tugged at that rope of tension I'd been fighting for weeks. The one that had wound my entire body, clenching around my heart. But rather than becoming more uncomfortable, this time it stretched and gave way, freeing my muscles to relax and my mind to quiet.

The brush of her lips against my neck reeled me back in. I tangled my fingers through her mess of wavy hair and backed her into the wall. Kissing her gently at first, before giving into the ferocity of my newfound freedom.

Rose cleared her throat and pulled back a bit. "I assume the rules are still in effect."

The damn rules. I wanted to keep myself from crossing the line.

She pressed against me, which only drew my attention to my growing erection—apparently that was her intent since she quirked an eyebrow and smirked.

"Ignore it," I said.

"That's going to be rather difficult," she snorted. "We should go downstairs and eat before one of us gets in trouble."

"If I'm not ready to eat?" I expected my stomach to growl to spite me, but it kept quiet and played along with my little game.

I pulled her hand from around my neck and pinned it against the wall above her head. Holding her other arm more gently at her side—since she couldn't move it much anyway. My restraint slid away, buried beneath the fibers of the knot she wove around my chest. A battle of control that I wasn't certain she even knew we were having.

I needed her not to move. Her chest heaved against mine, even as I stood there holding her. I pressed my lips to her neck and felt the erratic pulse beneath her skin.

A crash outside the bedroom door jerked me upright, pulling the tension agonizingly taut again.

"It's Trapper. She's been doing that all evening—practically since you left."

I blew out a long slow breath. "We should probably go rescue the food before she gets any crazy ideas."

Rose slipped from my loosened grasp, her incredulous look given away by her quiet laugh. "You left it out?"

"You messaged me that you were in the bath, I had other things on my mind."

"Ah yes, Mr. Innocent."

By the time we returned downstairs, Trapper had

wrecked most of the living room, but the food was miraculously spared, still in the plastic bag where I'd left it. I wasn't sure if that meant she wasn't hungry, or if carry-out dining simply wasn't her preference.

The whiplash of changing emotions left Rose and I quiet through dinner, but it was one of those moments where I yearned for some kind of ESP to give me even a subtle hint at what she was thinking. The silence left too much room for guesses and turning around on myself.

Too much time to contemplate the one thing I did know as truth. Part of me still wanted to tame her.

No, that wasn't an accurate explanation.

I wanted to *try* to tame her, and I wanted her to kick back and fight me for it. Like a purebred muscle car, she was strong but unpredictable, and that combination is where things get fun—when you put your foot down and the tail kicks out, threatening to propel you off the side of the road. My first car was a '97 Mustang that did just that.

More than once, and I never learned.

After we put away the leftovers and we cleaned up, I kept my promise and led Rose back up to her room. My conscious stuttered at the decision again, but I'd give her this even if it did drive me insane.

She snuggled under the covers, her form fitting against mine, perfectly cradled against me with her back to my front. I buried my nose in her hair, knowing the dangerous effects her drug-like smell had on my libido.

But instead of twisting me into knots, my body relaxed next to hers, and the dark room faded away.

———

I FELT A JERK, unsure if I was awake or asleep. Everything shook and shifted, and something thudded nearby.

I opened my eyes and shot up. It took me a few moments to remember where I was, but then I saw the bathroom door slam shut.

What the hell?

I sat in the dark silence trying to figure out what was going on. Had I hurt her? Did I do something in my sleep?

I almost couldn't get out of bed, afraid of what would happen if I knocked on the door to check on her.

Maybe it was nothing.

"Rose?" I called across the room.

"I'm fine."

I heard water running, so I waited, but she still didn't emerge.

"Rose."

The door creaked open, but she stayed near the sink. "It was just a dream. I didn't feel good." She dropped against the counter and rubbed the back of her neck. "Still don't feel good."

I crept across the dark bedroom, the light from the bathroom spilled out across the floor and stung my eyes. "Anything I can do?"

She closed her eyes and shook her head, before dropping it against the wall. "You think I'm—?" her question died away.

"What is it?"

"Why do you still want me?"

My throat and stomach collided. "Why wouldn't I want you?"

She tried to retreat backward, but I caught her by the waist. "You think that—Sugar, you know my reluctance right now has nothing to do with you."

I'd figured our earlier encounter had erased all doubts to that effect.

"But, you had to watch all of them with me," her knees gave way, and I leaned her against the sink for extra support in case her knees buckled while I held her to my chest.

"Rose, I——" I couldn't find the words. I was responsible for every man who touched her, violated her, and she thought I held that against her. "There's nothing wrong with you."

I reached to caress her face, but she shied away as if my touch burned her. Had my distance caused this? Watching her go through this was worse than my constant struggle for control.

"It's just the dream," she said.

"I hate seeing you hurt. Somewhere along the line, I should have prevented it from happening."

"Rule one, no sex. Rule two, stop apologizing for things we can't change. At least I'm alive to have nightmares."

I lifted her chin, her shiny eyes found mine and locked there until I sealed my mouth over hers. She relaxed into my touch, parting her lips so my tongue could mingle with hers.

Her taste filled my senses, waking every synapse and fiber in my body as the blood rushed in one direction. I pulled her harder against me, yearning for every inch of contact I could get.

She broke the kiss but didn't pull her body away.

"Don't do this just for me. It'll pass and I'll be——"

I caught the rest of her argument before it became audible. My mouth moved along her jaw and neck. Even though her mouth was free, she seemed to have lost interest in the protest.

"If you want me to stop," I whispered, "then say it.

Otherwise, let me have my way. Tonight I can only battle one of us for control."

Thankfully, she didn't ask what I meant, she went completely quiet, her body arching into mine as my hands and lips explored her exposed skin. Careful of her injured arm, I lifted her up, and she wrapped her legs around my hips, her left hand moving through the short hair at the back of my head.

I returned her to the bed, pulling off her pajama bottoms and shirt as I laid her out, the perfect sight. I watched her breasts rise and fall with every pant. She reached up to me, tugging at the hem of my shirt until I leaned over, close enough for her to remove it, adding to the growing pile on the floor.

"Sugar," I whispered, freeing myself from the fabric of my pants. Trailing my hands up her stomach, until I crouched above her. The soft skin of her inner thigh squeezed against my hips as I lowered to take her nipple in my mouth.

It had been so long.

Not long enough. I hadn't even lasted a week.

She lifted her hips, pressing against the head of my cock, and I bit in response to the sudden shock of sensations.

My hand tightened in the sheets below us, but Rose moaned and spurred me on. Her chest jutting up towards me, her fingers in my hair pulling me back.

I moved to her other nipple, trying to compose myself as she wriggled beneath me, but it was too much after weeks of nothing or angry solo jobs.

Her hand slid between us, grabbing me and pressing my cock toward her entrance. A bold move, even though her eyes met mine with a question. I pressed forward, taking in nothing but the sound of her gasps as I filled her, and the sensation of her squeezing around my cock.

I rocked inside of her, watching her chest move in quick breaths, and feeling her muscles work as she thrust up to meet my movements.

But my temporary respite from the war of emotions was short lived, and anger pulled free again. The wound on her arm. The look on her face, when I'd tried to console her in the bathroom.

My movements became frantic and hurried. Why the hell did I have to be losing it now?

"James." Her voice tethered me to the present. A weak and tenuous connection, but I held onto it with everything I had. I captured her mouth, letting myself fall into the sensations of her as the world drifted away.

One night of peace. We both needed it.

I slowed my pace, but she urged me on with a whimper and a tug with her leg.

Not so fast.

I returned to my deliberate assault of kisses. A trail across her chest, a slow thrust inside her.

Over her shoulder, with a little nip to her neck. Up her jawline, my lips dusted against hers, like static building between our bodies. I punctuated each set of kisses and nibbles with another slow thrust, until her body was taut, yearning for release, with her fingers digging into my back.

Her eyes squeezed closed, and her mouth formed a small oval. I wanted to kiss every inch of her but didn't have the will to pull out and explore the rest of her body. I didn't want to break away from whatever momentarily set me free.

My cock throbbed inside of her, the tingling build of an orgasm taunted me. I increased my pace until I was slamming inside of her, pushed onward by every moan of ecstasy.

Fingers moved down my spine, a delicate dance of pleasure laced with the sharp pain of nails finding my skin. I fisted my hand in her hair, pulling her up to meet my kiss, just as her muscles exploded around me and sent me flying after her.

I relaxed against her chest, the drum of her heart a ballad as I closed my eyes, and found my way back. My back burned, and I couldn't have cared less.

Maybe everything I had been running from was its own façade. The worries exacerbated by uncertainty and darkness. I rolled, taking her with me. Keeping her against my chest, as she moved freely with me—her tension washed away by pleasure.

The thrum of my own heart coaxed me back to sleep. That and the warm body pressed against mine.

———

ROSE WOKE ME, trailing her fingers down my chest, across my abs, further down until she reached my hardening cock and pulled. Then, she pressed her palm against the head and slid her fingers up the backside. She lifted her head as she moved to straddle me.

But it wasn't Rose who stared back from under the long brown hair.

Raini.

I flipped her off of me and rolled off the bed, keeping my eyes on her while I moved away.

"They'll kill us," she whispered, reaching for me.

It had to be a dream.

I spun, looking for an exit, but Rose stood in the doorway, taking my hands and wrapping them around her waist, pulling me down to reach her mouth.

"We have to go," I said.

"Don't you want to tie me up first?" She traced her fingers over my lips then down my throat. "Or maybe a butt plug, clamps.... A whip? Aren't those your favorites?"

I shoved her backward, waking with a jerk before she fell away.

It was nearly six in the morning, and Rose was still curled at my side, sound asleep as her hair trailed out in a satiny starburst across her pillow. I slid out from under her arm and pulled on my boxers and pants.

The dreams weren't real, but the shadows of emotion they imprinted were very real, and I needed to get some air. I made it as far as the living room before dropping to the couch and covering my face with my hands.

I needed a reset button. Or at least a map. Some way out of the endless loop. I sat back, staring up at the ceiling. Every time I tried to put myself back together, the pieces wouldn't fit right anymore. Everything was the wrong size and shape.

There were some moments when it felt like there were two opposing beings inside me, both seeking validation and hungry for power over my life. I had thought the endless hours of sitting on the couch at Dr. Combs office were coming to a final resolution, but the more I questioned who really had control over my life, the more I doubted ever getting rid of her.

————

"JAMES?"

I opened my eyes. The room was much brighter than I remembered. "Did I wake you?"

I thought for an instant that I'd woken her up when I climbed out of bed, but I wasn't even sure how long I'd been downstairs.

"It's almost seven." She yawned and covered her mouth. "Didn't really expect to wake up alone."

"Sorry."

She sat down beside me, her leg tucked up under her so she was facing me. "I don't want things to be uncomfortable."

"I know, Sugar." I squeezed her leg. "I enjoyed it. Don't worry."

"Yeah, but old ways won out—using sex to try and make everything better."

"Is that how you think of it?"

"You don't?" She scoffed and laid her head against the back of the couch. Even though she was looking right at me, her eyes were distant. "It was our distraction."

"Is a distraction what you wanted last night?"

She hesitated, her foot wriggling on the couch like a fish seeking water.

"Because a distraction isn't what I intended." I grabbed her thigh, hoisting her up so she straddled my lap and hooked her good arm around my neck. "I intended to show you how I feel. What you mean to me."

"But it's still too soon. I didn't mean for it to go there last night, I was just freaked about the dream and afraid you didn't want me. And then, I—" her mouth twisted as she debated over her words. "I noticed that you zoned out. Figured you remembered something. You just looked like you went somewhere else for a moment."

I nodded. "And you pulled me back." *This time.* "But sometimes the memories...."

"Are so real you don't know how to find your way back or what direction to even begin looking in. I know," she whispered. "I want you—but I'm afraid that I just want you to take the pain away."

"I'd love to do that." But I wanted more, too. Something real, something that I could keep.

And that's why I had to pull myself together first— reconcile the wants, needs, dreams, and fears until I could at least separate fact from façade. I needed to know I wouldn't hurt her.

Chapter Fourteen

WHO NEEDS A KNIGHT?

BY MONDAY MORNING, Captain Richards had ordered me back to work, and Trent filled me in on what I had missed—which wasn't much. The feds had basically cut us off, opting instead to concentrate on the rest of the organizations they had yet to take down and leaving us with a slew of girls to take care of on limited resources.

Richards was faced with a balancing act—trying to balance the high priority cases that required significant man hours with all of the new matters that came in daily. Detectives Winsor and Hudson were still primary on the newest missing girl, but we agreed to work the whole thing in tandem to keep fresh eyes on the developments as much as possible.

Even though I predicted it would be a dead end, Trent and I followed the A.A. lead, since they had an afternoon session on Mondays.

We waited outside until the meeting dismissed—giving them all their privacy and relative anonymity during the meeting. As they passed us by, one by one they either snubbed our request entirely or claimed they didn't know her without giving the image more than a subtle glance.

"Told you," I muttered after fifteen people had climbed into their cars and left. Two cars remained in the lot, in addition to ours.

"Still a couple of chances," Trent said. "Get rid of the glare and turn on the charm and we might get somewhere."

I leaned against the wall, staring off toward the woods as the door opened again. Trent cleared his throat and elbowed me. And I prepared my spiel again—until I recognized the woman standing in front of me. Apparently my ex, Claudia, had stuck with A.A.

She smiled and raised her eyebrows. "Looking for someone?"

My mouth opened to answer, but the shock prevented any sound from coming out.

Trent held up the picture and she plucked it from his hand, eyeing us both just as long as she stared at the picture.

"You guys know the rules."

"She's been missing for more than three days now," I said, hoping we could at least get some information—however simple. I hoped that however long Elizabeth had spent with the group, she might have picked up one or two who would put her safety above the rules.

Another man exited the building, and Trent left us to chat with him.

"That's a shame, but as I said, you know the rules." Claudia glanced over her shoulder and blew out a breath. The man gave her a warning glance, then headed down the path to his car, peeking back once more before climbing inside.

"I also know that sometimes bending the rules can save lives. What can you tell me about Elizabeth?"

"Didn't talk much. She came to one of the weekend retreats and a couple sessions through the week—more because it was ordered than anything."

"She got mandatory A.A. after only one offense?"

Claudia tightened her lips and shrugged.

Only one offense on record, I guessed.

"She hasn't been around in about two weeks," Claudia said. "I really can't give you much of anything else. Although, she pointed and made a tapping motion with her hand. "Last time she left here she was picked up. It was odd because I'd always seen her drive herself. He drove a black BMW, fancy thing, but I never was the car person."

Trent held up his phone—the drawing from Raini's session with the sketch artist on the screen.

"That looks like him. It was Friday before last, I believe. Just don't tell anyone in the group I told you any of this—especially her when you find her."

"You're confident," I said. So far, we hadn't been doing a brilliant job of finding the cracks in the case.

"You're determined." She tucked her hands in her pocket, keeping her eyes on me as Trent backed away to take a phone call. "You looked damned surprised to see me," she whispered.

"Well, you were pretty stubborn yourself, and you didn't seem interested in help."

"I wasn't," she shrugged. "But it has been a few years. You seeing anyone?"

"Yes." I didn't know her intentions, but I wasn't beating around the bush.

She smiled—her face remained relaxed, not forced at all. "Good."

Then, she held up her left hand, a gold band with diamond insets adorned her finger. "Me, too."

Married. It seemed she might have cleaned up for a good cause. "That's a little more than seeing someone, I believe. Congratulations."

"Thanks, and good luck finding Elizabeth. I hope everything works out."

We spent the next few hours back at the station, sifting through leads with Winsor and Hudson, before filing reports and making a few calls of our own.

"We're going out tonight," Trent said, pulling on his jacket.

I tossed my pen across the desk. "No offense, but I've spent all day with you and I'd rather see Rose."

"Or," he leaned over the desk, "we could go follow a lead."

I grunted. *Of course.* We needed something new to follow, so for that, I was thankful, but it felt like we were trying to get traction on a solid block of ice. And I realized, the overwhelming desire to run from everything that had to do with the Retreat had me wanting to run from my own job. How long until I wanted to run from Rose, too? "What kind of lead?"

He handed me a slip of paper with the name of a local bar on the east side of town—near the café where Raini and her missing friend had been approached by Kirk. I knew the place and it wasn't an area either of us would usually hang out at.

Or anywhere near.

"Seems our local escort service has been recruiting there," he explained.

"As soon as Kirk sees us, he'll spook—not that I wouldn't mind hauling his ass in, but if that's the plan, we might want to have backup."

"I asked, the men who have been showing up there

don't match Kirk's description. One of the servers called earlier to report a man who tried to pick up one of their waitresses—she thought it was hinky and wanted to know if there was anything she could do. He gave her a card that matches the one we found on the girl we picked up for prostitution. She said he comes in every Monday night at eight, sometimes meeting with other men. And she called him the 'desperate to get a date type', but she doesn't have a name."

"And what's the plan if he does come in? I doubt he'll be real enthused to chat with *us*. I don't think we're necessarily his type."

"We'll play it by ear," Trent shrugged and finished clearing his desk.

I went home, threw on an old pair of jeans and a T-shirt and sent off a message to Rose, telling her I'd be out late.

When I met Trent near his car in the busy parking lot, he was still in a dress shirt—with the sleeves rolled up to his elbows so the tattoos along his forearms peeked out, and a pair of carpenter khakis. It was his usual version of casual wear, but at least without long sleeves, no one usually pegged either of us for cops.

"Now a good time to bring up my unease toward loud, crowded buildings filled with drunks these days?" I shoved my hands in my pockets and stared toward the door. I could hear the music pulsing from the establishment, but louder than that was my pulse pounding in my ears.

Trent slapped my arm. "I'll be watching your back this time."

It was now or never, so I led the way across the parking lot and shoved through the massive front door. The bar was full, a sea of people, and the biting smell of alcohol wafted through the thick air. Music pumped through the speakers, it wasn't obnoxiously loud, but the bass was turned up so high, I could feel each beat from my feet to my head.

I scanned the room, looking for anyone who stood out— or more importantly, people who didn't stand out. "Is your girl on tonight?"

"Yeah, she said she'd give a nod, so we may as well belly up to the bar and get cozy."

"Perfect." I glanced back toward the booths near the entrance. It really was perfect. I elbowed Trent, and he spun around to look.

Rose was tucked into one of the corner benches, sitting across from another olive-skinned brunette I didn't recognize and a man with a similar, but slightly darker skin-tone than the girl. I took a step, but Trent caught my arm.

I nearly snapped his head off before biting my tongue.

"Charlene," he said in my ear.

I scratched the back of my head, attempting to shake off the bad feeling I had. Charlene was the girl Rose had been with when she was taken, but that didn't explain their male friend.

"He's her brother," Trent said. "They came to the station together after Rose was abducted."

Still didn't explain what he was doing in a booth with Rose—or why she hadn't mentioned anything to me about being here. *Get it together*, I reminded myself, but I still headed toward them. My feet were connected to the rash portion of my brain rather than the logical side.

The brunette's eyes widened when she saw me, but without a word I plopped down on the bench next to Rose. She startled for a second and visibly forced herself to calm.

"What are you doing here?" she asked.

"Getting ready to ask you the same thing." Even a few minutes around her did strange things to my body and mind. It didn't matter that we were in a public place, or that she didn't seem particularly thrilled that I was crashing her evening.

Trent leaned against the back of our booth bench and gave everyone a flip of his hand in greeting.

Rose forced a smile and kept her eyes on me. "This is Charlene and her brother Elijah. She called and said she was in town so I came over to meet her for a 'face your fears' type evening."

"So you choose the busiest bar in town?" It wasn't as if I was trying to spy, but the crowded room already had me itchy and paranoid, and her being here only multiplied the effect.

Rose glanced at the man, then down at the drink in front of her. "May as well jump in at the deep end."

"I wouldn't expect anything less." Although I would have preferred it, apparently I didn't have any say in the matter.

"You never answered me," she said, straightening her back.

I couldn't tell if she was incredibly uncomfortable with the situation or truly pissed to see me. I nodded toward the center of the room, "Dance with me."

I didn't want to discuss any of the details where anyone could hear me, even if they were Rose's friends. At least on the floor, I had a reason to stay close, and fewer people would be paying attention to what we were talking about. The booth made us the center of attention.

Her mouth flattened, and she rolled the glass between her fingers. "I'm not keen on dancing. Especially with stitches in my arm—I'd rather stay where people can't attempt to run me over."

Fine. I wasn't convinced it was the dancing part that

deterred her as much as the possibility of walking away from her friends with me, but I leaned to her ear, "We're following a lead."

Her eyes widened and she pulled her arms around herself, glaring at the glass on the table as if it had done something to offend her. That's how they had gotten to her last time—even though she said she'd never left her drink unattended.

"You're fine," I said. At least I hoped so. I could feel the accessing gazes of the two sitting across from us. Charlene didn't bother me, but Elijah taunted the primal part of my brain.

Trent tapped my shoulder and nodded toward the bar.

I had no interest in the bar, a drink, or the lead. I wanted to drag Rose out to my car and get more than an answer, but I reigned in the internal storm.

"Have fun, Sugar." I lifted her hand to my mouth and brushed my lips against her knuckles.

"You, too." She nodded to Trent as we stepped away.

He led the way to the bar, ordering us each a drink that neither of us would likely drink. "Leave her be. She's allowed to have friends and go out without your permission."

"What do you know about the brother?" I glanced over my shoulder again. Rose was still staring down at the drink, but the other two were leaning over the table as if engaged in conversation with her. "I don't like him."

"You don't like any person with a dick going anywhere near Rose. You didn't even talk to him, so keep your head on." He focused on someone on the other side of the bar. "Our mark isn't here."

"Then, we should blend in and chat." I wanted to head back toward Rose's table, but I resisted.

"You going to be able to do this with her here?" Trent gave me a sideways glance before scanning the room again. "He seemed the awkward type, not romantically interested in her. Relax."

Sure, relax. I went ahead and took a swig of my drink—couldn't hurt since we were just observing, but Trent still gave me a scowl.

"Look, man," I said. "If we're just going to sit here and stare at each other and our drinks, we may as well put huge signs over our heads to explain why we're here."

"Right, you're only drinking to blend in. Not because your girlfriend is sitting less than fifty feet away in a booth with her friend and her friend's brother."

"I may as well have spent a year drinking while working. One beer isn't going to kill me."

Something brushed against me and I tensed. Rose slid in next to me, planting her elbow on the bar. "I didn't want you to worry," she said. "But I guess I ended up with you here to check in on me anyway."

"That wasn't our intent." I glanced back at the booth that was now empty. "I wasn't trying to crash." I had to force the words out, knowing full well that was my reason for sitting at the booth with her. I wanted her with me, not her friends.

"But overprotective you couldn't resist." Despite the glint in her eye, she dropped her cheek against my shoulder. Her body remained stiff, muscles tight and twitchy under her skin.

"Everything okay?" I asked, rubbing her lower back.

"Yeah, Charlene and Elijah are dancing with some friends, over there," she nodded. "So, I thought I'd hang out here—if I'm not interfering."

Trent slid over, sniping the empty seat next to him and

leaving an empty seat for Rose between us. I pulled the empty chair closer before she sat, so I could still keep her as close as possible.

"The guy we're waiting on is a no-show, so far," Trent said.

"Do I get to ask what this is all about or should I just sit here like a quiet decoy?" she smirked.

"We don't know. We're unofficially trying to close in on some leads that may have to do with the missing girls," I said despite Trent's warning glance.

She'd kept my secrets before—whether or not I was supposed to tell her, I knew they wouldn't go any farther.

"Why didn't you tell me you were coming here?" I asked.

Trent cleared his throat, took a swig of his own drink, then slid away from the bar. "I'll be back."

Rose kept her eye on him as he disappeared into the crowd before answering me. "Charlene and Elijah were in town—they still have an apartment here, but Elijah is the only one actually staying there lately. I wanted to do this myself. Sometimes a girl wants to be her own knight in shining armor."

I squeezed her shoulder and smiled. That wasn't in the least surprising, but with someone targeting girls associated with the Retreat, I had no guarantee she wasn't on the list.

"Girls from the Retreat seem to be disappearing, and we don't know why," I spoke into her ear, so no one else could hear. "It may have something to do with an escort company who's been trying to recruit them."

"I came with friends," she said, but her glare quickly faded, probably realizing like I had that the friend she was with had also been with her the first time she was abducted.

"You said you believe it has something to do with the escorts—well, I'm not exactly going to volunteer."

"We don't know—"

"Stop it, James. I don't need to be *more* paranoid." She took a drink of my beer.

"Sorry. I—"

"I hope you're planning to say you're sorry for being an ass for no particular reason, but can we just drop it?" She raised her eyebrows and smiled, before sinking back into her shell as the voices of the frenzied room weighed down on us. Her small hands circled my forearm, and she laid her head against my shoulder again. "Maybe we can talk later. We're probably not going to stay long—I don't want to anyway. I was banking on a quiet evening with Charlene, but Elijah insisted in coming along."

"And bringing you two here of all places?"

"Don't be such an old fart. We do have friends who come here often."

"Sure," I nodded, kissing her temple. Friends I believed, but knowing what I did about Rose, I couldn't picture this being one of her top choices even before the Retreat.

Trent returned and took his seat. "You two done having it out?"

A blonde waitress behind the bar sauntered over and put a plate of fries in front of me. "Here you go, handsome."

Rose straightened as if she was about to leap over the bar—apparently she didn't need my protection quite so much.

"Stand down," Trent said bumping her arm as he reached across for a handful of fries. "She obviously meant them for me."

Before I could give him hell, Rose smacked him in the back of the head.

"Hey," he mumbled around a fry. "I figured something productive to fight about would keep you from clawing each other's eyes out. Although I admit it could have backfired and exacerbated the whole thing...." He trailed off, munching down on another fry. "Our guy doesn't seem to have shown up, and he's usually here by now."

"So, Monday night wasted?" I swiped a few of the fries. I should have eaten something substantive when I'd gone home to change, but I just grabbed a quick snack. The music and clamoring people were giving me a headache—and the lack of dinner wasn't helping. "Does that mean we can get out of here?"

Trent went uncharacteristically silent, staring at something or someone across the room, before ducking his head. "Yeah, we should definitely get out of here."

"No shit," I said. "What did you see?" I asked, barely resisting the temptation to tear through the bar to figure out what could make Trent look like he'd seen a ghost.

"Your doppelganger. If he spots us—"

It felt like all of the beer that sat in my stomach erupted into a fiery frenzy. *Fuck.*

"You should come with us," I whispered to Rose.

"What the hell is going on?" She shook away my hand.

I remained bent over the bar, keeping my head down. "I'll explain later, but we can't stay."

"Is it dangerous?"

Trent paid the tab. "She might be better off going back to her friends."

I glared at him for having the nerve. There was no way in hell I wanted to leave her in a building with *him*.

"If I'm leaving, I need to get Charlene and Elijah

anyway," Rose said. "I can't just disappear. If you have to leave, go. I'll meet up with you later."

A growl built low in my throat and I squeezed her hand. I didn't very well intend to let go. To let her stay.

There was too much to lose and more loose ends than I was willing to accept.

She flinched and tried to pull her hand away. "You're. Hurting. Me," she mouthed, not making a noise.

I jerked my hand away, fisting it against my leg, but her scowl didn't fade until she shook her head and looked toward her friends. "I'm going back to my friends."

Crazy. Obstinate.

"You can message me later if you want," she added. She didn't even look back at me as she slid off the stool and into the crowd.

My heart pounded in my chest so hard I couldn't breathe without shuddering.

"Come on," Trent said—apparently he'd missed half of the previous conversation.

"I don't want to leave her—"

"She'll be fine—we won't be if he spots us here. And we certainly don't want him to see her with us. Out." He pointed to the door.

I knew he was right, but it didn't stop the endless stream of expletives in my head. What if he had already seen us together? What if he targeted her? Kirk definitely had a bone to pick with me, whether or not he was living it up now.

I managed to keep my head lowered as we headed for the door. As soon as the cool, fresh, night air hit my skin. My legs urged me to go back inside. "We could just arrest him."

Trent spun and glared at me. We both knew it'd show

our hand. We didn't have any reason to hold him, so as soon as we set him free he'd go off the radar. He'd evidently gotten smarter and gained new connections since our last encounter, but there was a missing girl on the line who'd last been seen with him.

"Let's wait in the car. I have a full view of the front, so we'll know when he comes out, and in the meantime, I can call it in," Trent said.

Trent's phone beeped and he took a minute to fish it out as he headed toward his car.

I kept my eyes on the front door of the club. Where the hell was she?

"James," Trent said, a low grumble to his voice. "You've always been hard-headed, but it's getting infuriating. Stop fucking blaming yourself for everything that happened. Rose is with friends."

"I heard you," I yelled louder than necessary. "I know she's a strong girl. I know she's capable. But if there's any chance that something might happen to her—"

"And if he comes out here and sees us waiting in the parking lot? Get in the damn car." He threw up his hands and answered his phone. "Davis."

He unlocked his car, climbing behind the wheel and waving me toward the passenger seat.

My foot twitched as I waited and willed Rose to come out of the bar. I had a sick feeling we weren't going to be able to wait any longer. I listened as Trent explained our situation, but the conversation seemed to take a grave turn.

"We have to go," Trent said when he hung up the phone and slid it into the center console. "They found Elizabeth. We need to get to the hospital."

"She's in the hospital and we're leaving our top suspect

inside?" I was incredulous, grinding my teeth together to keep from saying something else stupid.

"Captain's orders," Trent sighed and turned over the ignition. "All we have is circumstantial."

I yanked on the door handle. "I'll meet you there. I'm not leaving my car here for God knows how long."

"You're not planning on waiting for Rose and standing me up, are you?"

I didn't answer, just slammed the door and crossed the parking lot to my own car, still staring at the front door to the bar. When I slid into my car and she still hadn't come out, I sent a quick message.

Got called in. Text me when you get to your house.

Her reply came back before I could put the car in drive.

ROSE: Please?

I clicked my tongue against the roof of my mouth.

Please, text me when you get home, Sugar.

I got a slight kick out of picturing her blushing face as she read the message in the middle of the crowded room.

ROSE: Will do. Elijah is finishing his drink and chatting with a friend. We'll leave soon.

The message soothed my nerves a bit—I wasn't happy that she was going to be there longer than necessary, but at least I knew that nothing worrisome was stopping her. And that she wasn't completely infuriated with me.

A second message came in.

ROSE: Whatever's going on, be careful.

And, she was still worried about me. I typed in a quick reply and dropped the phone in the passenger seat. If I didn't do some serious catching up, Trent was going to be the biggest threat when he ripped me a new one for leaving him hanging.

―――――

I ARRIVED SHORTLY behind Trent and we met one of the officers who'd responded to the call outside of Elizabeth's room.

"She hasn't regained consciousness," he explained. "They gave her naloxone and intubated her. They're running an EKG right now—trying to determine her chances at this point, but it doesn't look good."

"Where'd you find her?" Trent asked.

"Near the viaduct. Looked like she'd been sleeping there, but we cleared that area Saturday and there hadn't been a sign of her then."

Trent looked at me. The viaduct had been where I first took Kirk's place to meet Miles, but what were the chances Kirk knew those details since he was locked up before the final instructions came in. It was a common gathering place for vagrants and criminals anyway, lots of places to hide and shelter from the finicky weather.

"We gathered all of the standard forensics on her, and they've documented and collected all of the evidence at the scene. She was a Jane Doe until we got her to the hospital."

"Her photo should have gone around the department several times by now," Trent said. The bulging vein in his neck indicated he was ready to explode.

"Hers and about twelve other girls' photos. Besides, it wasn't immediately obvious since she's dyed her hair—jet black, even got fancy with eyebrows to match."

I pushed by him and through the door, ignoring the tech and nurse inside the room. I just wanted to see her face for myself. The facial features were all right—perfect match for Elizabeth—but on first glance the hair would probably throw anyone off.

Trent and I met the other detectives back at the station to go over the evidence found at the scene, but I just kept staring at Elizabeth's picture. Usually by now, I'd be hyped up on adrenaline and ready to go, but sixteen hours after arriving at the station the first time, I was running on fumes.

Detectives Winsor and Hudson picked up where we left off for the evening—fresh eyes and more rested bodies would give them an advantage for a few more hours. But we were chasing leads that were stretched thinner than dental floss.

And I had a gut feeling none of them were where we were supposed to be looking—except I couldn't quite put my finger on a better suggestion at the moment.

"I'm getting old," I said as Trent and I walked out of the building.

"Mind over body," he replied, even though he looked equally exhausted. He rubbed his forehead, then dropped back against a retaining wall flanking the parking lot. Aside from the sound of traffic, the city was quiet.

"I think that's my problem," I said, "my mind wants a vacation. Particularly from all of this."

"And yet it won't let you take one because you have this insane drive to set things right." He scuffed the bottom of his shoe against the rough concrete. "Not that I can talk since I seem to share it. Over the weekend, I ran an idea by Richards—setting up one of our uniformed officers to get inside the escort company as a customer."

My brain clicked right to the first one I'd ask—Ryan Corell. He was new enough that he shouldn't be well known among the ring, and even though I'd seen very little of his skill, his personality would be a good match. My only hesitation was putting the girls in the middle again—especially if it was one of the girls from the Retreat.

They were already skittish around cops, so much so that they didn't even trust our help, and that was a big part of the problem.

Trent cleared his throat, and I focused on him again.

"Stop racing through the possibilities," he said. "Richards turned it down. Said we'd risk spooking them too soon."

"To be honest. I think they already know we're on to something. And I don't think they're spooking, more like taunting."

"You don't think the viaduct was a coincidence?"

"Something doesn't fit." I shook my head, more to try and shake away the exhaustion. "I think we just walked away from a big chance. If they're a step ahead of us, we're not likely to catch another break."

I waved and headed for my car, my fingers wrapping around the newest key on my key ring. I hadn't put Rose's spare key back in the garden. It had been an hour since she'd texted me that she was home safe, and even though she'd probably be fast asleep by now, I needed to see her.

I drove like the all-around paranoid person I'd become, zigzagging up side streets and lollygagging about until I was too exhausted to keep up the charade.

Rose's house was dark and quiet.

You're going to scare the bejabbers out of her.

I tried sending a text message, but she probably turned her phone off before she went to bed, so despite knowing that it was a bad idea, I slid the key into the deadbolt and let myself in.

There wasn't even a sign of Trapper as I crept up the dark stairs and opened the bedroom door. Rose's quiet breathing set my heart back to a near-normal pace.

She's fine, I told myself, *leave her be and go home before you give her a heart attack.*

But I couldn't. I knelt beside the bed and whispered her name.

She moaned and her eyes twitched, but she didn't wake.

"Rose," I repeated, brushing my fingertips through a strand of hair that fell across her forehead.

Her eyes opened and she stared at me for a moment before jerking awake. "Is something wrong?"

"I needed to see you."

"In the middle of the night?" She dropped her head. "Must've been bad…. Whatever you were called in for."

"Another heroin overdose."

She slid over and pulled back the covers, so I kicked off my shoes and took the invitation. As we readjusted she winced and buried her face in my shoulder.

"Took my meds," she said. "Unfortunately, they also give me the false belief that I can move my arm."

I rubbed her skin, carefully avoiding the injured part of her arm until she relaxed again.

"Was it someone from the Retreat again?" she whispered.

"No. Someone who'd met Raini through a job workshop."

Every time her eyes reopened, it obviously took some effort, so I didn't explain further. It could wait for another day if we ever discussed it at all. She didn't need to know of further horrors courtesy of another day at my job.

Chapter Fifteen

SO MUCH FOR PRETENDING

FOR ONE LONG week after another, we chased down endless or dead end leads. Kirk—or Bentley, whatever he wanted to call himself these days—had disappeared, along with most of his known contacts.

The bastard either took a well-timed vacation or he knew we were onto him and went into hiding. Even Richards finally gave in and let us send one of our own out to request an escort for the night. After three attempts, he came up with nothing. Either the girls were also onto us or the whole thing was legit.

We had no line on the heroin, the missing girls, or their connections to the escort company, and every person we interviewed gave us just enough to keep us digging, but never enough to get us where we needed to be.

The only thing I looked forward to was the weekend—not that I believed I was going to get an uninterrupted day, but as burnout loomed even the promise of a brief lull was encouraging. I just needed a few hours to forget the frustration and reset.

On Friday night, Rose was waiting for me at her house by the time I finally escaped another endless day at the station. She was stretched out on the couch with Trapper laying across her stomach and the television on across the room.

"Hey, Sugar. How was your day?"

"Better before I spent the last couple of hours worried about what had happened to you." She tossed Trapper onto the floor and dusted the fur off her top.

"I texted you so you wouldn't worry," I said, distracted by the packed bags waiting in the hallway. "Planning a trip?"

"Really?"

I put my hands up and glanced around, to see if she'd left another clue laying around.

"I told you last week and again a few days ago," she said. "I'm spending the weekend in Rockhill. There's wedding planning to be done and dresses to try on." She ended with a sardonic eye roll.

Apparently, I'd been more distracted than I thought. "Sorry about that."

She snorted and shook her head, patting the couch next to her. "You can still check in on Trapper, right?" she asked. "Peter's coming up to—"

"Peter?" I fought to loosen my jaw as I spoke, but it didn't want to move. Since we'd gotten word about Elizabeth's death, the nightmares had worsened again, sending me back to the Retreat every night while every day gave me new fodder to add to the burning pit. I opted to stay in the doorway, away from Rose, where I hoped my anger would have room to melt away.

"Yeah," her eyes widened at my reaction. "The guy

who's marrying my sister. You're really going to be angry about it when you didn't even let me finish."

"Fine, then finish." The edge to my voice only made the situation worse, but I was too tired to put on a façade.

She jumped up to storm out of the room, but I grabbed her and spun her into the wall, holding her there with my bodyweight.

"Stop being an ass," she hissed through her teeth.

I knew she was right, but I didn't care. The thought of him, for whatever reason, made my entire body tingle with the need to remind her....

She has a right to friends, I reminded myself. Trent was right, and I was overreacting over every single man she mentioned, talked to, or sat in the same room with. Even though she'd never given me a reason.

"James," she said softly. "He's going to be up this way to pick up something for the wedding, and he's giving me a ride down so I don't have to drive alone. That's it."

She didn't struggle against me. Instead she stood there, right where I held her, and let me. Even then, for the life of me, I couldn't calm down.

My fist connected with the wall a few inches from her side. She closed her eyes but barely flinched.

"I let you go once," I whispered, then shoved myself away from her, and stormed through the hallway, grabbing my keys on the way to the door.

"James. Where the fuck are you going?"

"I'll be back," I called over my shoulder. I needed a place to blow off steam—I should have done it before coming home to her. Between the questions, rooting around through my memories, and imagining her with Peter, I felt like I could shoot missiles out of my fingertips.

I felt guilty for leaving her. Stupid even. But I would have been even stupider to stay.

I drove to the gym, it was the closest place with a punching bag. I didn't even have anything to change into, but I checked in, picked up some gloves from the shop and went upstairs to meet the punching bag.

I tore into it until my body couldn't take anymore and my mind finally started to clear—whether from exhaustion or blissful surrender. Collapsing against the wall, I stared through the ten-foot tall window to the blue sky outside. Now I had to do the hardest part. I had to fucking go back and face her—if she was still there.

Her car was still in the driveway—a good sign, but a familiar black car also sat out front, parked on the street. Trent met me at the door, closing it behind him before I could get inside.

"Before she rips you a new ass. What the hell were you thinking?"

"Which part?"

"You can't get fucking up in arms every damn time she's around another guy. How bad was the heart attack when you saw my car out front?"

I swallowed, but my throat was dry and sticky from dehydration. "I'm fighting to keep everything together, and…."

"You're still not sure that you're good enough for her?"

I turned on him. "I never said that."

"Then why are you, James Carter, so fucking insecure about her spending the weekend with her family and an old friend? She's yours, and if you don't see that, you have to be blind."

I didn't have an answer unless I wanted to admit to losing my mind.

"She called me because she was worried about you and wanted to know if I might be able to find you. I knew right where you were, so I decided to stay here and wait instead. I'm still not sure who the fuck needs protection from who." He sighed and pushed open the door. "Once you two make amends how about we all have dinner—we'll have Katie and Evan join us, too."

"Not sure about leaving us alone?"

"I think you both might need a chaperone or three. A low-key change of scenery might do you both some good."

"I'll ask, but I'm not sure she'll—"

Trent shoved me inside and closed the door. I turned and scowled at it for a moment—mostly because that gave me a short delay from the inevitable.

Let the sucking up of the pride commence. I walked into the living room where she sat balled up on the edge of the couch. Instead of sitting next to her, I knelt on the floor in front of her. "I'm sorry, Rose."

"Why are you on the floor?" She nudged her foot against me.

I rested my chin on her knee and she fought a smile, looking up at the ceiling instead of down at me. First point in my favor.

"Will you get up, crazy man?"

"Not until you're not mad. I didn't want to hurt you," I admitted.

"No, you punched the wall and still hurt me." Her fingers slid against my scalp, gentle in contrast to the power of her words. "Maybe not physically, but—"

"I know."

"You were already worked up when you got here— Trent kinda told me what's going on at work."

"It's a mess." I closed my eyes. "Everything's a mess."

"I know, but I need you to talk to me, James, and listen to me." She shoved me back with her knee and slid to the floor beside me. "I enjoy talking to my sister, hearing about Peter and the baby. All the little things he does for her—it's sweet and romantic. He's coming up here to get a special ring custom made by a friend of his."

There wasn't a drop of jealousy in her voice, just her gentle sweetness, maybe a bit of awe. It gave no reason for me to be jealous either—except the very things she spoke of were things I currently felt were out of my grasp.

"I don't know that I'm good at romantic."

"You are," she laid her head against my shoulder, nestling against me as she talked. "But neither of us are going to be good at any of this relationship stuff if we keep shutting each other out."

She said we, but it was clearly pointed at me. I'd made a habit of shutting down or turning to anger over every conversation that pushed my comfort zone.

Settling back into a regular routine was supposed to help me regain control over my life, but the last few hours told me otherwise. I could throw myself into a case all day, and shallow conversations with Rose at night. Even though we disguised it as getting to know each other better, I still kept up the façade, just to hide my remaining secret.

Come clean, tell her. Of all people, she deserves to know. "I'm not sure what I'm capable of, especially where you're concerned."

"I don't know what that means."

"I have dreams where I'm hurting you." I closed my eyes, unable to face her expression as I continued. "It's not always entirely unpleasant."

"As in?"

Wasn't that enough? I wasn't keenly interested in going

207

into a play-by-play. "As in wrapping my hand around your throat. Forcing you to do things you don't want."

"You want to choke me?" she asked. Her voice was smooth, barely any evidence of emotion behind it—utterly calm, and it knocked me off my guard.

"Choke—I," I was the one imagining it and I didn't even know what the hell I wanted. "I don't know what I want."

She climbed to her knees in front of me and lifted my hand to her throat, but I refused to play along, it was too real.

Staring me straight in the eye, she spoke with an even tone and no sign of hesitation. "You're not going to hurt me."

"What makes you so sure?"

She looked at me like I'd just asked the stupidest question she'd ever heard. "You've had every opportunity in the world. I've pushed you, goaded you, risked your life when you didn't have a whole lot of options, and if you didn't hurt me then, why the hell would I think you'd do it now?"

"I did at the bar, and almost today."

Her brows wrinkled and she shook her head. "You squeezed my hand too tight because you were thinking about something else. You weren't doing it on purpose."

"And that's the problem."

"Well, if you're ever in a bar looking for a fight, I'll be sure not to let you wrap your hand around my neck."

"Smart ass."

She tilted her head to the side and smiled. "Thought you were used to that by now."

Taunting. She trusted me too well.

I flattened my hand around her neck, just to see what she'd do—what either of us would do.

My hand tightened, but there was still no panic in her eyes. I grabbed a fistful of hair and pulled her down to face me, keeping my hand firmly around her neck, but she smirked. "What the hell are you doing to me?"

"You're still not hurting me." She took a long breath. "I'm perfectly capable of handling whatever it is that you need."

"I don't want you to." Keeping my hand around her throat, I pushed her down to the floor beside me.

Which one of us would crack first?

"I do, James." Somehow she remained relaxed under my grasp. "And if it's too much—if you get out of hand—I'll tell you."

"I'm bigger than you." I leaned over her face, pressing her into the floor. "How much do you think you can do if I really get out of hand?"

She shook her head—her lips pressed into a tiny line that I had the steadily increasing urge to kiss rather than fight.

"How badly have you really wanted to hurt me?"

"I don't," I said from pure instinct. I released her, groaning as I sat up again. "Remember—" I almost called it back. It was dangerous to ask her to dredge up memories. "In the kitchen, when you decided you wanted to submit—to give me what I wanted."

"And I called you out for getting riled up when I pushed back? That's what you want?" She crawled back to me, head slightly lowered, eyes half closed, and her green eyes peeking up through her lashes.

"All the stuff I couldn't wait to get away from—plugs, and clamps, and watching you fight it before giving in. I still want it and I can't reconcile all of that," my voice was thick and rumbled from my throat.

"You're still trying to convince yourself that Kirk is gone," she said. "Trying so hard that you don't realize that the guy in front of me is all that I want, and you can't understand what on earth would possess me to still want you after everything that happened."

I was frozen in my place. Where was this coming from? She'd been watching me as closely as I watched her in the Retreat, seeing through my avoidance and anger.

"You didn't take the easy way out," she continued. "Maybe not everyone will see it that way because not everyone was in our situation, but I've had a lot of time to think and as far as I'm concerned, you did the right thing."

I shook my head, but she held my face between her palms until I couldn't argue. Until all I could do was face her.

"Do you trust me?" she asked.

"Yes." I finally unlocked my body and pulled her closer, into my lap.

"Then, use that until you trust yourself again. Whatever war is going on in your head," she sighed, "you're just driving yourself crazy. I know because I've been there too. Telling myself that I never wanted to experience any of those things again, even though the thought of what you might do to me...," she closed her eyes, but her face remained lax—unadulterated by whatever she was going to say.

When her eyes opened again, they pulled me into their depths, letting me inside her in ways physical closeness couldn't accomplish. "You pushed me to put my trust in you —in ways I'd never trusted anyone. I still ache for that—for your ability to take me to places I never imagined. I'm not a big fan of pain, but what you give me is different."

"I'm not even in control of myself, and you trust me?"

"Are you out of control or just second guessing your instinct because you *think* it's off?"

I splayed my hands against her back and watched as she arched into me. Taking any motion and pressure I gave her, letting me control her body with a single touch. "Since when are you so good at reading *me*?"

"I had a month with nothing to do except study you," she came back down to earth and poked me in the chest. "Then a month to stew on those studies. And weeks with cranky detective you since then. I guarantee that whatever it is you think you're still protecting me from—I don't need it."

"No?"

"No, James. I stayed with you. I schemed with you. I played my part for you. For the other girls. I killed a man—" She shuddered and the tears began instantly.

"Rose." I wanted to pull her back out of the memories and chase it all away, but she put two fingers across my lips silencing me.

"Let me finish. I let Ross and his friends use me. I watched you get a blow job from the only girl there who was my friend. I sat on that table while Milo tortured us—while you drove the pain away in front of everyone. I chose *you*." Even though her chest shook with emotion, she raised her voice even more. "I chose to live. And I dare anyone to tell me that either of us made the wrong choices."

I cupped her face, wiping away the streaks of tears. "I went under because of the girls, because I wanted to see them freed and returned to their families. But the whole damn system didn't work. I stayed away to protect you and you got shot. Alley died. The other girls—they're not doing a whole lot better, and—"

"And it's not your fault. You can't fix everything." Her

fingers traced my shirt where the scar hid underneath, her breath sent prickles of sensation against my bare neck as she leaned closer. "I watched you enough to know which parts you liked and which ones made you miserable. You took me down to the lake on my birthday—you promised me a good day. I lost the battle that day and realized that I relished in your control. Even though it hurt to move the next morning."

She wet her lips, clenching her fists against my shoulders. "I'm afraid of the pain. I'm afraid of giving you control again. And, I'm afraid of how I'll react, but I *want* it. It is what it is."

I can be reasonable, but you need to stop considering the impossible. You can't go home, you can't escape, and I can't let you go. It is what it is.

How dare she use those words against me?

My anger swelled, vibrating through my muscles, but Rose didn't move—she didn't even look worried. Her head shook slightly, then she pressed her lips against mine. Coaxing me past the anger, and back to sanity.

I felt like a hundred pound weight sat on my chest by the time she finished. "Where'd all that come from?"

She dragged her hand through her hair. "I figured it was about time I give you a little reminder that I'm not so easily broken. Whatever it is you need, I'm game—I do like... watching you. The look you get when you're up to no good and can't hold back. I could get off on that."

With a nervous giggle, she dropped her head forward, her hair creating a curtain around her face. I brushed it back, then pushed her to the floor again, pinning her under me.

"God, I love you."

"What?" Her eyes popped open and she rose so fast, she nearly busted me in the nose with her head.

"Didn't quite think about what I was going to say."

Her shock melted into a smile. "You're serious?"

I nodded, pressing her into the carpet as I leaned in for a kiss. Then, something vibrated against my leg. "That'll probably be Trent about dinner."

"Let it go," she whispered.

I plunged my tongue into her mouth, silencing any other argument she had since I didn't need to hear it. Kisses became like lifesaving breath for a drowning victim, but it wasn't moving past that. Not now. Not after everything we'd been through.

Too much waiting, then rushing things along. I wanted this to be slow. I wanted to revel in the needy look in her eyes —in knowing that she ached for me as much as I did for her.

My cock was engorged by the time I pulled away, and I watched her eye it with a look of lust and hunger.

But I pulled out my phone and checked the message. "We're meeting at Evan's house in thirty."

She cocked an eyebrow. "Priorities."

"Family's important." Pulling her upright, I kissed her forehead. She was visibly off-balance, not knowing where the next touch was going to lead us. And she was fucking gorgeous. Her hair in a fluffy mess and clothes disheveled. "Tonight you meet mine."

"Family includes Trent?"

"You surprised by that?" Blood or not, Trent had always been my brother. Even though they were young, he'd been the love of my sister's life—and so far, I was fairly positive she'd been his as well.

"So it'll just be the six of us?"

"That's all there is, Sugar. Evan's parents live in Florida —his mom is my dad's sister, but they're—" I tried to hold back from explaining too much of my family history, but it was part of us, and something she'd eventually need to know. "She wasn't a carrier like Dad, so they never had to worry about it. My parents died a few years after my sister."

"You never told me her name."

"Taylor." I stared down to where our torsos touched, hugging Rose close. This battle I wasn't going to lose. I couldn't let go of someone who meant so much to me again. "You asked if Cystic Fibrosis was the reason I don't want to have kids."

She nodded.

"But you were a little out of it at the time and I didn't tell you everything. I never wanted to go through anything like that again, or watch someone I loved suffer so much." It was one of the reasons it was so hard to deal with Rose and her nightmares—the reason I always wanted to make things better. I couldn't stand the helpless feeling of not being able to do a damn thing—the same feeling this case was giving me, I realized.

"As soon as I turned twenty-one, I had a vasectomy," I said. I let the news sink in before I said anything more or tried to elaborate—even though I wasn't sure how to even begin.

Her jaw pulsed, eyebrows twitched—I just wanted her to say something.

"Okay," she finally said. "I'm uh—I have no idea how else to respond to that."

"Are you okay with it? I mean dating a guy with no chance of kids—a family of your own."

Her face twisted. "Are you forgetting how I am with kids?"

I laughed, but let it go. That didn't mean she wouldn't change her mind. Evan had, time and time again, given me a spiel about how I'd one day change my mind and regret it, but I just wanted it done—to never have to worry about it.

I stood and pulled her to her feet as well. Much as I hated to go, dinner with friends would be good for us.

"Are we supposed to be bringing anything to dinner?"

"Trent didn't say. I could go for a beer though."

Rose shook her head and slipped on her shoes while I stared out the window next to the door. The late-June evenings were bright and although the air was usually heavy and oppressive with humidity, tonight was fresh and crisp as if a storm had just passed by.

It was the first time I acknowledged the weather in a long time. The first time I could see past the fog of my own brain to enjoy the outside world.

———

AS TRENT PROMISED, dinner with everyone was a good change of pace for us. Rose and Katie hit it off, chatting out back while Evan, Trent, and I sat in the kitchen with our beers. Jack had passed out after dinner, and was slung over Evan's shoulder—apparently all of the company was too much for him.

I tossed my empty bottle into the recycling bin and peeked out the window. Both women were sitting on the porch swing laughing. I hated to think what they might be talking about.

A few minutes later, Katie came inside. "Want me to take him?" she asked, pointing to Jack.

As if he'd recognized the sound of his Mom from deep sleep, Jack lifted his head and slid to the floor and ran across the kitchen. But he didn't stop at Katie. Instead, he breezed right past, into the living room, around in circles, and back again.

"So much for that long nap," I said, ducking out the door Katie had just come in.

"I guess Trent didn't have such a bad idea after all," Rose said, leaning against my shoulder as I sat down next to her.

There wasn't much daylight left, and the sky was turning a bright shade of red. The door opened again, and Trent offered me another beer, which I happily accepted. He offered the second bottle to Rose, but she shook her head and took a couple of swigs of mine instead.

We all sat for a few moments, enjoying the peaceful silence of the beautiful evening until the screen door shook with a loud bang.

"Munchkin wants out," Trent said.

I used my foot to push closed the baby gate on the porch stairs. "Let him run—he might sleep through the night."

Jack had a yard full of toys, but I think Evan had more fun with most of them than the kid did. He also had about half of the large back patio dedicated to his little sheriff's station and rocking pony.

As soon as Trent opened the door, Jack ran straight for the pony, throwing himself over its back. He laid on his stomach, draped over both sides, looking like a cowboy who had one too many nips at the whisky bottle.

Then he jumped up and smacked the horse in the head. I would have laughed if my stomach didn't drop at the same time. The horse rocked back and knocked Jack flat on his back.

I was on my feet before he had a chance to make a

sound, but by the time I picked him up, his eyes were red and he'd broken into a full bawl.

"You shouldn't pick on horses, kid. They have a tendency to buck."

Jack's bottom lip jutted out and he buried his face against my shoulder.

I caught a glimpse of Katie and Evan watching from inside, but I waved for them to go back to whatever they were doing. In five minutes, he'd be fine and back to playing.

When he went quiet, I swiveled back and saw that Trent had taken my seat, his arm resting on the back of the swing behind Rose.

I lowered my eyes to Jack, making sure that he was okay, and trying not to pay attention to what I assumed was an attempt at baiting me.

"Everything's okay," I whispered, rubbing Jack's back. Nearly as quickly as it all happened, he was kicking to get down and ready to go again.

Now I had nothing to help me avoid facing Rose and Trent. Why'd he have to go and ruin a perfectly good night?

She handed me back my beer—which I didn't even remember passing to her. Trent didn't even offer to get up, and I knew that nothing that came out of my mouth was going to be positive.

It wasn't just jealousy—it was pain and anger, betrayal —loss of control. So many emotions surged through my body.

Trent had called it insecurity, and hell, that may have played a part in it.

I claimed her at the Retreat—claimed a living human being to keep her alive. Even Ross called her mine, but I had to wake every morning and go through my day knowing that she wasn't really. Knowing that someone could take her away at any moment.

"James?" Rose sat forward.

I shook my head, picked up Jack and went inside, handing him to Katie as I passed. "Sorry."

Her face was questioning, but before she could say anything Trent followed me in.

"I need a few minutes. And if you follow me—" I pointed at Trent as I marched backward through the living room toward the stairs "I will rip your head off."

"What the heck did you do?" I heard Katie whisper not so quietly to Trent, but I barricaded myself in the bedroom before I could hear the rest.

I pressed my forehead into the wall. I knew I had no reason to be angry, and it just made it worse. Trent was pushing me, and I fully admitted that on one level, I needed to be pushed. To see how irrational my anger was.

But the whole situation made my skin burn like I'd been dunked in acid.

"James," Rose called, knocking on the door. "Can I come in?"

I didn't answer. My muscles ached under the strain, and my eyes burned with overdue tears of every emotion.

"I know you don't want to talk—"

I slid down the wall. I didn't want to see anyone either. Not until I could pull myself together.

"Can you at least knock on the door, so I know you're alive in there?"

I sighed and opened the door.

Without unnecessary words, she sat down next to me and laid her head on my shoulder. "I get it."

I closed my eyes as the hot trails burned down my face.

Rose wrapped her arms around mine but didn't move or speak until the sun had set and the room darkened.

"I don't have to leave tomorrow," she whispered.

I kissed her head and swallowed all of the crud that had collected in my throat. "Go, Sugar. I want you to. You should see your family and have some fun."

"Remember what you said earlier?" She squeezed my hand.

"I've said a lot of things." I'd regained the ability to formulate sentences, but I still felt raw and empty.

She snorted and shook her head. "Well, I love you too."

I squeezed her until I thought her bones were in danger of breaking, and then we moved to the bed, sitting in each other's arms in silence until she fell asleep.

Chapter Sixteen

TARGETED

TUESDAY NIGHT, I let myself into Rose's empty house to feed Trapper. She'd already called to tell me that she wouldn't be back until late Wednesday—three days later than she originally planned.

She needed more time with her family—I could give her that, but it didn't mean it was easy.

I tapped her number on my phone while I straightened up in the living room where Trapper had once again played bulldozer and wiped everything out. It was an uphill battle to clean up after her, and usually useless, but it gave me something to do.

"Hey." Her voice was light and chipper when she answered. "You should come rescue me before they try to put me on baby duty again."

"Uh huh. And how long did you last? Five minutes?"

She made a sound but didn't respond.

"Well, you can come relieve me from cat duty. Trapper's a bigger pain in the ass." I squinted toward a window at a car creeping down the road in front of the house. I couldn't make out any details through the curtains, but I hit the light next to me, darkening the room.

A blast filled the air, leaving me surrounded by the sounds of shattering glass as I hit the floor.

The cellphone landed on the ground next to me, but I could still hear Rose's voice. "James? What the hell?"

I picked up the phone, still unable to talk and surveyed my body. I didn't feel pain, but everything was so shaky and numb I wasn't sure.

No blood. No pain.

Rose yelled again.

"I'm okay," I said, staying close to the floor. "I need to call Trent. Can I call you right back?"

"No. Something exploded. Tell me what the fuck is going on." I had to hold the phone away from my ear to keep from being deafened again.

"Someone just shot at me, and I need to call it in." Despite my best efforts, my voice still shook uncontrollably.

"What?"

I knew the onslaught of questions was coming, and I felt guilty for leaving her hanging. "I promise, Sugar. Give me ten. I'm safe."

Unless the guy decides to come back and finish the job, but I wasn't going to be the jerk to give her that idea if she hadn't already considered it.

Rose was still speaking when I disconnected. I called the station first, then Trent.

"You okay?" he asked immediately. "I just heard it come over the radio."

"Fine, he missed by at least an inch or two."

"Amateur," Trent said. "I'm on my way. Rose is still out of town?"

"Yeah, but she might not be for very long if I don't call her back and convince her to stay where she is."

The phone barely had a chance to ring before Rose answered. "What the fuck, James?"

"Calm down. I haven't had a chance to figure out the whole story, but as you heard someone tried to shoot me."

"In my house?" she shrieked.

"Through the living room window. The shot came from the street, but the car's gone. Squad cars are on their way, and so is Trent." I locked Trapper in the bathroom in case she got any ideas about escaping through the broken window or running through the broken glass. Then I sat down on the stairs, with Rose still on the line.

We both waited quietly as if anticipating that the other would have something to say, but my mind was too busy racing through the possibilities to speak much.

If they were after me, they knew my schedule and could have attacked at any time, but they chose to use my girl-friend's house. The alternative was that they were after her, but any good hired killer worth his salt would have done enough research to know she was gone.

He was after me, I reasoned—I hoped. But either way, he now knew where Rose lived and could come back for either of us if he figured out he missed. Unless even that was intentional.

If all the noise hadn't given me a headache, the slew of possibilities would have.

There wasn't anything else I could tell Rose, but she refused to let me off the phone until the other officers had arrived seven minutes later.

Trent pulled up behind the cruiser and ran up to the porch where we were all standing.

"I need to go, Rose," I explained. It was difficult to keep up with her and everyone else at the same time.

"I'm coming home tonight," she said.

"No, stay where you are until we figure it all out."

"James," her voice squeaked. "I don't want to sit down here and worry between phone calls. I'll stay out of the way, I just—"

"You're safer there," I said, but I knew that argument wouldn't work. Safer for her wasn't her concern.

Trent sniped my phone. "Rose?"

He paused a second while I watched and considered knocking his block off.

"I'm going to make sure he's safe, but it's much easier to keep track of one person and keep him guarded, rather than two. I know you want to help, and I know you don't want to be out of the loop, but I need you to stay there so I can keep him safe."

He waited for her response then handed the phone back to me.

"I'll stay put," she said quietly, "but if either of you get hurt, I'm coming after someone."

I couldn't help but laugh. "I have no doubt. I'll call you later."

As I began explaining what had happened, Trent's phone beeped.

"Davis," he said, stepping away from us. "Where?... We'll be right there."

He pointed to the officers. "Get the house secure, and let me know what you find." Then, he motioned for me to follow. "A cell phone was left for you at the station. All it had was a post-it note with your name. They're running fingerprints and reviewing the cameras to see if they can determine where it came from."

"You think it was dumb luck that it turned up the same day as the shooting?" I asked.

"Let's find out."

———

WE MET the techs downstairs where they were discussing the cell phone with Captain Richards.

"Are they trying to bomb us now?" I asked.

"No, it's just a standard camera phone that you can pick up at any store. It's never been used except to take one picture."

I had to school my features when I picked it up to see a picture of a group of women in a bridal store. "That's Rose and her sister."

Dragging my hands through my hair, I marched around the room. I couldn't stand looking at it. "Any way to tell when it was taken?"

"According to the timestamp," the tech said, "yesterday afternoon."

Trent intercepted me. "You just talked to her, so you know she's fine."

That didn't matter. It didn't take long for everything to begin falling apart. Within seconds, I went from a quiet day stopping by her house to feed the cat and ended up getting shot at.

I took the phone from the tech, scowling at the image on the screen, and started dialing my own phone.

I dropped into a chair, relieved when Rose answered on the first ring.

"Everything okay?"

I was probably going to give the poor girl a heart attack before the end of the day. "Where are you right now?"

"Um," I could tell the question threw her off guard. "My parents' house, we're having dinner."

"Who all is we?"

"You're not going to flip out again, are you?"

"No, Rose, just answer." I was already flipping out and Peter was the least of my worries.

"My parents, Chey, Laney, and Peter."

The other phone vibrated—I'd almost forgotten I was holding it, but when I looked down, I saw a new image had automatically opened. A blue house. The area was dimly lit, taken outdoors—my eyes went to the window.

The photo perfectly matched the current evening light.

I lowered my head, praying that I was wrong. "Describe your parent's house."

"Um, light blue, cape cod. What the hell is going on, James?"

"Make sure everything is locked." I handed Trent the phone with the image, and he stepped away to make his own call. "Keep everyone away from the windows, and don't let anyone in or out."

"James?" Her voice was desperate, but I didn't know what else to give her. She was two hours away, and whatever these bastards had planned she was long out of my reach.

They'd been waiting for this. Someone had been waiting for us to separate.

Trent tapped my shoulder, then pointed to his phone. "I'm talking to a detective there, he and an unmarked squad car are on their way over there."

I assumed he'd already had their address and contacts in their area from when Rose was missing.

"We're in Dad's office," Rose whispered. "There aren't any windows and the house is locked up. What's going on?"

I heard a baby fussing in the background. "You're being watched."

"Does this have anything to do with what happened to you earlier?"

From the vagueness of her statement, I assumed that meant she hadn't told her family about the shooting. I wouldn't want to find out what they'd think of me if they knew all the details. "Probably."

"Won't do me any good to say I want to come home, will it?"

I didn't know how to answer that. Fifteen minutes ago, I was convinced she was safer with her family, but now I wasn't convinced of anything.

Trent got the call when the police arrived. It took only five minutes. Even that wasn't fast enough in my opinion, but nothing would be.

"Trent has a contact down there," I explained to Rose, "Detective Stephens, he should be walking up to your front door now, so go answer it."

"Okay."

I heard movement through the phone, then some kind of debate.

"Stay here," Rose said. "It's a cop. I'm going to let him in. It'll be fine."

The fear was nearly completely gone from her voice— whether it was just for show for me or her family. I took a deep breath. "Rose."

"Yeah, I'm heading to the door."

"I love you, Sugar."

I heard her breath across the microphone. "I love you, too, even though I'd rather tell you that in person."

"Hi," her voice was faint, and then I heard a male voice, but couldn't quite make out the words. I rubbed my hand through my hair. Their conversation was faded and near impossible to keep up with.

After a few tense minutes, she came back on and I put her on speaker phone so Trent and Captain Richards could hear. "They're clearing the area, but haven't found anything suspicious. You're sure he's watching?"

"Sent a picture of your parents' house. Looks like it was taken in the evening, right about this time, but we can't be certain. He also had a picture of you and your sister in a bridal shop." I didn't want to alarm her, but she needed all of the facts to keep herself safe.

"We've been there the last two days. What the hell am I supposed to do? I don't want my family in danger, too."

"They're putting a protective detail on the house," Trent said.

"So, I'm just supposed to sit here and wait—what about everyone else?"

It was me they wanted, and if they could use her, they could use her family. "Stay together. We'll get you more information as soon as we can."

"For now," Trent said, "get ahold of Stephens if you need anything."

He gave her the direct number to call, and I said my reluctant goodbye before hanging up the phone.

"You're going to a safe house," Captain Richards said.

I began to argue but recalled it within the same instant. I wasn't living alone, and I sure as hell wasn't going to Evan's house with someone gunning for me. I should have started apartment hunting when the thought had first crossed my mind—but then, my request to the universe for more hours in a day had yet to be granted.

I had a feeling I was about to have far more hours with nothing to do.

"Evan and Katie have been thinking about taking a trip to see his parents," Trent said. "I'm going to see that they get on a plane and get out of here for a few days."

I nodded and watched my grasp on the situation slip impossibly away. We'd been worried about the wrong enemy coming back to bite me in the ass. I couldn't believe that Kirk had gotten so powerful or made this many ties. He'd only been out months.

Maybe we'd discounted my enemies too quickly. And I hoped the dread—the overwhelming fear that they might be joining forces—was unsubstantiated. The Retreat had been hard to bring down on its own, but whatever was going on now was running with the same level of efficiency.

If they controlled every lead and every piece of information we'd received, we'd spend years digging before we figured out what might lead us in the right direction.

"They know Rose is my weakness…. Waited until she was out of town and out of reach. But… why?"

"You," Trent said. "If this is the real Kirk, he's putting you out of commission, just like you did him."

Richards picked up his phone. "I'll make the calls to get you set up in the safe house, James. Don't make me order you to stay there until we get this worked out."

"Just find me the bastard. I've had enough of this shit."

Chapter Seventeen

RELEASE THE DARK

TRENT PROMISED I'd be in the safe house a few days max, but faster than I imagined, that turned into weeks. Evan and Katie were home and back to business as usual, and although the authorities were keeping an eye on Rose and her family, they couldn't stay on lockdown forever.

And neither could I.

I sat on the living room floor, going over the copies of everything that Trent brought over most evenings. The quiet was the only reason I hadn't begun demanding to leave the safe house. Surprisingly, it wasn't as intimidating as I feared—especially since I had plenty to keep me busy.

A board creaked on the front porch and I reached for the gun I'd stored under the couch.

"It's me," Trent called.

I relaxed, returning my attention to the files as the lock unfastened and the door opened. But, as he entered, I noticed a second set of footsteps.

Trent rounded the corner, leaned against the back of the chair and smirked. "Don't shoot me."

I scowled. What the hell was he up to?

Rose stepped through the doorway. "Apparently I can be a pain in the ass."

"That's an understatement." I jumped to my feet and lifted her with a crushing hug.

"I have a meeting to get back to, but I figured you could use some company. And maybe she'll keep you in line," he winked and headed right back out.

"Couldn't handle it anymore," Rose said. "Maybe it's all over, and he just wanted to fuck with you."

"We can hope, but either way, no one is trusting anything until we get to the bottom of it. And considering it has been weeks since I've seen anything outside of this house, I'm beginning to wonder if it's possible."

She hooked her arms around my neck—the first time she'd been able to do it since being shot. "Trouble is almost healed," she said with a wink. "But that's about the limits of my skill right now. Sometimes rehab is worse than the initial shot."

"You'll get there. You did survive me for a month."

"Mmmh, yes. I guess you'd like to get back to your work," she said waving to my makeshift workstation on the coffee table and floor.

"I could think of better things to do." Hands on her ass, I lifted her up to kiss me.

She slid back down to the floor, a smile plastered on her face. "Anything I can do to help?"

I glided my hand up the back of her shirt to rest on her bare back.

"Rules," she whispered, but it didn't bring me back down.

Captain Richards had made arrangements for Dr. Combs to come to me once a week to continue our sessions, but I still hadn't admitted to her all the things I'd told Rose. The dreams were still relentless, but it was becoming easier to disconnect with them.

Pushing her back toward the couch, my lips crashed against hers. Needy and hungry for her taste, her touch, even her voice. I wanted her, and for a moment, I wanted to forget everything that kept getting in our way.

After two steps, Rose stood her ground, slipping from my grasp. "Nice to see you, too. Maybe we should talk first."

I caught her again and spun her against my chest so her back was to me and her ear was near my mouth. "Really want me to stop?"

"Are you doing this for a distraction?"

I released her and dropped my hands to my sides. *Distraction? Fuck yes,* I wanted a distraction. But that wasn't all I wanted. "Fine. I want to think about my girlfriend more than this stupid case and my current situation."

I reached to grab her arm, but she ducked away again.

Her mouth twitched, and she took another step backward. She was intentionally goading me.

Springing toward her, I grabbed her by the waist and pulled her down onto the couch. I landed on my back, holding her tight to my chest. My mouth sealed around hers igniting a searing pulse through my veins. My body wanted free from the rules. Free from everything to concentrate on only one thing.

But she flipped to the floor again and scampered away. "We shouldn't, James." She put out her hand but had a smile on her face the whole time.

I chased after her again, slamming her into a wall—it vibrated so hard a picture frame fell off. I froze as soon as it happened, but she reached back up to kiss me.

Too much. I straightened and pulled back. "What the hell are you doing?"

"Giving you something else to think about."

"Not throwing you through a wall—that's a brilliant alternative."

She pursed her lips and fisted my shirt deterring me from retreating any further. "Well, if you get close to that point, I'll let you know."

I wanted to push, and she wanted to be pushed.

And that gave me an idea. Kissing her to keep her attention, I held her there and reached over to my suit jacket that was thrown over a nearby table. I felt heavy metal against my fingers, and for a moment, I second guessed my intention.

I couldn't go my entire life second guessing everything.

Her eyes opened as I tightened the cold cuff around one wrist.

"Still game?"

She looked down at the cuffs, then up at me. "I really hope you have the key."

"You'll find out." I twisted her cuffed hand behind her back. Kissing her neck and pulling her shirt down to trail my lips along her collarbone. "No sex," I muttered.

I could indulge in my fantasies, or I could let go of my rules, but I wasn't willing to do both yet.

"No being rash this time?"

"I wasn't rash last time." *Not entirely.* I needed control, not rash, impulsive lust, if we were going to test this out. I hadn't wanted to justify my dark fantasies. Leaving it as some foreign part of me was easier to accept. Chiefly because I associated it with the Retreat—not with my real life, but it kept slowly creeping back. It pained me to admit that Rose was right.

She tilted her head and smiled. "Do your worst."

"You don't want to tell me that, Sugar," my voice growled as I spoke, moving toward her again. "You're just fine with me acting out my fantasies without sex?"

She rubbed her lips together. "Delayed gratification, I guess."

"Any limits?"

Her eyebrows wiggled. "We'll figure it out when we get to it."

I put my hand to her throat. All the times in life I'd been told to face my fears—I didn't think anyone would have anticipated my applying that to strangling my girlfriend.

Her eyes locked on me, slightly distant, but still aware of every motion.

I hooked my finger through the empty ring of the hand-cuff and led her toward the kitchen. No plan in mind, I'd just have to see what I could come up with.

I started to pull up her shirt, but she brushed away my hands.

"You first."

I groaned and pressed her backward over the table. "My fantasy. Take your shirt off."

She jutted out her lower lip for a second, before slowly pulling up her shirt and dropping it on the floor.

We were about to see how far my control could go.

"Don't I even get some eye candy?" she asked, tugging at my shirt again.

"No," I flipped her legs onto the table and twisted her around to lay across it long ways. "You might not be seeing much of anything."

I fastened the other end of the cuff to the leg of the table. "Can you lift your other arm over your head?"

"Not even close," she slid it up the table until it was

nearly straight out. "That's about the limit for my shoulder."

"Don't move," I kissed her bare stomach before I stepped away. There had to be a few things around the house we could use for fun. I grabbed a length of clothesline and clothespins from the laundry room, and a couple of ties from the suitcase I had never unpacked.

I used one tie on her right arm—leaving her plenty of room to keep it comfortable and not strain the healing muscle. Then, I slid off her shoes and jean shorts.

"You're quiet," I said.

"I'm enjoying watching you." Her voice was already light, yet rough.

My first big surprise—she really did enjoy it.

I took the scissors from the knife rack and cut the clothesline into smaller sections so I could secure her ankles. I was sure to leave enough room that the harsh line wouldn't cut into skin, but I didn't imagine she'd be flailing around too much anyway.

Then, my second tie. I held it up, loosely hanging over my finger. "I'm going to cover your eyes."

"That's no fun," she pouted, testing each of her restrained appendages before she nodded. She never took her gaze from my face, but her neck and arms strained.

I made a loop with the tie, then slid it over her head and tightened it. Without being able to see me, she wouldn't know what to expect, and I could have some fun watching her reactions and seeing how far she'd let me go without stopping me.

I rubbed my fingers down her body, leaving a trail of goosebumps that tightened her skin up to her breasts, pulling her nipples into tight points. I pinched one and she

234

arched, a moan beginning deep in her chest and sticking in her throat.

Rolling her breasts beneath my palms, I squeezed again. Switching between soft caresses and harsh pinches at a random pace until she squirmed and gasped for air.

I moved down the table and smacked the inside of her leg, gently at first, but I increased the power behind each swing.

She fisted her hands and curled her toes.

Then, I picked up the clothespins, stretching them so the springs would be a bit looser. I snapped the first one over her left nipple, and she squealed, sucking in her lower lip and biting it. Her body remained tense, probably preparing for the second pinch, so I stepped back and waited.

I searched through a few kitchen drawers and found a basting brush. Starting just below her bellybutton, I drew the silicone bristles gently up her stomach, across her collarbone, and then I trailed it around her other taut nipple.

She shuddered, then relaxed—just what I was waiting for. I snapped the second clothespin onto her nipple.

"Son of a—" Biting back the words, she arched off the table. Air hissed as she forced slow breaths through her clenched teeth.

I opened another drawer, searching for something else and grabbed a butter knife—blindfolded, she'd have no idea what the cold surface was. I dragged it down her sides, across her neck, and between her legs. Each whispered gasp spurring me onward.

I pressed the heel of my palm to her sex. I was slipping dangerously close to breaking my rule, especially as I heard her moan and watched her muscles twitch for more. My cock jumped in reaction to her movements.

I dragged my nails up her body. She still arched toward my touch, mewing quietly as I reached her neck. Standing at the head of the table, I kissed her. Holding my hand around her neck while my other hand twisted and pulled at her nipple.

She took in a long shaky breath when I released her and stepped away. "What do you want, Sugar?"

"Your fantasy," she spoke as if her tongue stuck to the roof of her mouth. "Your worst. Push."

I flicked one of the clothespins, and she gulped in a rough breath of air.

As I started to step around the table again, her fingers brushed against my belt.

She couldn't.

I unfastened the cuffs and untied her other arm.

She sat up and pursed her lips, yanking the tie off of her head and snapping it at me. "That all you got?"

I caught the end of the tie and pulled her to my face. "Not at all."

I untied her legs. "Roll over."

She didn't move, so I smacked the inside of her thigh, and she finally rolled over, a smile on her face the whole time.

"Oh, Sugar." I fished through the open drawer again and came up with a spatula.

I can't believe I'm really doing this.

But it was damn fun. Especially after being locked up on my own for weeks on end.

The spatula slapped against her skin, and she squeaked, grabbing ahold of the side of the table. "How about this? Zero means you feel great and want to keep going—"

"Zero."

I raised an eyebrow and smacked her again. "Five

means you can't take it anymore, and the rest is if you need something in between."

I wanted to move slow—even if she wanted it, one of us could just as easily slide into a flashback that would not only ruin the mood but the entire week.

"Zero," she said again, this time in a teasing sing-song voice.

I brought the spatula down again, one strike to each ass cheek and one on the back of each thigh. She took a deep breath when I paused, but her body was still.

"If I didn't know better, I'd say you enjoy far more than just watching me." I winked, kissing her shoulder.

All I got was a moan in return that grew louder as I brought the spatula down four more times. I continued beating out a variety of patterns while I listened to her mix of moans and squeaks. She pressed against me as I rubbed a hand across the pinkened skin.

"More, Sugar?"

"Yes," she breathed.

Where would either of us draw the line?

I took off my belt and folded it over as she watched, biting her lip.

"Where do you stand?"

"One."

I smiled at her honesty. The belt cracked against her skin and she squeezed her eyes closed. My second strike was a bit lighter, giving her a chance to adjust. After three more strikes, her body—of all things—started to relax.

"Number?" I asked, taking a moment to rub her skin again.

"Zero," her voice was almost drowsy.

I scoffed. "After all that, you went from one to zero?"

"Mmm," she took a deep breath. "It's starting to feel… fuzzy. Good. Very good."

My next few strikes were harder and swifter, but she didn't tense again until the third, and then she relaxed again immediately. I sat my belt down on the counter.

Caressing and kissing all of the warm, tender flesh, I moved up her body. Even her shoulders and neck were free from tension as if I'd just given her a long full-body massage rather than a beating.

"Don't stop," she said, voice barely verging on a whisper.

"I think you've had enough, Sugar." I kissed her forehead, but she glared back at me. "And so have I, for now."

Suddenly, she shivered and goosebumps broke out all over her skin again. "How about we just cuddle for a while?"

I helped her to her feet and wrapped her in a blanket as we settled on the couch, her laying between my legs and against my chest.

As much as the whole thing turned me on, my cock had resolved to the fact that it wasn't getting any attention, and I was finally beginning to feel in control of it all.

Chapter Eighteen

FRIENDS, LOVERS, AND FIENDS

I STARTLED at the sound of Trent's voice.

"About damn time you wake up," he said.

Still laying against my chest, Rose groaned and pulled the blanket tighter around her.

The room was darker as the late afternoon sun moved to the back of the house. The main source of light came from the lamp Trent must have turned on when he came in.

It took me another second to remember what we'd done.

"We really need some new rules for you barging in here," I said.

"Right, well if you would have answered the door the first three times I knocked—I was beginning to worry." He stood above us, hands on hips and oblivious to Rose's condition beneath the blanket.

"How about you step back *out* the door?" I raised my eyebrows and cocked my head.

His eyebrows pinched together, then his eyes widened, and he stepped back without another word. I sat up with

Rose as the door clicked closed, stealing a final kiss before she dashed off to the kitchen to gather her clothes.

I followed behind at a more casual pace, stowing away all of the implements I'd gathered. "You still okay with everything?"

"Us, yes. Trent, not so much—can I go hide now?" At first, I thought she was kidding, but her eyes were miserably pleading.

I hooked my arm around her neck. "No hiding. Let's go see what our intruder wants."

"You see what he wants. If I can't hide, I'm at least going back to sleep." She dropped to the couch as we passed and pulled the blanket around herself again.

I opened the door and gave Trent a flat look, but he just laughed in my face. "Next time hang a tie on the door."

"Didn't have one to spare."

Trent gave me a second look as he passed. "Well, I mostly came to see if you wanted anything for dinner. Bad news—"

"Nothing new on the case?" I guessed and Trent nodded. "Why am I not surprised? I'm about to start subscribing to conspiracy theories."

Rose squinted at something on the table where I'd left my copies of the case files strewn out. She slid over a piece of paper and picked up the sketch of the second man Raini had described.

"You recognize him?" I asked.

She nodded slowly. "Remember when I said Elijah was talking to an old friend at the bar? This is him," her voice barely made a sound with her final statement.

Trent and I flanked her—I felt like we were swarming her, but it was the first big break we had.

"You know his name? Anything?" I asked.

"No. He had a wicked scar down his arm, but that's all I know. Elijah stepped away to talk to him, and Charlene said she didn't know him either." She dropped the picture and stood. "Oh god."

I tried to pull her back, but she shook me off.

"I um…. It's just that. Elijah knows where my parents live. He's been there. I told Charlene I was going to be there. That you were taking care of Trapper. I sent her a picture of where we were shopping for dresses. James—" she spun back toward me "—tell me I'm overthinking it. Tell me I'm wrong, being paranoid. Something."

I stared down at the picture and shook my head. "I don't know." I wanted to ease her fears, but couldn't convince myself to lie to do it. "We need to find him."

Trent sat against the couch arm. "Charlene said you two went to school together before her family moved to Oklahoma. Then, you both moved here a couple of years ago."

"Yeah, we always stayed in touch. I never really talked to Elijah though. He had the whole overprotective brother thing down, but not really the social thing. He moved in with her a few months back after a big tiff with his roommate."

She rubbed her forehead and I pulled her into my lap.

"We need to find out what all he knows," Trent said.

"No," I said, and they both looked at me. "I know how you think—" I pointed to Trent "—and Rose is staying out of this."

"You know how I think because it's how you'd think too if you didn't have puppy dog eyes."

I straightened, nearly shoving Rose back to her feet.

"Guys," she jumped up before I had the chance. "If I can help, I'll do it. It's better than waiting for them to make the next move. Everything has been silent since the threats, maybe going into hiding is what they wanted. Maybe...." She looked back at the photograph. "It's all a misunderstanding and he can just give us a name."

"And if he's willing to kill to protect that name?" I asked. Given what we were dealing with—the level of deceit from whoever was playing us—we'd be insane to ignore that possibility.

"He hasn't done it yet," Rose said, holding her head high. "And he's had the opportunity. You drag him in and you throw up all the flags, but if I go over there looking for Charlene—"

I cut her off. "And you'll randomly ask about the guy he spoke to in the bar? I think by that point he'll be on to you."

She shrugged, her gaze moved from me to Trent and back again. "Lucky my guards will be waiting close by."

Why did I have to go after a girl who was at least as gutsy as me? It had to be against the laws of the universe. "That won't do us any good if he shoots you first."

"I doubt he'd know how to aim a gun if he had one. If he goes for something, I'll drop everything and duck. You know I can do this."

It was one thing watching her put herself on the line at the Retreat, I didn't want to do it again. But I also knew she could handle it, and that there was no arguing when she put on her determined face. "Fine, you be the knight in shining armor."

She smirked and put her hand on her hip.

Trent chuckled. "Sometimes, I question my sanity for encouraging you two. As if you're both not crazy, intimidating, and stubborn on your own.... I'll work on getting everything set up."

"Only if I'm in that surveillance van," I said through clenched teeth.

———

TRENT and I got Rose set up and wired. According to Trent, Richards had been out of the office and unreachable, so, yet again, we'd opted to take our chances and run with the plan ourselves with only a couple of officers who agreed to go along as backup. I called Detective Winsor to drop Rose off at her own car so she could drive herself to Elijah's apartment. Then, with my gut tangled in several dozen knots that I wasn't sure even time would ever undo, Trent and I headed over to the location to set up surveillance.

"If you don't stop freaking out and bouncing her foot, people are going to think we're in here having sex," Trent said.

"It'll make a good cover," I said. As much as we tended to quibble and fight, push each other's buttons, and threaten to rip each other apart, we never had a problem settling back into our usual banter and rhythm.

Trent nodded to the driveway about five hundred feet away from our SUV. "She's here."

Rose's voice came over the receiver. "Hope you guys can hear me."

I sent her a text: *Take it slow.*

"Right," she said.

My phone buzzed.

ROSE: Love you.

She climbed out of the car and headed up to the apartment complex without even looking in our direction.

"She's good," Trent said. "Calm, not fidgety—"

"You have no idea how good she is." I couldn't imagine that confronting an old friend—even under the current circumstances—could be as intimidating as facing Milo or staring down Ross with his gun pointed to her face.

Over the receiver, we heard the mutter of people passing by, doors opening and closing, and then three solid knocks.

"Rose," he sounded surprised. "What's going on?"

"I was hoping Charlene was still around. I've been out of the loop for a while."

"No, she left last week. Everything okay?"

"Yeah, sorry." There was a pause. "Hey, that guy you were talking to at the bar the other night, I started thinking that he looked familiar and it's been bugging me. Does he bartend? Pufferbelly maybe?"

"Why would you think that?" He already sounded tense and defensive.

"Just curious. We used to go there all the time, you know."

"He doesn't."

Come on, Rose. I tapped my fingers against my thigh, unable to sit still.

"I'm sure I know him from somewhere. What does he do?"

"Why do you care?" Elijah's voice rose.

I heard the door close and my heart clenched.

"Like I said," she kept her voice even and slow, "it was bugging me. How do you know him?"

"Leave it alone," he said in a hushed voice.

"No big deal, right?" She matched his tone.

My hand clenched against my thigh. I wasn't sure if she could get anything before he sounded the alarms.

"What do you know?" Elijah asked.

"I asked first. One simple question."

"You and your cop friends just need to stay out of it."

Almost there.

"Stay out of it? I wasn't doing anything when I was threatened last month."

"It wasn't a threat," he growled.

I reached for the door handle—it was enough for me, and with his rising anger, I wasn't sure how much longer she'd be safe.

Rose snorted. "So you told them where I was? How to find me?"

"No." There was a long pause, and Elijah's voice sounded more distant as if he'd moved away from her.

Trent didn't budge, but I was about to crawl out of my skin. "I don't like not having eyes on her."

He put up his hand, staring intently at the receiver. "You said that I have no idea how good she is—maybe you should trust in your own assessment and give her a minute."

"I didn't tell anyone where you were," Elijah said. "They never knew."

"You arranged the pictures?"

There was silence.

"How dare you," she yelled so loudly the mic crackled. "Were you also the one shooting up my house?"

"I didn't expect anyone to be there," his voice rose again. "They were going to kill Charlene if I didn't take off some of the pressure."

"How did you get involved with them in the first place?"

"Long story. I, uh, they got something on me. I just kept going deeper and they—they said they'd kill Charlene and my family."

"So, much better to threaten *my* family."

"I'm sorry, Rose. I had nothing—*Please*. I knew nothing bad would happen to anyone. They were just pictures."

"You're begging me now. You could have come clean."

"Not with everything they had on me. I made stupid

mistakes. They weren't—you weren't supposed to get hurt. B-but I screwed up—I had to save my sister. I didn't mean for you to get hurt."

"Oh...."

Something rustled against the microphone and my body coiled, ready to spring out of the car, but Trent caught my arm and held up his finger for me to give it another minute.

"Please," her voice wavered, "tell me you didn't set me up."

"They'll never let me go. They won't let you go either now."

"Elijah, wait. We can fix it we can take it—"

"No," he shouted and something rustled against the mic again.

"Just give me five minutes—"

Five. That was our cue, we signaled for backup to move in and sprinted toward the front of the building.

No noise. No shots. My skin tingled with anticipation.

Just keep him talking, I mentally urged her. Keep him talking and not attacking.

We flanked the door listening for a brief moment to gauge what was going on. Trent tried the knob, turning it slowly, then he nodded to me and flung it open.

Rose was in the corner of the room, hands raised in a defensive posture while Elijah stood a few feet in front of her with a kitchen knife.

"I just need to keep her here," he said.

Trent and I edged around him until I had a clear line to Rose. Keeping my gun pointed at him, I held my hand out to her. "I'm not going to let you do that. How about you let her come to me?"

"They're going to be coming for us," Elijah said, the knife in his hand shaking. "They know everything. Always."

"They have the place bugged?" Trent asked, somehow managing to keep his voice com.

"No. They just know." Elijah's hand shook even harder.

A parade of officers entered the room behind us.

"Drop the knife, Elijah," Trent said, moving cautiously toward him. "They're the least of your worries at the moment."

Elijah shook his head and charged toward Rose, but Trent caught his arm and in a swift move twisted his forearm around until the knife clattered to the floor. Trent used Elijah's momentum to then slam him into the wall and held him there long enough for one of the officers to cuff him.

Rose straightened and ran straight to my arms. "What the fuck took you so long?"

I kissed her forehead and lifted her to her toes. "We came as soon as you said five."

"Well, that seemed like an hour ago."

"Sweep the place for radio frequencies," Trent ordered. "We need to find out quick if they were already listening or if he's just paranoid. In the meantime, let's get you two back to the station, too."

Chapter Nineteen

TRAITOR WITHIN

"TOLD YOU I COULD HANDLE IT," Rose said with a wink.

We were waiting in the same interview room I'd been shoved into while Trent handled Raini's interview, but at least this time, I had far better company. Rose came over and sat in my lap, curling her arm around my neck.

I clasped my hands around her waist, content to keep her there. "You didn't seem so cocky when I walked in."

"Decided to let you play the hero," she whispered, her nose grazing my cheek.

"Uh-huh," I muttered. There was something off about her—more than the scare she'd received from Elijah. After the long nap she'd had, I didn't think even the afternoon was intense enough to make her that sleepy, but she sighed and sagged against my shoulder.

"Sometimes, I quite enjoy having you rescue me." Every sentence was lighter than the last.

I pushed her upright to see her face, her forehead and neck were tense, eyes half-hooded. "Headache?"

"It's fine." She tried to brush me off, but I'd be stupid to let her. We were both good at downplaying what was wrong. Trying to shove it to the side and ignore it rather than deal with it—rather than let someone help us deal with it. I pulled the chair next to me closer and motioned her toward it. Then, I turned mine sideways so that she could sit across the chair and lean back against me.

"Close your eyes," I said. Starting with her temples, I pressed small circles in her skin.

"Can't believe Trent just walked in today." Her brow furrowed again as she spoke, practically undoing my work.

"If it makes you feel better, I can tell you plenty of embarrassing stories about him."

"No thanks," she made a quiet noise in her throat. "Rather not know since I'd probably never be able to look at him again."

Right on cue, Trent opened the door and Rose giggled softly, sitting up in her seat again and leaning her elbows on the table.

"What did you tell her?" He asked, eyeing us both cautiously before letting the other officers in the room.

"Nothing of interest, yet. What'd you find in the apartment?"

"There were no radio frequencies, so I don't think anyone heard the conversation, but I wouldn't be surprised if news hasn't spread yet. We did find a list of meeting times, though. The next one is tomorrow night, same bar."

"He said something about always knowing what's going on," Rose said. "Any way there's you know—a leak?"

"I've considered it," Trent mumbled. "Much as I hate to admit it."

"It'd explain how they're so far ahead of us every time," I agreed. I hadn't wanted to consider the possibility either— the times of questioning everyone behind me were supposed to be over. "But most of this stuff is big, there have been multiple officers working on it—practically the whole station gets updated."

Rose slumped against her upbent arms, and I rubbed her back. There was something else familiar about how she was acting—something more than a tension headache. "You didn't eat this morning did you?"

"Not a breakfast fan, it's too early."

Breakfast? It was evening, and I'd been a major reason she hadn't eaten all afternoon. "Why didn't you say something?"

She glanced at Trent, then back at me. "I had other stuff going on."

Saving her from further explanation, the door opened and Captain Richards entered. "Wilson and Hudson are checking in the evidence and looking for contact information on anyone involved. We should get started."

"Rose needs a snack," I said. "A can of pop." Not the healthiest, but it'd keep her going until I got her a proper dinner.

Richards lifted his eyebrows and stared at me for a moment, but like hell I was going to budge and leave her in there to be questioned alone. I was going to be there for everything she had to say.

"Pop machine has been empty for days," he said, finally.

"Coffee?" Rose suggested. "And yes, I realize it's probably horrible, but better than nothing."

"Corell was just up there putting on a fresh pot," Captain Richards said. "I think he lives on the stuff, but I'll see if he'll bring some down when it's brewed." He stepped back into the hallway and waved someone down, sending someone else to relay his message.

"Now," Richards sat in the chair across from me. His

eyes were narrowed slits, and I didn't think it had anything to do with the delay or requests for food or drink for Rose. Then again, I assumed we all looked somewhat cranky these days. If it wasn't one thing standing in the way of this investigation, it was another. "I guess now isn't the time to discuss your little stunt. What do you know about the guy you just dragged in?"

Rose shook her head, her movements already slowed by the effects of the headache. "Like I said, he generally kept to himself. Not the social type, but it was him who suggested that particular bar the night we went out. Charlene and I wanted to hit Diggers—it's far less skivvy. But we figured having a guy with us would keep some of the creepers away." She gave me a sideways glance and smirked. "It didn't entirely work."

"He seemed fairly paranoid. He always talk like that?" I asked. His rants about the people he was working for stood out in particular. However, given the group's propensity for staying under the radar and avoiding us it, unfortunately, didn't seem like a stretched assumption.

"We did find a stash of marijuana," Trent said. Someone had sent the image to his phone and he slid it across the table. "It'll be a while before we can get results from his blood test to see if he was using, but that could explain why he thinks they're keeping such a close eye on him."

"I've never seen him use," Rose sighed and leaned back. "I'd love to help you figure him out—especially since it seems like he set me up in the first place, but I really don't know that much. Last I heard, he worked for a construction company. He's not talkative and I never pushed."

"Did he ever make you uncomfortable?" I asked.

"Yeah." She blew out a puff of air. "But not like he was

creepy or anything, just awkward. I thought he was really shy, but he seemed better the handful of times I'd seen him when he came out here to visit Charlene over the past couple of years."

Detective Winsor knocked on the door and peeked in. "Guy's lawyer's here."

Then, he held up a foam cup and bag of chips. "Corell said these come here too."

Richards was closest to the door so he stood and took the cup and chips, setting them on the table next to Rose.

I peeked through the blinds. "I assume I'm not invited to the interview."

"Go for it," Captain Richards said, giving me a flat look. "Caution hasn't served us fantastically in solving this case."

I closed the blinds and left Rose with her snack. I passed Corell in the hallway and gave him whispered instructions to keep an eye on the room. If there was a mole somewhere in the station I didn't fully trust anyone, I only had my gut feeling to rely on.

I opened the interrogation room door, and let Trent enter first so I could hang back, but Elijah stared in my direction, keeping his eyes low so as not to make eye contact. "Officer Carter, I presume."

"Nice to put a face to the person you were shooting at, huh? I guess attempted murder on a cop is a great place to start the conversation."

He shrank back, shaking his head violently. "No, like I told Rose, I didn't know anyone was in the house."

"And the living room light magically turned off right before you pulled the trigger?" I didn't actually mean to sound so sarcastic, but it was all I really had left.

Trent pulled out a chair and sat down. "Now would be a good time to start explaining."

Elijah fidgeted, picking at his fingers, the table, the cuffs around his wrists. He kept his body stiff, and his gaze indirect. "I told Rose."

"Did you set her up to get abducted?"

"No," he yelled. "That isn't what was supposed to happen. I—I screwed up. They took my sister—I had to get her back."

"So you bargained with them to keep her friend instead?" My voice rumbled in my throat. Anger sprouted like a thorny vine, twisting its way through my body and leaving every part of me burning and raw.

"They caught me," he squirmed around, tracing a line on the metal surface of the table and looking more pathetic with every damn excuse. "With one of their girls. Said if I didn't do what they wanted, they'd make me pay. At first, it was simple stuff, but they used it all to get more on me— they found out where my family lived. They found out what neither Charlene nor Rose know…. I've got a kid, in Oklahoma. The mom wants nothing to do with me, but I pay my child support."

"With dirty money?" Trent asked with a mocking tone.

"Not at first. They sent me pictures of the baby. They wanted me to recruit some women for them."

"Who gave you the orders?" I asked.

"Sometimes Drisco, and sometimes a blonde guy, Alan, and sometimes a few of his friends. I haven't seen them around in a while though. Now it's just Drisco."

Alan, he'd worked security at the Retreat, and had not only been there when Rose was abducted in the first place —he'd also helped Gabe abduct her from my room and sneak her away to rape her with a few of his buddies.

"And what does Drisco want you to do now?" Trent asked, sounding as impatient as I felt.

"He told me to bring Rose to the bar. He said nothing bad would happen to her. I wasn't stupid enough to question him again."

I nearly exploded, but instead I shoved my fists in my pockets and let Trent take it.

"Is that what Alan told you, too?" he asked. "Did he promise you Rose wouldn't get hurt?"

Elijah shook his head. "I didn't set them up. I wasn't going to do it, so they tracked Charlene and Rose down and took them. What would you do if they threatened your family?"

I stepped forward, placing my fists on the table. "*You* threatened Rose. In my world, that's close enough. Would you like to hear what they did to her?"

Rose would kill me if she ever found out, but I didn't intend to ever let her anywhere near him again. "How they beat her and stripped her of everything before raping her?"

His face paled and his eyes fluttered side to side. "I—"

Trent sat down across from Elijah. "If you knew who took her, why didn't you ever tell us?"

"I wouldn't have done you any good," he whispered. "And what difference does it make now? He—" Elijah thrust his hands at me "—was there and you still couldn't get her out."

"No," Trent said. "But then we'd have a reason to trust you. To help you, but you gave us nothing. You just kept letting them threaten your family and helped them gain footing to become stronger and do it all the more."

Elijah sat back, dropping his hands into his lap.

"Do you know a guy named Kirk or Bentley?" I asked.

Elijah glanced at his lawyer, and she nodded, urging him on. We had him on enough, the only way we were getting anywhere is if he gave us everyone else. "Bentley, he's Drisco's boss."

"Is that all you can give us?" Trent asked pressing his palms into the table and leaning forward. "You understand that we're not just going to open the doors and let you walk out after everything you've done?"

He twisted in his seat, then leaned over the table and whispered, "What if they go after my family?"

They had him terrified—that I could understand, but it pissed me off that he put everyone in even more danger by keeping his silence and helping the criminals who threatened them. A line had to be drawn. "When all of your buddies are sitting in jail with you, your family will be perfectly fine."

"Drisco was my roommate for a while before I moved in with my sister. I thought I had gotten rid of them, but then they came after me again. Said he wanted to make amends, and I was skeptical but I talked to him. He told me he had a deal set up, all he had to do was deliver one more thing and he'd be free—he asked me to help him deliver. I backed out, and the next night they took Rose and Charlene." He closed his eyes and swallowed. "They told me to choose—whoever I didn't choose would be my reminder to never cross them again."

I shook my head. I didn't have any more questions in me—and I couldn't listen to any more of his explanations at the moment. Richards shouldn't have ever let me in the room because as much as I hated to admit it—I was too close. I didn't care why he did what he did, his actions hurt Rose and he didn't do a damn thing to rectify it. For that, I wanted him to pay. I stepped away from the table and opened the door.

The lawyer made a sound in her throat and followed us

out of the room. "Look at him," she said. "Listen to him. Threats aren't going to help at this point."

I scoffed, "Keeping him locked up where he can't make any more threats of his own will."

"He needs help," she said.

"So do we," I said, throwing up my arms. Then, I spotted Rose in the hallway with Corell and Captain Richards and my stomach sank.

"We have the date and time of his next meeting," Trent said. "Maybe we can luck out and Drisco will still show up."

But I wasn't entirely paying attention to him. Outside, Rose was leaned against the wall, Corell's hand on her arm. Then, the trio, led by Corell came toward the observation room where we were gathered.

Trent started to speak again, then followed my gaze. "What the hell now?"

Corell pulled open the door, and as soon as she saw me, Rose broke away.

"She said she's not feeling well," Corell explained. "I really think we should get her to the hospital."

Her eyes were heavier than before, every movement was sluggish. She put her hands around my neck, wrapping herself around me in a hug, so she could whisper in my ear. "Someone spiked my drink."

How? I kissed her neck to hide my expression.

Over Rose's shoulder, Elijah's lawyer gave us a flat look.

Too many problems to solve, and too few people to trust. Someone in the damn precinct had drugged my girlfriend.

"I'll give you all a few minutes," the lawyer said. Then she mumbled under her breath, "To get your shit together."

There were too many eyes in the room, so I took Rose outside, and back down the hallway to the other room. Even with her tucked against my side, I had to practically carry her and guide each step. She sank into one of the chairs and covered her face with her hands.

"Who all came in here?" I asked.

"Just who you saw." I could barely hear her since she didn't lift her head, and her already quieted voice was muffled by her hands.

"Corell and Winsor are presumably the only ones who touched your drink." Maybe my instinct had been wrong.

She shook her head. "I don't think it was Corell. Your captain touched it too."

But we'd all been in the room for that. He'd only had his back turned for a few seconds—if that. The realization that I was even considering it was just as unsettling. I knelt in front of her, holding her chin up—she was speaking so quietly that I could barely hear her otherwise.

"Corell doesn't fit," she whispered. "What good would it have done to drug me in the middle of the station and bring me straight to you?"

"Raise suspicions."

She bit her lip. "I know. I can't be sure, but--" She closed her eyes, and her head lobbed to the side.

Trent stepped inside the door. "What's going on? I figured you wanted a minute alone, but Richards is launching the inquisition out here."

Why would he be so upset if he only thought she was feeling ill? Unless he knew something more.

"We need to take you to the hospital," I whispered, tucking her hair back.

"It'll wear off and I'll be fine. Just like every other time."

Trent leaned over the back of her chair. "Are either of you going to answer me?"

I didn't—not directly. I knew he'd get the picture soon enough. "We need a blood test, Rose. Evidence."

She dropped her head back and it landed against Trent's arm.

"You've got to be kidding me," he said, staring wide-eyed down at her. "How the hell does someone slip her a mickey *here*?"

"Your guess is as good as mine. Have you seen Winsor?"

"Yeah, he's at his desk," he looked me in the eye, glare as hard as steel. "He wouldn't."

I returned his gaze with a flat look of my own. "Well, we're down to about three options; Winsor, Corell, and the Captain. Unless there was someone else in the line of delivery Winsor failed to mention."

"Or someone drugged the entire pot of coffee."

I knew he meant it sarcastically to begin with, but the growing hardness of his face indicated that he was seriously considering the proposition. "I'm going to run upstairs."

"Well, I need to get her to the hospital."

"I'll meet you there."

"What about Elijah?" I asked. I didn't want to think about the uproar his lawyer was probably going to cause after everything that she saw in the observation room. We weren't coming off as the most well-prepared team—and I was sure she was going to fight for me to be pulled from the case. "The D.A. is going to want to talk to someone, and right now there are only about three people I trust."

Rose lifted her head and smirked. "Hey, that's an improvement."

"Come on, Sugar," I pulled her to her feet, then lifted her into my arms.

"I'd ask for someone to go with you since you've both

been threatened, but at this point, I don't know who the hell to ask." Trent threw up his arms.

"Corell didn't do it," Rose said again.

"You stop to consider maybe they're trying to force your hand? You two together and *alone* on the way to the hospital. An ambulance might be safer right now."

I stared down at her soft face, resting against my shoulder. Backed against a wall, I had to make yet another choice that could mean life or death if Trent was right. The chances of that were too high for comfort. "Do it," I whispered, keeping her in my arms and taking her seat.

It wouldn't take the ambulance more than five minutes to pick her up since the dispatch garage was only a couple of blocks away from us.

Captain Richards burst through the door. "Are you going to explain what's going on? The D.A. and Elijah's lawyer are both waiting."

"She's extremely sick," I said. "Trent was just going to call an ambulance."

Trent nodded and stepped out. I presumed that he was also intent on checking the pot of coffee while he made the call.

"I'll assume you're going with her," Richards said, neither his voice nor his face revealing much emotion.

I kept my head lowered unsure of what I'd feel or do if I looked up at him. I couldn't even control my facial expression. Rational or not, my boss just earned a top spot on my suspect list. Not that everyone in the building didn't make that list at the moment. "I am."

Richards approached the table reaching for the trash Rose had left after finishing the chips and coffee.

"I can take care of that," I said, thinking there might be

residue of whatever she'd been given still in the cup, but Richards snatched it up anyway.

"Nonsense. It's quite obvious you have your hands full."

I brushed my chin against her warm forehead, and she stirred.

"Stay with me, Rose."

She lifted her head, her nose brushing against my neck. "Always."

Within a few minutes, Trent led the paramedics into the room where we waited. I squeezed her even tighter, realizing I'd have to relinquish her—if even for a few moments.

The paramedic set his bag on the table, looking at me as much as he looked at Rose. "I'm just going to take her vitals. Then, we'll get her loaded up."

"I'm going with her," I said.

He gave me a tense smile and nodded. "I figured."

Trent came around behind me and slapped a hand to my shoulder. "You might want to tame the glower that says you're going to kill everyone."

He dropped back and sat on the table. "I promise he's not as bad as he looks."

"Mmm," Rose snorted, then she pressed a kiss to my jaw. "Yeah, he is."

"Her vitals are stable," the paramedic said, repacking his equipment. "You want to bring her out?"

I expected more questions, but then I suspected that Trent might have covered that on the phone. I shifted her so that I could stand and followed the paramedics toward the door.

"I'll meet you there," Trent called after us.

———

ROSE SLEPT all the way to the hospital while I fielded the paramedic's questions.

Age. Symptoms. Medical history.

What the heck could I tell them about her medical history? Most of it, I didn't want to think about, so I stuck with the basics—including the shooting.

The hustle of the hospital was actually a relief since I wasn't the sole focus of their inquisition. They pulled her into a private room and checked her vitals again. Rose didn't stir until the phlebotomist came in to draw blood. It took two attempts to rouse her, but she remained on the edge of semi-consciousness until the needle pressed into her skin.

"Easy, Sugar." I tried to hold her still until the procedure was complete, but just as quickly as she'd woken and tensed, sleep reclaimed her.

I dragged my fingers through her hair, gently tugging free the small tangles around her face. Since we weren't entirely sure what she'd been given, they couldn't give her anything to counteract it yet.

Fortunately, she wasn't experiencing any severe side effects aside from extreme fatigue.

Trent snuck quietly into the room, taking up his position on the opposite side of her bed. "I may have pilfered the cup from the trash can after everyone left."

"You sneaky bastard," I whispered. "Glad you're on my side."

"Now we just have to figure out who isn't." He leaned his arms against the railings and stretched out his neck. "I also got a sample of coffee from the coffee pot. I dropped them both off with a lab tech, who I'm fairly confident isn't the mole."

He twisted his mouth and shook his head, keeping his

eyes on Rose as if he expected the answers to come from her unconscious body.

But, it felt like answers were slipping farther and farther away. It was one thing being in the Retreat and having to watch my back. I knew I was out for myself, but now things were supposed to be different. We were supposed to be a team, working in tandem to save girls, not drugging them and aiding the criminals.

What the hell were we coming to?

"Any theories?" he asked.

I stared down at the cotton blanket—all of the tiny threads intersecting, strengthening each other, creating the larger structure. "Who's in the best position to get away with it all? To keep track of everything we know, and play the pieces just right to make it look like we're digging as deep as we possibly can without actually finding anything to go on?"

Trent's mouth hung wide open for a moment. "If you're implying what I think, you either just signed your own death warrant or resignation."

"Did you report that we were going to the bar the night that Elizabeth OD'ed?"

"Of course…. And our guy didn't show up, then we got called out of there damn quick." He rubbed his chin and stepped away from the bed, shaking his head as he paced slowly around the room. "I can't even believe I'm considering this. We're going to need damn good evidence. He'd have to seriously fuck up—"

I nodded to Rose. "I think he already did."

A knock sounded at the door, and a doctor stepped in with Rose's chart in hand. "We rushed through the tox screen on her blood. There's no GHB or any related substance in her system—"

"Then—" I gestured toward her. She certainly wasn't having a typical reaction to drinking coffee—not even the coffee at the station house was that dangerous.

The doctor put up a hand to quiet me. "I wasn't done. She had high levels of muscle relaxers in her system. Not dangerously high, so she'll probably sleep it off."

"She said she was on muscle relaxers for tension headaches."

He nodded. "I saw that in her chart—it's actually one of the reasons we tested for it. She takes a fast-acting, but short-lived muscle relaxer, metaxalone. A more extensive test would be able to confirm whether that was the culprit, but if so, she took triple the prescribed dose."

I clenched the bed railing, debating over how much to tell him—if I said foul play was involved, it wouldn't be long before word of it got back to the station.

"If that's the case," the doctor said, "I'll have to recommend we keep her for psychiatric evaluation."

"That won't be necessary." If I couldn't leave her for more than twenty minutes in the station, I wasn't leaving her in the hospital.

"We'll keep an eye on her," Trent said, maintaining a slight smile until the doctor disappeared. Then, he leaned over the bed toward me. "What's the plan?"

"Know of any nifty ways to find out who in our department is on muscle relaxers?"

Horrible start to the plan because it'd never work, but I needed a few more minutes to think.

Trent's phone beeped, and he glanced down at the messages. He raised one eyebrow as he read and I had to steel myself to the bed to keep from jumping over and reading it myself.

"It's not really news," he said. "There was nothing in

the coffee sample, but there was residue on Rose's cup. Tizanadine," he grimaced at the word. "Brand name is Zanaflex—clearly not what Rose was taking. But here's the brilliant bit, it's available in a capsule."

"Easier to spike your drink with." I tried to focus on coming up with a solution, but as I stared down at her, the only thing I could think of was how much she'd been through.

Waking up from a drug-induced sleep surrounded by Gabe's men, and thrust into life at the Retreat. I had to force her to put her trust in me—a man she didn't know. All she knew was that she'd become my new sex slave—just a new toy, like all the others.

But she'd never been like them. She fought for everything. In the end, she fought to save herself—and me.

Choose to die or fight to live, I'd told her, after threatening to drown her in the bathtub. *It is what it is.*

I trailed my fingers down her arm and took her hand. The rest of her body remained perfectly still, except for her slow breaths, and her fingers squeezing mine.

It's what we make of it, I decided. Whatever fate or anyone else wanted or expected us to be was irrelevant. We'd made our own way—so far off the original plan. It all shouldn't have come together, but it did.

She may have been a stubborn thorn in my side who threatened both our lives in the beginning, but she became exactly what she needed to be to survive. I'd told Trent not to underestimate her, but I'd done just that myself. She was smart, intuitive, stubborn, and a damn sight brave. Hell, she could probably have done my job as well as me.

Trent cleared his throat. "You're smiling, and if we're honest, it's kind of creeping me out."

I snorted and straightened my back. It was starting to

kink up from staying hunched over the bed so long. "Just thinking."

"About whatever it was—that I shouldn't mention—that you two were doing before I showed up at the safe house earlier?"

My smile widened. "I am now."

"Plan?" he reminded me.

I scratched the back of my head and stared toward the dark window. "Hell if I know. Richards already knows about everything we got off Elijah, so—if he is the mole—he's probably already informed the others to cover their tracks. So, any plan to intercept Elijah's friend tomorrow will be shot. We're right back at square one. How do you play a cunning game when there's someone standing over you who can see your cards and your opponent's cards? He'd know every possible move before we could even consider acting on it."

"If we force his hand, we're likely to get shot in the back —or fired. In this situation, I'm considering 'fired' a best case scenario. And we still have no proof it's him."

I silently sorted through the possibilities. Maybe we weren't supposed to have discovered Rose after she'd been drugged—he'd fucked up there, but it wasn't enough to get him. We could prove there had been foul play in the station, but we'd probably end up spinning in circles again.

Chapter Twenty

TENUOUS GROUND

AFTER A COUPLE of hours in the hospital, the effects of the muscle relaxers were fading from Rose's system, but she was still groggy and nestled on the couch with her legs across my lap. "I'm never going to sleep tonight."

"You can keep us company, then," I said, squeezing her thigh.

Going back to the safe house was useless if we had someone on the inside ratting our every move, but it provided a quiet place to think. Trent joined us for the quietest brainstorming session I'd ever been a part of.

Rose sat up and adjusted until she was curled at my side with her head on my shoulder. "Right. Nearly forgot that you hardly ever need sleep. What'd I miss?"

Trent scoffed and flicked a stack of papers across the coffee table. "Absolutely nothing."

I blew out a long breath that hissed through my clenched teeth. "In theory, we could try to trace the drugs back to whoever decided to slip them in your drink, but that'd require us opening an official investigation which would tip off whoever we're looking for."

She pressed her lips together and looked up at me. "You mean your captain?"

"Why would you say that?" Trent asked, looking down at his phone and acting disinterested.

"I don't know. How else—Elijah said that the people he's working for would know. Maybe we were wrong to think he was paranoid just because there weren't any transmitting devices in the apartment."

"But how do we prove it?" I asked. "We need more than intuition and guesswork."

"Is Raini still around?" Rose asked quietly.

Trent and I both dropped what we were looking at to turn our full attention to her.

Raini wasn't ever the social type, she just did as she was told—her own version of survival instinct. "Did you ever talk to Raini?"

Rose shook her head. "But Alley...." She trailed off, fussing with a string on the blanket that pooled around her lap.

All we needed was one little string to pull. Then we could let everything fall apart.

"Alley was friends with nearly all of the girls," I finished her statement. "So, Raini might be willing to help find out what happened to her."

Trent stood and popped his back. "I can try to track her down tomorrow. We have her address, but I can't guarantee she's still there. I spoke to her briefly after Elizabeth's death, and she seemed okay."

"Raini suspects that I was the traitor," I said. "She wasn't there that night, but I'd assume the girls who were didn't keep quiet about it." And knowing that Rose was with me, Raini might be suspicious of her as well.

"I can handle it," Rose said. "She can't be much harder than Elijah, right?"

I nodded. At least I didn't have to worry too much about Raini attacking her. I just had to worry about who Raini knew and who she might report to. "Except this time we're doing it completely off the record. No backup."

"I can rig up a wire, though," Trent said. "We can stick close by and listen in case you hit trouble. I'll make the calls and set everything up, but it's getting late and we'll have to wait until tomorrow."

Which meant we'd also have to balance keeping Richards and the rest of the department off our asses.

———

TRENT FINAGLED a call to keep us out of the station, leaving Winsor and Hudson to work the official case. Then, he called up Ryan Corell and asked him to meet us near the café where Rose and Raini were meeting.

If all we had to go on was instinct, I assumed that we all couldn't be wrong. He showed up—even though it was his day off—as requested, in plain clothes. Since he wasn't expected at the office anyway, it all happened to work out in our favor.

"What's going on?" he asked. "Is Rose okay?"

"She's fine," I looked at Trent and then took a running leap off the cliff. It was time to spill and let everything land where it may. "She was drugged, by someone in the station."

Corell's face went pale as the clouds in the sky. "A cop?"

He stepped away, taking a moment to breathe and let it

all sink in. "That'd explain why y'all aren't getting any traction, but why'd you call me?"

"We're banking on you not being the one who did it."

He scoffed and rubbed the back of his head. "Well, um, thanks. I guess."

"Rose is inside," I nodded to the café on the corner. "She's waiting for one of the girls from the Retreat. The girl was with Elizabeth Watkins when she disappeared, so we're hoping she might be an in."

"She's the girl who came in the night you were hiding out in the interview room?" He waited for my confirmation, then nodded. "Your girlfriend's a brave girl—getting wrapped up in all of this. She knows what she's getting into?"

I glanced back to Trent again, unless he was a damn good actor, Corell definitely wasn't the mole, since he apparently hadn't followed our case closely.

"Something amusing?" Corell asked.

Forcing away my smirk, I shook my head. Where the hell do I start on the abridged version? "I met Rose *while* I was undercover. She was brought into the Retreat, she definitely knows what she's getting into."

"Hell," Trent said. "Give the girl her credit, since this was her idea. We're bringing them down, along with whoever's leaking information from the department, but that means we can't launch an official investigation yet. We'd be tipping our hand too soon. It's important that you also know what you're going into."

This time, we were taking it upon ourselves to fly under the radar.

Corell took a moment, and I thought he'd tell us to shove it, but he pressed his lips together and nodded. "What do you want me to do?"

Trent handed him a cell that would let him take video without anyone noticing. "Go inside and order a cup of coffee. Don't make eye contact with Rose, but get set up somewhere you can see her."

"We'll be in the car across the street." I pointed to Trent's car. We parked almost a block from the Café, but we'd have eyes and ears on Rose. "Her danger word is 'five'."

We got settled in the car and turned on the receiver so we could hear Rose in the café. After she picked up her order, the only thing we could hear was the clinking of glass and the distant mumble of people around her. Trent cued up the video on his phone, but it was still dark.

Raini's smooth, quiet voice came through the speakers. "You had Trent call me?"

"Yeah, I wanted to check in with you," Rose said.

"Me?" Raini made a noise and mumbled something I couldn't make out.

A picture popped up on Trent's screen. Corell was sitting several booths away, but we got a clear image of both girls.

Rose leaned toward her. "I wasn't sure how to talk to anyone, but after Alley died," her voice crackled and she paused. "I heard about your friend and—"

"She wasn't my *friend*," Raini snorted. "You really think people like us come back out here and make *friends*? How many do you have?"

Raini had hardened even more over the last few months.

"I had one from before, but I've met a few new people I like."

"Oh, right. But you don't see how different it was for you. You were there, what? A month?"

Rose nodded.

Come on, Sugar, I urged. She'd gone quiet as if uncertain about how to keep pressing.

"It was long enough," she said, her voice wavering again. "I have nightmares almost every night, and no one to call when I don't even want to leave my house."

Raini's shoulders sagged. "Don't get me wrong—it's just been a long week—I'm glad to be out. Every day's a struggle, but I don't have any assholes forcing their... you know," she shrugged and left the rest of the statement to the imagination.

"Yeah, I know," Rose whispered.

We'd never stop reliving it, but at least if we turned the damn memories into a strength we got something positive out of the whole situation.

"Have you talked to Kirk since then?"

Rose straightened, her gaze flickered to Corell for a split second.

"I saw him at the police station," Raini continued, "no idea why he was *there*. The detective seemed a little ticked with him, but I assumed that's how you knew."

"Yeah, he told me."

"Well, tell him thanks. If he wants to hear that from me. It probably doesn't—" She started to slide out of the booth, but Rose caught her arm.

My heart raced, but my mind quieted for a moment, waiting to see what Rose would come up with.

"Wait," Rose said. "I need your help."

"What on earth can I do for you?"

"I need to get to the guys who killed Elizabeth—I think they were involved in Alley's death as well."

"Just leave it," Raini hissed.

"There are other girls in trouble—girls from the Retreat. Innocent girls."

Raini scratched her forehead and abruptly sat back in the seat. "What are you doing? Is Kirk going on some crazy new rescue mission? What the hell is he getting out of this one?"

Trent bumped my arm and nodded toward the café. "What do you think she'll do if we just come clean?"

"Run," I said. That's what I would have done, but I knew better.

"Worked on Miles," Trent said with a sly smile.

I shook my head and reached for the door handle. No point in wasting time on an argument I couldn't win.

As we entered the café, Trent motioned for Corell to hold his position—no need in spooking her more than necessary. Rose's eyes widened when she saw us approaching and Raini spun around quickly in her seat. I slid into the booth, next to Rose, resting my arm around her shoulders. Trent pulled up a chair from a nearby table and sat at the end.

"What the hell?" Raini whispered, keeping her eyes locked on me in particular.

While everyone else was quiet, I launched into a brief explanation. "We need to find the people who are recruiting the girls so we can bring down their operation. We're running out of people to trust who might be able to help."

Raini's forehead crinkled and her gaze moved to Trent. "You're all working together?"

Trent looked down for a moment, then nodded. "He's my partner."

"Partner," she choked on the word.

"I'm a cop," I said. "Have been the entire time and *I'm sorry*."

"A cop," she repeated, barely making a sound. She fidgeted and played with a charm bracelet that hung loosely around her wrist. "Sorry. You're sorry?"

I straightened, preparing for an outburst.

"You got me away from Ross," she said. "I don't care what else you did or how you did it."

I laughed because I was so nervous I didn't know what else to do.

Raini smiled and nodded to Rose. "She was in on it?"

"Not intentionally, but she's not easily deterred," I looked over Trent's shoulder and motioned for Corell to join us, too. We had five people to possibly bring down a crime ring, and a dirty officer, but I'd done more with less, I supposed.

"Anyone else?" Raini asked, scooting over to let Corell join the discussion.

"This is it," I said.

She shook her head and laughed. "More protectors than I've ever had."

"Well," Trent said, "that's not true anymore, but I know we're asking a lot of you."

"I'm not entirely certain *what* you're asking," she said.

Trent slid the card for the escort company across the table. "For you to change your mind. Give them a call."

She exhaled loudly, then stared down at the card for a long quiet moment.

Rose straightened, her green eyes on me. "I could go, too."

I shook my head. "They know you. We don't know what information anyone has given them on you, and judging from yesterday—"

She put up her hand to stop me.

Raini picked up the card. "I can do it. Then, what? How long?"

Despite the high-tension situation, calm flooded through me. We were finally on the right track—possibly about to lose our jobs, but everything finally felt whole. "We'll make arrangements to have eyes on you when you meet them. Tell them you're desperate—you can't pay your bills, the utilities are threatening shut off."

She nodded.

"Um," Corell put up his finger. "What about the... *internal* problem?"

Trent smiled and slapped his shoulder. "I have a plan. You two get her set up and ready to go, and I'll go set up part two."

"Any idea what he's planning?" Rose asked as Trent put his chair back—giving us a simple nod as he left.

"Nope. But I think you're stuck with me since I rode over with him."

"Smart." She lifted her cup toward me. "Want to be my taste tester?"

"And what are you going to do if I pass out?" I peeked in the cup at the light brown liquid. "How much cream and sugar did you put in this?"

"I like it sweet." She swirled it around in the cup and took a drink. "I watched them make it, and I'm still paranoid."

I grimaced and put the cup back on the table. "Speaking of coffee—"

Corell shifted uncomfortably, predicting where the conversation was about to go. "It had just finished brewing, I poured a cup, grabbed the chips and headed back to the interview room. I crossed paths with Winsor right outside the door and he said he'd take it in with him." He put up his right hand. "I swear, that's it. But if you thought I had anything to do with it—"

"I didn't. Just wanted to know the details."

Corell's eyes widened. "But that leaves—"

"A couple of possibilities," I said. "Neither of which are brilliant. If you want to bow out, do it now."

Raini stared at us wide-eyed as we talked, but she stayed quietly tucked into her corner of the booth.

"You ready to make the call," I asked her.

She shook her head, staring down at the card she'd left on the table in front of her. "Yeah. I can do this."

I pulled another card out of my wallet and handed it to her as well. "A cell number is written on the back—it's secure and untraceable, so you can send me a message if you need me."

"I'll put it in my phone," she said, "with a fake name, just in case."

"They come off as a little crazy," Rose said, giving me a sardonic look. "But they're good at what they do."

Raini glanced at me then dropped her head, focusing on her phone instead. "I know."

I didn't have to look over to know that Rose was glaring at me. I felt the heat from the entire room absorbed into my body.

"Should I make the call now?" Raini asked, taking the most intense of the attention off me—off our past.

"Yeah. All we need is a meeting place. We'll make sure you're safe until then and have someone waiting nearby when you go to the meeting. There will be someone in range the whole time."

She snorted and shook her head. "You say that as if they won't outnumber and outgun you even if you are close."

"So we out-strategize them." I squeezed Rose's hand under the table. "I need to pick up my car. Corell, you okay staying with—" I almost said Raini. I guess I had to amend that part of my brain, too. "—*Fiona*."

She smiled. "It takes some getting used to after a few years, but it's particularly strange hearing it from you."

"My real name is James, by the way, I think I left that part out."

"I'll stay with her," Corell said, turning to Fiona with a faint smile. "And you can call me Ryan, you don't have to be all formal like this guy."

I didn't want to leave her at all, but I also had plans to be made before we went in—mainly making sure that Rose was safe and that we'd have the supplies we needed. I gave Corell an address for the safe house and told him to meet us there in an hour. Hopefully, Trent would be done setting up whatever the hell he'd planned by then.

Rose and I climbed into her car, but she didn't start the engine. She kept her hands tight around the steering wheel and stared through the window. "I want to help."

"You just did."

"You can't go in there—just the three of you and keep an eye on everyone and everything."

"I don't intend to. Once we get there, we're calling in backup."

"But—"

"We'll put them in a bind and it'll be too late for Richards to do anything about it."

"You all are going to end up fired."

I huffed. I didn't want to be going over this again. We already knew this part, but every way we went about it was a loss game. "Yeah, we've discussed that."

"With Ryan? How long has he been with the force?"

"Yes, with Ryan." My voice rose. This was my job—the one I'd done successfully for years, and although I anticipated her concern, we didn't have time to sit and debate it out again. "We gave him the option to back out."

"But why would he if his sense of moral obligation even matches a quarter of yours?" She banged her head against the headrest and reached for the ignition. I had a feeling that whatever had her flustered didn't have so much to do with our plan.

"We don't have a lot of options, and Corell knows how to handle himself."

"So do I," she yelled.

"Can we have this argument later? I need to pick up my car, I have some things in the trunk that we'll need."

She started the car, but still didn't move to put it in gear. "Did you sleep with her?"

It felt like everything inside my chest suddenly vanished, leaving an empty throbbing hole that threatened to collapse on itself. "Yes. Once."

"She has feelings for you."

"She doesn't *know* me. I saved her from Ross, she spent one night in my bed."

"Come on, I know how dangerous that is," she said it like she meant it to be funny, but there was no humor on her face. Her eyes were moist with tears yet to fall, and her chest shook with each breath.

I pried her hand away from the steering wheel and kissed her knuckles. "I have a girlfriend, Sugar. One that I'm very happy with, and intend to spend a long time enjoying."

She covered her mouth, muffling a sound that was a cross between a laugh and a sob.

In some twisted way, it was actually comforting to know

that the jealousy problem went both ways. At least I wasn't the only irrational one—but I wasn't about to use that word to her face.

"I kept telling myself not to get jealous over you," she whispered.

I wasn't sure if she was talking about in the café or at the Retreat.

"I knew it was inevitable. I wanted to claw Kat's eyes out, and then, Alley—Ross was a sick bastard."

He'd wanted to make sure that her initiation made a statement—that we were all his toys. While he and three others forced her to perform oral sex on them, he ordered Alley to do the same to me.

She tried to pull her hand away, but I didn't release it. "You were the only one I enjoyed being with—and you have no idea how badly I hated myself over that sometimes."

"Oh, I think I do." Jerking her hand away, she put the car in gear and reversed out of the parking space. "Falling in love with you... definitely the hardest thing I've ever done in my life. But it turned me into a fighter, and I don't intend on letting anyone take any of that away from me."

Her not so subtle way of telling me that she wasn't sitting at home while I went out on this operation.

———

TRENT EYED ROSE suspiciously when we all met up at the safe house an hour later. She slipped off to the side of the room to talk to Fiona. Then, Trent directed his inquisitive gaze on me.

"What would you have had me do? Slip her some more drugs?" I said as quietly as possible. "You think it's so easy, you convince her to listen."

"Welcome to my world," he said, tipping his head to the side.

"What the hell is that supposed to mean?" I reached for him, but he ducked away and laughed.

"It means," he got in a smack to the side of my head, "I think you're rubbing off on her."

I had no doubt that everyone was watching our exchange—a mix of pre-operation jitters getting worked out and excessive frustration. I motioned for Rose to come over. "I need you to wait here."

Her mouth dropped open. "You already gave me a long spiel on the consequences involved here—"

"With the arrangements Trent made we're back on the grid and I can't take you."

"Fine," she said. "Did you have to wait until now to tell me that?"

"I wanted a witness," I grumbled.

Trent threw up his hands and whistled as if there were a herd of people he was trying to control. "Okay. Now that we have that sorted. Fiona, you said the meeting location is the Franklin Street Hotel?"

"Yeah." She had her arms wrapped around herself, and although she looked up at Trent for a split second when she answered, she kept her head angled down.

I had no right to ask her to do this while expecting Rose to stay at home.

"Corell and I will head over there now, so we'll be nearby the entire time. If something makes you uncomfortable and you need us to pull you out, say dodge."

"How are you going to explain all of this when it's over?" Rose asked.

"We're going to tell the truth—banking on discrediting Richards and then showing that we had no choice."

"Is this even legal?" Rose asked.

"I pulled some strings," Trent said. "Richards isn't where the chain of command ends. I explained that we had a mole, but we couldn't identify who. I told her the plan."

Rose raised her eyebrows, giving him an incredulous stare. "And she just believed you?"

I put my arm around Rose's shoulder and pulled her away from the group. "Remember the 'fuck buddy'?"

Her mouth formed an "O", but she didn't say anything else. The expression made me want to kiss her, but I held back, so I could explain and prevent further questions. "She's a deputy chief—knows damn well how to play the political side. That's not something we're brilliant at so she can be quite helpful. He turned over all of the information on what happened to you last night, so our case looks good, we just need proof pointing to who did it."

"How is all of this going to accomplish that?"

"She'll watch and see who squirms the most," I smirked, pulling her back toward the others.

Trent struggled to keep a straight face as we rejoined them. "Everything clear now?"

"Yeah, I'll follow Fiona over and stay out of sight," I said. "If they decide to move the location once you get there, Trent will be ready to follow, and we'll hand off so they don't suspect anything."

We retested Fiona's wire and suited up. Trent and Corell left first to get into position, and then I followed Fiona to the hotel.

"Heading in," Fiona said over the speaker.

Trent came over the CB. "Richards is out of the office, so Libby has backup standing by. We're not on the primary frequency just in case. I'll call it in as soon as I know we're not moving."

"Got it," I replied, "Fiona is in."

I tucked the handset in the center console, waiting to hear from Fiona, but the receiver was still silent.

"Fiona." The familiar voice drew out her name. We had my "*doppelganger*" as Trent like to call him.

"We were sorry to hear about your situation," another man spoke, "but I think we can help you out with that. And, I'm sure you already know some of our girls, so I think you might find you enjoy working with old friends."

"I appreciate anything you can do for me," Fiona said softly.

I really didn't want this to go down at the hotel. Trying to track them if they moved her would be a pain in the ass, too, but a less public location would keep innocent people out of the mess.

"Follow me, then," Kirk said.

The mic rustled with their movement, and I saw them emerge through the front door. Kirk looked around, then directed her to a black BMW.

I picked up the CB handset. "They're getting into the BMW Claudia mentioned."

"My car—" Fiona pointed back toward the rest of the lot.

"Don't worry, darlin'," Kirk opened the back door. "We'll bring you right back after we finish up. We're just going for a ride. I've been cramped up all day and I need some air and scenery."

They both climbed in the back door, and the other man, Drisco from the looks of him, got into the driver's seat.

I waited until the car cleared the lot to follow it to the end of the block. Trent was already waiting down the street and picked up their tail as soon as I turned off.

"Not so bad, right?" Kirk asked. "Here, we have some paperwork that we'll need to go over."

Papers rustled and the receiver cracked and popped as they moved out of range from me. I sped around the next corner, taking the road that ran parallel to the one they were on.

"Why do you need to know about my medical history? Birth control?" Fiona asked.

"Just a precaution," Kirk said. "We like to know that our girls are healthy in the event that anything should happen."

"But you told me that this isn't about sex."

"Now, darlin'—" Something moved against her and I hoped he wasn't getting handsy. She didn't need to be put through that, and if he happened to find the mic we were all going to be in a worse situation. "It's about relationships, being there for someone, and showing them a good time— sometimes that leads to other things that are beyond my realm of control. Some girls go for it, and others don't. If it makes you uncomfortable, maybe we should reconsider."

"No, Sir," she said quietly. "I just wanted to know."

Trent came over the radio again. "They're heading up Ninth Street—looks like they're heading toward the river overlook."

I reached for the handset just as Corell came on. "I'm on them."

"I'll head up and cut you off," I said.

I stared at the receiver—Fiona and Kirk had gone too silent, even if it had only been a few minutes.

Finally, Fiona spoke up again. "Where are we going?"

Kirk chuckled. "I have a friend who wants to meet us down by the river."

I gunned my car on the empty back roads, running parallel to Ninth Street until I caught a glimpse of their car.

Then, I shot ahead and turned on the next street, and pulled onto Ninth behind Corell.

We kept driving until we hit the edge of town—a popular overlook for the river, but the only place I could think of nearby was the old motorcycle club building. "I think they're heading to the MC building. Take Front Street and hang back until they're in."

The building was surrounded by overgrown lots and hadn't been used regularly in a couple of decades. It was isolated, yet convenient for anyone who wanted to use it for private activities that they might not want interrupted by passersby.

Trent and Corell agreed, and when the road branched off, I went up to the overlook, while they followed the curve around to Front Street.

"They're heading your way," I said.

Before I could back out, a black SUV passed behind me, heading in the same direction. My nerves grated under my skin, sending impulses of panic to my muscles. "How long before backup gets here?"

"Three minutes," Trent said.

"Well, they've got backup too, it appears. An SUV just passed. I'm changing over to my ear piece, are we good on the primary channel?"

"Yeah," Trent said, then the radio went silent, but I heard quiet voices on the receiver from Fiona's mic, and then Kirk's voice rose. "Get out of the car."

"What's wrong?" Fiona asked. Her voice was so light I could barely pick up the tremble of fear—but it was there.

Fuck. I jammed my car into park and left it to go on foot. A huge red car was going to be obvious to anyone standing around. At least I could hide behind the bushes. When I was just around the corner from the building, I drew my gun from the holster around my ankle and peeked through the bushes.

Kirk pushed Fiona toward Drisco, who led her inside.

Bastards. We were going to owe her hugely for this.

Then, Kirk approached the passenger side of the SUV. He nodded and opened the back door, pulling out a brunette girl bound at the hands and feet.

My heart stopped. *God, no.*

"They have Rose," I growled into my mic. "How the fuck do they have Rose?"

Chapter Twenty-One

NO ROOM

"STAY BACK," Trent warned me.

Kirk sat Rose down on her feet and she bucked against him, elbowing him in the side. The man from the passenger side of the SUV stepped out and they pinned her, one grabbing her feet while the other carried her upper body.

"What the hell is going on with Fiona?" I asked, assuming that one of them was still in a car listening, but all I got was silence.

I grunted and ducked through the bushes, working my way up to the side of the building where I hoped I could hear something.

"Keep your distance," Trent said. "Backup will be here soon—they're coming in silent so as not to spook them."

I tried to keep an eye on everything as the radio chatter filled my ear. I pressed my back to the wall of the clubhouse inching my way toward the window and hoping to hear something through the walls.

A muffled scream contracted all of my muscles and sent my heart into a tailspin.

My phone vibrated in my pocket, but the only one I had on me was the one that very few people had the number to —Rose, Fiona, and Trent.

I fished it out and squatted against the wall. Trent's name flashed on the screen, so I assumed it was something he didn't want everyone else on the radio hearing. I pressed accept but didn't speak.

"No one can find Richards. He used his bank card at an ATM near the safe house forty minutes ago. Apparently he got suspicious when neither of us came in today."

I shouldn't have left her there alone.

"Libby had a couple of cops watching the safe house. They're both dead. I'm assuming you're close to the building and not chancing it by talking, but so far both girls are okay."

I disconnected the phone, leaned my head back, and took a long deep breath.

A slap and a thud echoed through the building. I could rip their appendages off for touching her.

Sliding along the building, I risked a peek through the window. Rose was on her knees—her lip bloodied and shirt torn, with Fiona next to her. A total of five men stood around them.

That was easy, except for the hostage situation.

I ducked down and focused on the radio again. Backup had arrived and they were getting into formation to approach. I moved farther along the wall to check out the back of the building and heard a vehicle pull up and the engine cut out. The back door to the building creaked open.

"He's been taken care of. We made it look like he ran," an unfamiliar voice reported.

I assumed he was talking about Richards.

"Good," Kirk said. "Any sign of our other cop friends?"

"No," another man said. "Wasn't anywhere near their useless safe house."

"We have the girls," Kirk said. "So, the rest of our loose ends should be tied up shortly. He couldn't help risking his life for them before, I doubt he'll be able to resist now."

"We could have some fun with them in the meantime." The men chuckled, and I barely held back my growl.

Keep it under control, I told myself. If I blew this and didn't get myself killed, Trent would finish me off—especially if the girls got hurt. I knew backup was closing in, so all I had to do was wait a few more minutes. Rose would be able to keep them distracted at least that long.

At least they didn't seem to know about our plan. When the noise ceased and the back door closed again. I finished walking the perimeter of the building, sliding under the windows. I crouched under the final window and waited, listening to the voices inside. There were seven, maybe eight people now, but creaking floorboards dominated much of their hushed conversation.

"We're coming up on the East side," Trent reported. "You better damn well not have done something stupid."

I laughed silently. The team moved up through the bushes coming toward me, and I slipped away from the window to meet them while they were still undetected.

"Seven men—at least," I reported. "And they have two girls. Didn't notice guns, but I didn't get a good look."

The Sergeant leading the team nodded, keeping his eyes on the building.

I noticed movement in the building, and we ducked into the weeds. "There's a back door that might be less notice-able—no windows back there, and it leads to a back room that might give us some cover if we can get inside, but we'd have to get around."

"Until then, we'll stick to the bushes," he said. He held up his hand and motioned for one group to get in position to watch the front door. Corell joined that group while Trent and I followed Sergeant Dales and a group of six other men around to the back.

I joined the ranks next to Trent as we moved around the building.

"She'll be fine," Trent whispered.

It seemed like we had this conversation on a nearly daily basis—and yet, she always was fine, just like he said. "I know."

Sergeant Dales tried the handle, and the door opened freely, so one by one, we slowly slipped in. The back room was cut off from the room where I'd seen the men and girls. Once it was cleared we moved into the main room. Dales and four of his men went first, but the room was empty. The boards under my foot squeaked as I crossed the threshold.

They weren't magicians—they still had to be here. I looked down again, catching a shaft of light from between the boards. If I could see between the thick floorboards, so could they if they were watching from below.

I froze in place and put up my hand. When I had Dales' attention, I pointed toward the floor. He glared at me and shook his head, but before he could take another step, the floor erupted with bullets. Trent and I ducked back into the back room where the floor seemed to be solid.

"Officers down," the voice came over my earpiece, but I was too lost in the scene to know who said it. "We have six officers down. We need paramedics and backup."

Blood soaked the hole-riddled floor. Bullets and floor had both shattered on impact, leaving the room—and the men within it looking more like a grenade had gone off.

The front door burst open, the rest of the group ready to move in, but Trent motioned for them to stay back. A lone bullet came through the floor, shattering the wood into tiny fragments that pierced the group leader's skin. He fell back, the others pulling him away from the doorway.

No one in the main room moved, not a flinch, not a breath that I could see. Maybe they did know our plan— certainly enough to set us up with a death trap. We couldn't even move around the room to check on our men.

How the hell were we supposed to fight back? We couldn't fire blindly when they had the girls.

Trent and I held our position with two other men, all four of us hugging the floor so they wouldn't be able to shoot toward our shadows. The front group fell back.

A message came over the radios. "We're gearing up for tear gas. There's a duct to the basement at the corner of the house."

Trent and I didn't have masks, so we pulled back while the other two men suited up and prepared. I stared at the back door, running my hand through my hair, then doubling over, putting my hands to my knees.

"What the hell were we thinking?"

I heard them launch the tear gas and we backed farther away from the house as it came up through the floor and was carried in wisps through every opening. I charged toward the open door, but Trent grabbed my vest and whipped me around.

I twisted and broke free, but another pair of hands caught me before I made it to the door. Together, Trent and Corell held be back, my feet sliding in the slick gravel as I tried to get into the house.

"Rose is in there."

"And they'll get her out," Trent said. "She'll also be

shaken up and she'd probably prefer you to be in working order to take care of her."

I still shook with anger as they released me, but I gave in to Trent's point. I could barely make out what was going on through the cloud of thick yellow smoke that now permeated the ground floor, too.

"We've got four men detained," the report came over the radio.

There were more than that.

"Make that five. We've covered the room. There's no one else here."

No, there had to be.

"Prohibition," I said.

Trent and Corell both gave me looks like I had lost my mind. "The motorcycle club was here during the prohibition. They might have a secret passage or secret warehouse. If they didn't, who would?"

I held my sleeve over my face and headed back inside, searching the back room. There was a small closet that we'd cleared on our way through, but unlike the rest of the room, the floorboards felt loose. Trent and I managed to pry up one end using the edge of a curtain rod while Corell radioed the others for backup. We moved slowly down into the dark passage, trying to be as quiet as possible despite the old wooden stairs.

Five up front left us with at least two men to deal with. I led the way through the tunnel until we came toward a lighted opening. I crouched, sliding along the wall while Trent took the wall opposite me.

A muffled scream vibrated the air in the tunnel, and I squeezed the handle of my gun even tighter.

A thud and a series of scraping sounds followed.

"Don't even think about it." It sounded like Drisco's voice.

My feet moved faster than my brain. Training and precaution thrown to the wind as I moved closer to the opening.

Drisco stood at the back of the room, holding Rose in front of him, the gun to her head. "Not too shabby."

Fiona was crouched in the middle of the room, motionless, with her back to the opening.

"How about you all drop your weapons and get out of here," Drisco said.

Rose closed her eyes and shoved the arm around her neck upward, throwing him off balance long enough for her to dodge to the side. The arm holding the gun straightened, first aimed at her, then he swiveled around toward us.

I fired before he could regain his balance, and he slumped against the wall.

Rose huddled with Fiona in the middle of the room, while I kicked the gun away from Drisco and the team swept the rest of the enclosure. Once the room was secure, one of the officers following us tended to Drisco, while we got the girls to their feet.

"Where's Kirk?" I asked.

Fiona looked up at me in shock, but Rose pointed toward another door in the ceiling—Kirk would have needed a boost to get up there.

Damn paranoid people and all their secret passages....

I heard gunshots above us.

"Suspect down," came over the radio.

"That makes seven," I said, tucking away my gun and cutting free the cord tied around Rose's wrists.

She nodded. "That's all of them." Her voice throaty and horse.

I lifted her off her feet into a hug.

"Ow," she moaned, even though she squeezed her arms around my neck just as tightly as I held her. "I'm a little bruised."

"You look a lot bruised, Sugar."

Next to us, Corell tended to Fiona, while Trent reported in.

By the time we surfaced, the paramedics had already arrived and the main building was being cleared. We directed the girls through the back door, blocking their view of the bloody mess through the other doorway. A group of officers stood off to the back—I assumed that's where they caught Kirk.

"What about the rest of the operation?" Rose asked, clinging to my side. "What's going to happen now?"

"We have five guys, so we convince one of them to roll before the other four do. The only reason they seemed so tidy is because they had help from within the department." And Kirk's men had taken care of that problem—though I would have preferred to take Richards alive and find out what the hell he was thinking.

My wants didn't really matter to the bigger picture. Lives were lost, the grotesque scene embedded into the collection of nightmarish images in my head. I hugged Rose closer. The smell of her hair, feeling of her warm body pressed against mine, and her arms around my waist where the only things keeping me grounded.

I still had her—the rest I could deal with. And I felt selfish for thinking that, considering the lives that we'd lost —the men who wouldn't go back to hug their families or friends.

The sounds and movements of the scene around me faded into a dull roar. I stepped back from Rose, keeping my hands on her arms as I assessed her injuries. Something that happened far too often for us.

"I'm okay," she said. "Just a bunch of bruises and a few cuts. I got the worst of it when they barged in on the safe house. I heard them talking though, I think they followed Richards out there, but I never saw him."

One of the paramedics rounded the building and approached us. "We're ready to take the girls. It shouldn't take long to get them checked out."

But it was going to take far longer for me to get cleared. "Officer Corell is staying with them."

Corell's eyes widened, but he nodded. "Sure."

Rose's reaction wasn't quite so easy, her grasp digging into the edge of my vest.

"I'll be with you as soon as I can," I explained. "I fired my weapon. I'm going to be navigating bureaucracy for a while."

I walked her up front and got her securely to the ambulance with Fiona and Corell. I felt antsy watching her leave, stepping back and running my hands through my hair as the ambulance pulled away. But she was safe and had thoroughly proven once again that she was quite capable of handling whatever anyone threw at her.

Once we cleared the area, it was time to head back to the station to finish the administrative portion of events. After I turned over my weapon, I had a short lull and called Katie to see if she'd go over and sit with Rose, since she'd probably be discharged from the hospital long before I got to go anywhere.

Chapter Twenty-Two

ALL THAT'S LEFT

I FELT like I'd aged a few years by the time I got done retelling everything I knew and fielding questions for the second time. I sat back in my chair, rubbing my temples, and relished in the momentary quiet while a group of people stood outside the room debating my fate.

I knew it was a good shoot—Trent knew it was a good shoot, and everyone would probably agree, but it was the whole procedure that wore down my nerves even further.

The door opened and Libby stepped in. She wore a perfectly tailored skirt, with a matching suit jacket over a pink blouse—and her long blonde hair was twisted up in a formal looking style. Even before she took the role of deputy chief over our department, she usually looked the part—now she had the power to go with her look and abilities.

"Please tell me you're here to say I can go."

She smiled. "Your girlfriend was discharged from the hospital a while ago, along with the other girl, Fiona.

They're both fine aside from minor injuries. I don't even know what to say to you all."

Shaking her head, she closed the door and took a seat across from me. "It worked, I'll give you that, so I'm not even going to ask what you would have done if I hadn't agreed to support your little coup."

"It wasn't technically a coup. We weren't trying to take power, just finish this—" *Charade, farce...* a dozen words sprinted through my head, none the exact one I wanted to say in front of Libby.

"Maybe not," she snorted, "But we still need to find a new leader for the department. We found a bottle of pills in Richards desk after he disappeared. Capsules of Zanaflex— your instincts were dead on."

"Why? I just want to know why Richards would go through all of this."

Libby glanced at the door. "I have a theory, but for now, it can't go beyond us. He had no retirement left. Nothing. His wife had been sick for the last couple of years—he kept it a complete secret. I only know because of his dealings with the insurance company. Regular treatments weren't working. They had some benefits from some experimental stuff, but insurance wouldn't cover it. He spent everything he had, and then some."

I shook my head. There were always reasons or excuses— however they should be categorized. Anger and disgust created a cage around my chest. Even though there were very few things I wouldn't do to save Rose—even considering every horrible deed I'd committed in the name of justice—I couldn't wrap my head around either Richards or Elijah putting everything on the line to support the bastards who were ruining people's lives in the name of power and material gain.

"We got some more information out of Elijah," Libby said. "And, managed to use that to turn the five men you picked up against each other. They're duking it out to get the best deal. Prostitution. Heroin. It's all coming out," she continued quietly.

It would have felt more fulfilling without all the bloodshed, and months of drawn-out anxiety. But I was too exhausted to enjoy our victory.

"Well," she slapped her hands against her thighs and stood. "Fiona wanted to see you, and apparently everyone decided not to let her come alone, so you have quite the reception waiting for you in the break room. From what I hear, there's even pizza. The independent investigators will want to talk to you again, but until then you're free to go."

"Whatever their decision—" I stopped.

"If you want time off, take it," she said. "I think your comeback was a bit rushed, all things considered. However, I'm also glad you were here, so I'm not complaining. Whatever you need to do, do it. But I want you on my force."

I managed a half smile. "I just need to fix Rose's house since it got shot up and—" I closed my eyes, unsure how much longer my body would even function "—*move* out of my cousin's place. It's been *months*."

"Get your life back together, Detective. We all need something to go home to."

Libby walked with me down to the lounge, a chorus of voices—and even laughter—spilled out of the room. I paused before we reached the doorway, listening to the sound for a few moments.

"Oh," Libby said. "I got word on the Federal case and Miles' hearing. Seems Richards was doing some strange finagling there, too—or at least trying. There will be a hearing next month to review his case and sentence, you should be there. You said you'd like to see him moved somewhere for rehabilitation—where he'll still be safe from any retribution from the other members of Milo's ring. I think you're the best person to make that case."

"I will. I feel guilty for not going to check on him in a while. But—" I groaned and slumped against the wall.

"A lot of the other retreats are dropping like flies. It's all going to work out." She squeezed my shoulder and pushed me toward the doorway. "Go on, you have a lot of people waiting on you."

Despite the number of people in the room, my eyes went straight to Rose. She dropped a slice of pizza to her plate and stood. Her left cheek was darkening with a bruise, her lip swollen from being busted, and she probably had a dozen other injuries I couldn't see at the moment. I moved toward her, but she held out her arm, the other hugging her side.

"Easy. Bruised ribs."

I took her gently, and she nestled against my chest.

"You never go easy, do you?" I whispered.

"Oh," she held up her hand, the knuckles as busted and bruised as the rest of her. "You know me."

I shook my head, took her face between my hands, and pressed my lips to hers—much to the amusement of everyone gathered in the lounge. Katie whooped while others clapped, whistled, or laughed.

Rose buried her face against my neck while I surveyed the room. Corell, Winsor, and Hudson stood by the counter holding plates of pizza. Katie sat at the table with Jack in her lap, and Fiona next to her, while Evan and Trent sat along the side wall on a long couch.

I swallowed the swell of emotions and stole Rose's seat, pulling her down into my lap. She and pizza were of the few things that could monopolize my attention—I was starving.

Small talk filled the room as everyone ate. At the table, I was stuck listening to Katie grill Rose on the details of her sister's wedding. Under normal circumstances, I would have left them to it, and went off to join another conversation, but I was perfectly content with not moving.

Once the pizza was gone, Trent cleared the empty boxes and stuffed them into a trash can while Winsor and Hudson gave their nods of goodbye and disappeared.

"You coming back to the house, now?" Katie asked.

I nodded toward Rose. "Can I bring a guest? I believe I still owe her a living room window."

"I—" Rose started to object, but one look from Katie silenced her.

"No problem."

Trent sat another can of pop in front of me. "I'll help you fix the window this weekend. Then, I can get rid of my feline roomie."

He patted Rose on the back of the head. "You're going to owe me a new vacuum cleaner."

Fiona had sat quietly for most of the conversation, only throwing in a few comments about the wedding, so as the room emptied, I opened up her opportunity to speak.

"Libby said you wanted to talk to me?"

She nodded but didn't much look up from under her curtain of long bangs. I patted Rose's leg and asked her to give me a minute while Fiona and I talked.

We moved to a quiet corner of the room. Fiona kept her hands in her pockets and her gaze down. "It's no big deal. You should be with your friends and family."

She was shy, but it wasn't hard to figure out that wasn't her only problem around people.

"I am." I was done running from the Retreat. It always found its way back into my life in one way or another. "I think you've found your way into that group. I'm sorry—"

"No. Don't be sorry." Her eyes glassed over. "Rose... nothing stops her, does it?"

I shook my head and tried to keep from laughing. I had a feeling I was about to turn slaphappy. "Not for long."

"I just—" Fiona twisted a strand of hair, staring off across the room. "I wanted to say thank you—for caring about us."

"You shouldn't have to thank me for that." Caring should just be the norm expected of everyone, not something that needs accolades.

"Okay then," she said lightly. "Thank you for trusting me today."

I opened my mouth, but she kept going.

"Maybe you don't believe I should thank you for that either—especially considering how badly things went—I suppose they could have been worse though." She took a deep breath but kept her head down. "But you really don't know how much it means. Maybe my part was small and terrifying, but I did it. It kind of gives me a different impression about everything—about myself."

I looked up at the lights for a moment fearing the universe was dead set on seeing me cry in front of everyone. *Not happening.*

I scooped her up into a hug and looked over expecting to see a glare from Rose, but she smiled and went back to her conversation with Katie.

Fiona wiped the tears from her own eyes as she stepped away. "Ryan's waiting to take me home."

I nodded. It seemed we might be adding two new regulars to our group. "Call me if you need anything."

She didn't move. Instead, she looked me over like she'd never seen me before—or I'd recently sprouted a third hand growing out of my head. "It's just hard to take it all in. You... being who you are. You called that guy Kirk—that wasn't a coincidence was it?"

"No," my voice dropped so low it rumbled more than normal. "Trent and I arrested him, and I took his place to get into the Retreat."

"Well, I'm glad of that." She tucked her hair back and peeked toward Corell, who took it as his cue to approach. "I should get going."

Corell extended his hand to me and we shook. "Today was uh—" he wobbled his head "—I'm glad I could help. Definitely didn't see this coming when I tried to arrest you out on the west side a while back."

Rose and Katie turned to look at the same time, their eyebrows raised in similar questioning expressions.

"Maybe—," Evan scooped up Jack in an apparent attempt to use the boy as a barrier against his mom. "—we should plan an all-boys camping trip. Very. Very soon."

Crossing his arms, Corell smirked—a brave expression for a man who'd just outed our minor indiscretion to two feisty women. "We should go," he said to Fiona.

"Nothing happened," I said, but even Trent was giving me a skeptical gaze. Maybe he was the most entitled, but I assumed Evan had told him at least. "I was having a shitty night. I went to see Rose, and got deflected."

I purposely left out my partner in crime, in case it didn't need to be brought up, but Katie flattened her lips and turned to Evan. "And you were there?"

"Kinda gave myself away with the whole camping thing, eh?" He shifted a squirming Jack to a different position. "I wasn't going to let him run off alone, and I didn't intend to actually take him to Rose's house. But, the stubborn ass jumped out of the car at a stop sign."

"Thank you," I said sarcastically.

"My boyfriend," Rose murmured, "the hopeless romantic."

Trent snorted and punched my arm. "I think hopeless is the key term. I'm going home and crawling into bed so, if anyone needs me, wait five days until I'm alive again."

"We'll see you at the house," Katie said, grabbing Jack and giving me a kiss on the cheek as she passed. "Told you it'd all work out."

Evan also patted my arm on the way out, leaving me and Rose in the now empty room.

"I have one more thing I want to take care of tonight," I said, nodding to the door. I took her hand and stole an extra-long kiss.

Libby was still in the captain's office as we passed, so I knocked on the door frame. "I know it's late, but can I ask one more favor?"

———

MILES SQUINTED at me when I entered the room. "Should I ask how you got in here after visiting hours?"

I stayed near the door, arms folded over my chest. "I had to pull a lot of strings. I wanted you to be one of the first to know—we caught seven men in connection with the missing girls and heroin. The investigation will continue until we're sure, and hopefully, we'll get some answers about Alley along the way."

Miles nodded. He made a sound in his throat, but it took him a few moments before he spoke. "I figured you'd get 'em."

The sole of my shoe scuffed against the floor. "I uh—brought another little surprise, too. Hope you don't mind."

His eyes widened, but aside from that movement, his face looked dead.

I pushed open the door and Rose stepped inside, staying close to my side as the heavy door closed again.

"I'll be damned," Miles whispered. "You let him drag you here, and what the hell happened to your cheek?"

"He told me where he was going and I asked to come along. And—" Her fingers brushed the purpled skin "—you know me. Trouble everywhere."

"I think it might have something to do with your company," he whispered with a smirk. His solemn silence replaced with a new light in his eyes—more like the man I used to know. Except—I hoped—this version might be a little less trouble.

Rose took the other seat and I leaned against the back of the chair. "I was just informed that they're pushing to get you a hearing next month. Apparently, there was someone throwing a few kinks into the plan, but they're going to reevaluate your sentence and contribution to the federal case. Maybe we can get you some less severe living arrangements."

"What the hell am I supposed to do when I get out of here?" he asked. "You really think the system is going to help me?"

"If they won't, I will." He'd still have a few years at the very least, but I didn't care how long it took. He'd saved my life, the very least I could do was help him get his life on track.

He grunted. "Have you tracked down the girls? How are they doing?"

"My partner and a couple of other detectives have been

checking in on the ones we have locations for, but there are still a few missing," I admitted. "Raini—her real name is Fiona—she helped us with the case. Lured them out so we could find them. It all went a little hinky, but I think she's doing better."

"Hopefully, she doesn't look as bad as your girl," he motioned to Rose and smiled, but the skin around his eyes wrinkled with a touch of worry.

"Nah," she chuckled and held her side. "I kept most of their attention."

A guard knocked on the door, and I grabbed Rose's shoulders as she almost jumped out of the chair.

"You're time's nearly up," the guard yelled in.

Rose bent her head back and stared up at me.

"Well," I said, "go on then."

She jumped to her feet—faster than I expected anyone as busted up as her to move—and rounded the table. "He said I'm allowed one hug."

Miles watched her, his forehead wrought with lines, then his gaze bounced to me, and I shrugged. He slowly climbed to his feet and held out his arms, letting her come to him.

"Watch the bruised ribs," she whispered and stepped into his embrace. "Thanks for not letting Ross shoot me."

"Stay out of trouble," he said. His voice wavered, but he didn't take his intense gaze off her until she was by my side again.

Chapter Twenty-Three

CONSUMING THE DARKNESS

I TOLD Rose that I felt guilty for missing her sister's wedding, but in truth that was a minor exaggeration. I couldn't miss Miles' hearing, so it gave me a good excuse, but I was in no mood to sit through a long ceremony *and* reception surrounded by people I didn't know—who probably questioned the safety of my presence, given everything that had happened.

That wasn't the only reason, though. I needed to keep moving, keep talking—anything to avoid thinking. If I let my mind wander, I was afraid I'd talk myself out of my own plans.

After her most recent injuries, I'd been giving Rose time to heal physically before officially rescinding our rule.

Weeks before the wedding, I'd booked our cabin at a lodge near the ceremony. And then, I went shopping for a few things to keep us entertained. She had no idea what I had in mind—the images that were racing through my brain as we sat with her family during the reception. All entirely inappropriate for the circumstances, but I kept it to myself, forcing myself to smile and talk.

The sight of her in a bridesmaid dress didn't help either. I don't know what all of the horror stories are about because it fit her perfectly, and the soft purple fabric made her green eyes stand out.

As if I needed the extra nudge of enchantment.

I took advantage when Rose's family left her in charge of wrangling her five-month-old niece. It was quite an amusing sight, but I decided to relieve her just to have something to keep me occupied and deflect the attention from myself. Even so, the two-hour reception passed so slowly I could barely sit still by the end of it, but we finally slipped out early and pilfered a bottle of champagne.

The drive to the cabin only took a few minutes, but Rose seemed just as worked up as me by the time we got there. I kept it contained though—first, it was all about her, so we sat down on the back porch and sipped our champagne.

I sat my glass down next to the chair and dragged my fingers through her hair. Things as simple as touching her— the feeling her skin and hair—looking into her green eyes, hearing her voice—everything I got from being around her, twisted my body into knots. It could be agony, but not an entirely uncomfortable feeling. She also kept me grounded.

I'd begun to feel empty without the buzzing tension she created beneath my skin.

And, quite possibly the most frightening thing, I'd begun to accept the things I desired doing to her. I wanted the taut battle that brought out the determination in her eyes. Determination that slowly melted into acceptance and submission.

I craved the way she looked at me in those moments.

The darkness was still there, but I'd made it mine. I collared it and brought it to heel, but tonight I was letting it out to play.

I gave Rose the early lead—control to dictate what she wanted. Using my tie, she pulled me down to capture the first kiss, it began slow but built into a stormy battle as my erection grew against her.

I pulled her against me while she loosened my tie and began unbuttoning my shirt. We were on a screened in patio and I glanced to the sides to see if any of our neighbors seemed to be out. "You want to do this here?"

She flipped out the lights. "They won't see anything."

After another long kiss, she jumped to her feet, leaving me throbbing. I tightened my muscles to keep from going after her, I just had to last a little longer, before I had my way.

"Wait here," she said and disappeared into the cabin. I dropped my head against the back of the wicker chair until I heard her hurried footsteps returning. She threw a comforter on the floor, and with one look I didn't care where we were or what anyone else heard.

I kicked off my shoes, then pulled her against me, sliding the straps of her dress down slowly as my lips explored her skin. Her hands went to my belt and I swallowed a groan as she unzipped my pants and they slid to the floor. Our clothes made up a growing pile on the floor as we devoured each other with kisses and touches and moved to the comforter.

Her skin felt hot and every moan and gasp expressed her growing need. I traced the scar on her shoulder, the delicate pink mark before moving down her body. She wrapped her legs around my waist, trying to hurry me along.

Then, she grabbed my hair, forcing me to face her—it was going to be the last time she'd be on that end of the hair pulling. "I'm. Fucking. Losing. It," she grunted.

"Good." I considered making her wait, but I wasn't sure I could hold out any longer, and if I was going to cum, it was damn well going to be inside her.

I pressed my swollen cock to her entrance, sliding slowly inside as she rocked her hips forward to meet me.

My plans to go slow and savor each extended moment were lost to the chorus of groans and gasps. I watched her beneath me as the burning tingle started in my back, radiating through my nerves and unlocking a flood of pleasure that spread through my heated body.

She trembled beneath me, and I captured her mouth at the moment the orgasm claimed her. I slammed into her harder, driving my cock deeper as she shuddered around me until my release took away my control with a long groan.

The taste of her kiss lingered in my mouth—a taste that I could easily live on.

We laid there for a few moments, catching our breath and finding our mutual peace.

Bend, don't break. Over and over, I had reminded her of that, but it was something we'd both had to learn. Maybe me more so than her. I'd struggled for months trying to figure out how to put the pieces of my life back together— to make sense of everything that I had become after the Retreat. But I'd become so rigid in my expectations and beliefs that I'd tried to throw out pieces that still belonged.

"I love you, Rose," I whispered, pressing against her. I expected her to be quiet—at least somewhat sated for the time being, but she smirked.

"Good, then you can show me in all of the other rooms of the cabin."

I intended to, but I wasn't making it too easy. "You should have told me I'd have to pace myself."

"Then, let's hop in the shower and you can recover. Now that you're fully warned, you can pace yourself for the rest of the night."

The rest of the night—I could do that, but she'd be the one who'd have to pace herself. I smacked her thigh, and she moved her lips to my ear and whispered, "I love you too."

I took her hand and led her to the bathroom, stopping along the way to grab the suitcase from near the door. Since she hadn't known we were staying over for a few days, she'd have to deal with the clothes she brought down in her overnight bag, and what I'd packed her—which wasn't much since I didn't plan on leaving the cabin too often.

That wasn't going to be her only surprise. I pulled a black bag out of the suitcase—it looked like a large toiletry bag, but I'd filled it with a few amenities of my own choosing.

I opened the side pocket and handed her the bath set.

She shook the plastic case that held the small collection of bottles and soap. "I'm assuming that whole bag wasn't just to hold this."

"Get the shower started, Sugar."

She huffed and shook her head, hanging the bath soaps on a hook inside the shower. Then, she leaned over to turn on the water. "I feel you staring at me," she said, glaring at me over her shoulder.

I wiggled my eyebrows and turned back to the toiletry bag, I began pulling out my new assortment, placing the lubes in a collection along the back of the sink. Then, I then cleaned all the vibrators and butt plugs and sat them to the side on a towel to dry.

While my hands worked, I observed Rose through the mirror. She eyed me suspiciously but stayed near the shower where she couldn't see my new collection until I turned and leaned against the wall.

I licked my dry lips as I watched her eyes move from object to object.

"I guess my razzing you about pacing yourself was utterly useless." Her voice had gone from light and peppy to low and rough, seeded with passion and yearning.

I closed the distance between us, tangling my fingers through her hair, and pulling her face up to meet mine. "Still trust me?"

"Yes." Her answer didn't rise above a whisper, but the conviction in her eyes told me all I needed to know.

We climbed under the hot water of the shower, our hot bodies pressed together, searching, exploring, finding new points of pleasure to exploit. The tingling pressure in my groin indicated that my cock was already fighting to come back to life, but it was going to have plenty of time to wait, and I intended to indulge in every bittersweet moment.

I washed her body from neck to feet, then traded off the soap so she could do the same. Every movement sent tingles running through my skin, all demanding one thing.

She dunked her hair under the water and doused it with shampoo to get rid of the remaining hair spray, while I stood in front of her, tracing the suds down her front and fondling her breasts so I could watch her squirm.

Once all the soap was washed away, I stepped out first, grabbing a towel to wrap her in before she climbed over the edge of the tub. She squeezed the excess water from her hair and twisted it up to finish drying off. Turning away from me, she reached to hang up the towel, and I grabbed a fistful of her wet hair, pulling her back against me.

I still expected some ounce of trepidation in her eyes every time I seized her, but I had yet to see it. Instead, her eyes locked onto mine, waiting for me to do as I pleased or order her to do it.

"Lean on the counter."

It was strikingly familiar to our early encounters at the Retreat—intentionally so, but not because I longed for that —I wanted to prove how far we'd come. To prove how different it was when the actions were built on trust and desire.

She did as I asked, giving me full control of her slender form—mine for the taking.

I shoved her legs apart, my fingers exploring her exposed pussy—already hot and wet for me. I grabbed the first bottle of lube and clicked it open, and letting tiny drips fall between her ass cheeks and roll down. The next drop landed on her puckered hole and she jumped slightly.

I let another drop fall, then dragged my finger through the liquid, slipping it gently inside her. She moaned, and readjusted her footing as her head dropped to her hands.

"Eyes in the mirror," I said, pulling her hair back with my free hand. "Watch."

She kept her head up, silently obeying as I returned my concentration to exploring her. I reached around to her front, capturing her clit between two fingers and pinching and stroking in equal measure until Rose gasped for air.

I picked up the smaller of the plugs and added a few extra drops of lube before pressing it to her hole and gently working it back and forth until it fell into place. Rose groaned and grasped at the counter, her eyes were wide and her mouth hung open.

I pulled her upright, holding her against me as I washed my hands and packed up the rest of the toys and lube to move to the living room.

"I think I'd like to see you crawl," I growled, biting her ear.

Her eyes hardened, her lips puckering. "Would you?"

I patted the base of the plug and she grabbed the counter to balance herself. Her neck muscles tensed as she clenched her jaw and stared at me through the mirror.

"What was that?" I asked.

"Bedroom?" She raised her eyebrows and licked her lips.

"Living room. Go get the blanket from the porch and lay it over the couch."

She dropped to her knees, taking my breath with her as she crawled out of the room. I followed close behind, watching her ass sway from side to side with the black base peeking out from between her cheeks.

Leaving the bag on the side table, I waited until she had the comforter spread across the couch. I took a seat and pulled her up to straddle my lap with her warmth pressing against my cock. I twisted her hands behind her back and fastened a soft piece of cloth around them. In that position, her chest jutted forward—perfect for my mouth to explore her already erect nipples.

With every moan, she pressed harder against me, arching her back and increasing my access.

I stopped and her head fell forward. Her chest heaved as she raced futilely to catch her breath.

"How long do you think I can keep you going?" I whispered.

"Please," her mouth moved in the shape of the word, but barely more than hissed air escaped.

I patted the couch next to me then lifted her so that she stood on her knees in the center of the couch, facing the wall. I pushed her down to lean against the back of the couch and fished through the bag for my next implement.

Switching on the vibrator, I pushed it to her clit and she shrieked and wriggled.

"Still," I said, smacking her ass. She groaned and squeezed her eyes closed as the impact jarred the plug nestled in her ass.

I could see the concentration in her pinched expression as she tried not to move, but the involuntary spasms won out.

She clenched her fists as her breathing continued to increase and her toes curled against my knees. Her moans and mews filled the small room, louder with every second she closed in on her next orgasm.

Her back bucked and she lifted away from the back of the couch, her body jerking as the orgasm tore through her muscles. Dropping her head to the back of the couch, her body relaxed again—except for the small trembles that ran under her skin every few seconds.

"Don't tell me you're done already," I teased, untying her arms and pulling her hips back to meet mine.

Rose straightened and then leaned back against me, reclining her head against my shoulder. Her fingers caressed my neck and gently moved along my jawline. "That all you got?"

I chuckled and shoved her forward. "Lay down on your back."

She moved gingerly to disturb the plug as little as possible. I laid my hand against her side taking in the smooth feeling of her sweat-dampened skin.

I grabbed a pair of nipple clamps, and as soon as she

caught sight of the silver trinkets in my hand her mouth twisted into a pout. "I don't like those."

"I do." I twisted one nipple into a sharp peak again, and she bit her bottom lip but didn't move to stop me—even when I tightened the cold metal clamp over the sensitive nub.

Her breath shook jiggling her breasts as I repeated the same process on her other nipple.

I slipped my hand between her legs, and she jerked as I found her clit again. "Can you tolerate the clamps?"

"Mhh hmm," she moaned as I continued stroking her clit with my thumb and inched two fingers inside of her. Slowly, her muscles relaxed again as she gave up the struggle and pleasure overwhelmed her discomfort.

Leaning over her, I kissed and sucked at her neck until she bucked against me. Her nails dug into my shoulders, pulling me closer, and she nuzzled my neck. The gentle sensation turned into soft nips and one final bite.

I stiffened and pulled away, a twisted smile played at her lips, balanced by the mischief in her eyes.

"Oh, Sugar." I twisted one of the clamps and she screamed, lifting her hips off the couch.

Her scream turned into a guttural moan. "Still worth it."

My breath rumbled in my throat. My neck still burned, but the sensation sent blood streaming to my cock. Apparently part of me didn't mind taking it as well as dishing it out—mainly because I enjoyed the twisted clash of our wills.

And in the end, I knew mine would win out. I grabbed the bag and moved it to the side of the couch so I could reach its contents more easily. Then, I drew a single finger down her throat, over her sternum and down to her belly button, plotting what I'd do to get rid of that smug expression she still wore.

"Pull your knees up to your chest."

Her eyebrow twitched as she obeyed, revealing the nub of the black butt plug. I picked up the lube and a larger plug, laying them on the comforter next to her. She gasped as I pulled the plug free, but instead of removing it, I slowly slid it back in.

I watched as she strained to hold her knees in place while I moved the butt plug in and out a few times. Then, I dropped the used plug into a bag to be washed later and prepared the larger pink plug.

This time, she whimpered as I pressed it against her entrance.

"Relax, Sugar," I stroked the inside of her thigh and her stomach as I worked the plug inside her. She cried out and bit her bottom lip when it popped into place.

"Oooh," she held the sound out. "I don't like this one."

"You will," I said, entirely confident of it. I crouched over her, pressing my cock against her entrance and sliding in slowly.

Even with the plug creating extra pressure, she thrust up to take me in. She grabbed the comforter near her head, squeezing it until her knuckles whitened.

"Don't come," I growled, pumping inside of her gently.

She nodded, keeping her eyes on me.

"Enjoying the view?"

"Yes," she breathed, then licked her lips. "Very much."

I sped up my motions, feeling the build start again. The pulsing ache built spreading out from my balls and heating my cock.

Pressing her head into the couch, she lifted her hips, her body shaking under me as she grunted under the strain of holding back. I sat back and grabbed her hips pulling her up and tightly against me until my cock was buried inside of her.

She gasped and pressed her hands upward into the arm of the couch.

Rose gave me back myself—everything I'd lost during the year I spent at the Retreat. Every ounce of strength and willpower that had been slowly wrung out of me over the months. She was mine as much as I was hers. I took control and took her body, but only because she gifted it to me. It was that balance that made every moment delicious and breathtaking.

Her jerks became more violent and she tightened around me.

"Oh, please," she said, on the verge of a sob.

One more slow thrust and I leaned over her again, pressing my hand around her neck.

Her eyes were glassy but focused. She knew exactly what was happening, but she'd given into the physical sensation.

I held her throat tightly but still allowed her enough breath to keep from doing damage.

"Please," she croaked again as a shudder wracked her body.

"Now, Sugar," I whispered in her ear, the word tangling in my throat and coming out as worn and ragged as I felt.

Her hips slammed up against me and her insides shuddered against my cock. Her eyes fluttered closed, but her mouth widened, gasping for air.

I thrust harder, riding her waves of pleasure until I hit my own release and came inside of her. My own body shook, and my arms nearly refused to support me as I released each of the nipple clamps and dropped them into the bag. I laid on top of her, resting my head on her chest while her fingers wound through my hair.

After I removed the second plug, we both stumbled toward the bedroom, curled up together under the remaining blankets, and fell asleep before another word could be spoken.

Epilogue

THERE WERE times I tried my damnedest to imagine a happy ending after the Retreat. It was forced and generic— some fairy tale happily ever after that I knew was a mockery of life. I lost people I cared about, worked with, and respected. There were days I never thought anything would get better.

And yet six months after the raid, I found myself leaving work to visit the woman I loved.

Not only that, but I also had a surprise—and I hoped to the heavens that she liked it.

Rose was in the kitchen putting away groceries when I walked in.

"I talked to Fiona today." Her voice was high and perky. Between Katie and Fiona, she was always gossiping with someone lately.

"Ah, yeah?" I picked up an apple from the fruit bowl on the table and took a bite. I had a feeling I already knew what her news was going to be since I had crossed paths with Ryan earlier in the day.

"She had a date last night." When Rose turned around, she was smiling ear to ear, but after studying me for a minute, it faded slightly. "Ryan already told you, didn't he?"

"He may have alluded to it," I admitted, pulling her closer and brushing her hair back. "But I'll assume from your smile she enjoyed it."

"She did. It was dinner and a movie, but it was the world to her. It's nice to see her happy."

I chuckled. I wasn't intent on letting her go yet, but she wriggled out of my grasp and started putting away a new bag of groceries.

"That the last one?" I asked.

She nodded and chucked a box of cereal at me. "You could be a gentleman and help."

"I may have to do something about that bossiness."

Making a sound in her throat that twisted my core, she turned on her heels. "You do that. *After* dinner."

I flipped her around and pressed her forward into the refrigerator, twisting her hands behind her back and securing them in one hand. "See what I mean about the bossiness."

The more I threatened, the more her smile grew—it was useless, really.

But damn fun.

And it'd have to wait. "I have something I want to show you. Then, we'll discuss dinner and pleasure."

"Well, that's no fun," she stretched her head back against my shoulder and I nipped at her neck. Holding the pinch of skin until she squirmed.

Definitely damn fun. I was too tempted to follow through with my threat immediately, but I reminded myself that the anticipation would be just as much fun—especially when I got to watch her writhe.

Plus, I was just as anxious to show her my surprise, and if I had to put that off much longer, I'd be the one fidgeting through dinner.

I released her, and she packed away the last of the groceries and shoved the bags into a bin under the counter.

"What are you so intent on showing me, then?"

I shrugged and backed out of the kitchen. She caught up with me by the time I'd reached the door, grabbing her purse and keys along the way.

My surprise was about a fifteen miles out on the highway road that wound through the state forest.

Rose watched every sign and landmark we'd passed. I figured she must have been out this way at least once, since the lakes, picnic areas, and hiking trails were fairly popular during the summer, but she reminded me quite astutely that she was not a country girl.

I didn't want to change much about her, but that was something I was keen on working on.

"Seriously, James, if I hear banjo music, I'm bailing."

"We're on a main highway." I squeezed her thigh just above the knee until she twisted to get away. "We'll be there in about five minutes."

"Does this place have food?"

"No. Just enjoy the ride, Sugar."

She snorted and slumped against the window.

I followed the hills and curves until I spotted a little bridge tucked away in the trees. I held my breath as we crossed the creek—it was nearly time to face her reaction.

She sat up in her seat looking around at the creek and surroundings as I parked the car in front of a small red house.

"You found a place," she gasped. Jumping out of the car before I could turn it off.

I climbed out, too. Leaning against the roof and watching her take it all in. "I started looking for a place to buy and, well, I've had my eye on this one for a while. What do you think?"

"It's very you."

I snorted. That didn't tell me a whole lot. I fished the key out of my pocket and herded Rose toward the front door.

The house was a little musty since it had been empty for a few months, but some cleaning and a few days with the windows open would take care of that. The structure itself was sound and well-maintained.

"It's small, just a kitchen, bathroom, bedroom, and living room." I led her through the open area.

"I think the whole place could fit in my current living room." She smirked, wandering through the living room and into the bedroom.

I took a deep breath. "Is that a bad thing?"

"Nah." She peeked in the closet. "I don't know what to do with half the space in my house."

My heart pounded so hard I could hear it over her feet as she moved across the hardwood floors. *Now or never.* "So, you wouldn't mind living here with me?"

She stopped in her tracks with her mouth wide open. "You're asking me to move in with you?"

I nodded. My mouth agonizingly dry as I waited for her response, and I think she intentionally kept me waiting.

She looked out the bedroom window and let out a long sigh. "Really intent on turning me into a country girl, aren't you?"

"No—maybe—I don't want to turn you into—"

Grabbing my hand, she pulled me over to the window. October had made its mark, and the back window looked out over the lush colored hill. Reds and yellows with touches of greens and browns as far as I could see. The area was quiet and beautiful—the perfect place to relax and unwind.

Rose leaned against me, pulling my arms around her. "Think all three of us will fit here?"

My peace shattered. "Three?"

She turned and gave me a dumbfounded look. "Trapper, silly. What the hell else would I mean?"

"I thought we could give the—"

"No." She pressed her finger over my lips.

I yanked her hand away and countered with a kiss. "I think we'll all fit perfectly. I thought we could get a dog to guard the yard, too."

"*We* could." She laughed quietly and peered out the window again. I held her against me, tucking her head under my chin.

I knew we'd still have plenty to work through, new challenges every day, but at that moment, I had everything I needed and wanted. "You want to know the best thing about it?"

"What?"

"No neighbors." I pressed my lips against her ear and whispered, "I can make you scream as loud as I want. And I intend to do it very often."

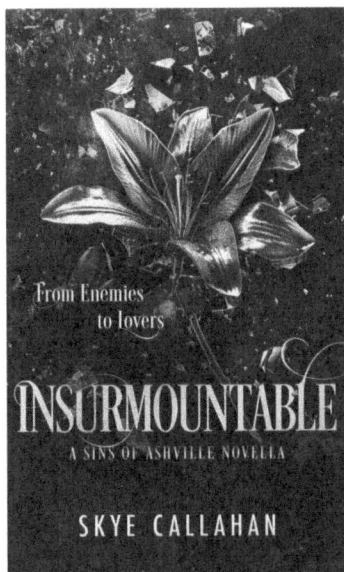

vinci-books.com/skyinsurmount

Bound by darkness, driven by desire—together, they'll defy the rules to find their freedom.

Turn the page for a preview…

Insurmountable: Chapter One

SCAR TISSUE

Miles

I NEVER STOOD A CHANCE.

Not once in my entire life did I ever know anything other than *this*.

Sex. Slaves. Drugs. Trafficking. Parties. Alcohol. Money. Extortion. Beatings. Blackmail. Pain.

And exquisite pleasure. Every fantasy at the snap of a finger.

"Miles," Gabe grunted my name as he pounded on my apartment door. I wanted to punch him in the face every time I heard his voice. Unfortunately, he worked for my security team—the most experienced dickhead I had. In more ways than one.

"New girls are here," he yelled.

New girls, or *fresh meat* as many of the men around the Retreat liked to call them. Everyone loves when the new girls show up. Clients, employees, especially the boss, Ross. I, however, dreaded the days when they showed up. The men went wild, and depending on where the girls came from, I could have a near crisis on my hands.

Our organization was made up of multiple sex trafficking rings and brothels around the world. Some were high-class establishments with money to throw around on the girls. Expensive costumes, elaborate facilities, and medical treatment for the women. Others were more questionable, using drugs and violence to subdue the women.

Punishments. Rewards. The scales could tip drastically in either direction.

I snapped my keys onto my belt loop and opened my apartment door, walking past Gabe without so much as a word. He was an asshole. Pure and simple. An asshole who didn't listen to jack shit. And I was the poor, unlucky fool strapped with being his boss.

Most days he was lucky I let him live.

We climbed aboard the elevator and I punched the button for the fifth floor—The Commons—where we processed all the new girls.

"You're in a mood today," Gabe said.

I didn't look at him. If I did, I might have punched his smug face in. I straightened the collar and cuffs of my shirt instead. "I'm not in a mood."

When we stepped off the elevator, twelve new girls were standing in the middle of the room; blondes, brunettes, redheads, and everything in between. I assessed them all within seconds of laying eyes on them. The bold girls, the timid girls, experienced and unexperienced. It's always in their eyes, their posture, and their nervous twitches. They were all dressed in street clothes to make their transportation less suspicious.

"Take off your clothes," I said.

Some of the girls grinned as they pulled their shirts over

their heads and dropped their bras to the floor. Others simply did as told, keeping their eyelids lowered. They all obeyed without hesitation.

Major perk of the job—looking at all the beautiful women.

"You'll all be examined by our doctor." I strolled past the line of women, checking them each out from head to foot. "He'll make sure your birth control is up to date and you're in good physical condition."

I circled around the last girl and walked up the backside, checking out their other assets. The redhead on the end arched her back, pressing her ass toward me as I passed. Then she peeked over her shoulder and winked.

I knew she'd be trouble, but the patrons would fucking love her. A lot of the girls did anything they could to get their five seconds of recognition. They needed attention, Yearned for it. After all, attention was quite possibly the only thing they lived for.

But it wasn't that cheeky redhead that caught my attention. It was the willowy blonde in the middle. The girl with her hair falling over her face, struggling not to make eye contact. Struggling not to stand out. Not to be pulled aside or singled out. But everything about her made her stand out to me.

"You're first, Little Dove." I pulled her forward. "What's your name?"

"Alley." She lifted her blue-green eyes, peeking out from under her long, bright lashes.

"Follow me to the infirmary." In this case, being chosen first was not the worst thing. We all knew what would happen as soon as I turned my back.

The guards and men lining the back wall smirked at us as we passed, waiting for their opportunity to pounce. You'd think that eventually they'd get enough. They'd get bored. Obviously, they hadn't seen as much as me. Done as much as me.

Even new girls were boring.

But then, I'd been involved in this world for as long as I could remember. That's a long time to develop tastes and get your fill.

––––––––

IT SEEMED like my days never ended, and, unfortunately, they blurred into weeks that also went on forever. I spent all day Monday processing the new girls and getting them settled with only a few minor incidents from my men. Tuesday through Thursday, however, I'd spent twenty-four hours a day merely keeping my team out of trouble. An impossible feat without new girls floating around. And Friday only meant it'd get worse. We had a hundred and six girls and ninety customers booked in for the night, starting at seven when we opened the girls. New girls, new visitors, and a security team with libidos of sixteen-year-olds meant my life would be a living hell until morning.

And then I'd start the process all over again.

At eight thirty—after having already dealt with enough crises to last an entire week, I pushed open the security room door, hoping for a quick update assuring me that all was under control. "Dig, what's the…"

The room was empty. The room was *never* supposed to be empty, especially on a packed night.

Damn incompetent fools. Lazy bastards.

All they cared about was getting their rocks off. Having their cocks fluffed. If replacing a single person didn't involve jumping through so many damn hoops, I'd replace them all in a fucking heartbeat.

I scanned the cameras. The lobby looked good. The grounds were fine. Every room. Every nook and cranny and foot of the yard. They're all monitored—at all times. More than two hundred cameras in the place that the security team are trusted to watch to protect our assets and our reputation.

In theory anyhow. Obviously, a flaw had developed in the system.

Some dipshits just couldn't take it. They got all hot and bothered and wander off to find an available girl for a quickie.

I scanned the third-floor rooms.

"Fuck," I yelled, slamming my hand down on the keyboard. The chair soared across the room, thumping against the back wall just as the door opened.

"Miles, I—" Dig stuttered. "I uh—"

"Shut up and call the team to room 329."

I bypassed the elevators—where any of the current customers would see me, and inevitably slow things up—and sprinted up three flights of stairs, ran down the hallway, and busted through the door of room 329.

The patron—a man I hadn't encountered directly before—was standing over Alley with his shoe in his hand, wailing on her. He was so busy with the beating that he hadn't even noticed that I'd entered the room until I had my arm around his neck. I twisted, throwing him off balance, and slamming him face first into the opposite wall.

"What?" he growled through his clenched teeth. "You stick me with a useless piece of shit then come in here to fuck me over?"

His shoulder jerked, but he didn't stand a chance of

throwing off a two-hundred-forty-pound, six-foot-nine man. "Don't even give me that. You don't rough up our girls and expect not to pay the price."

Finally, backup arrived, and I shoved the bastard toward Dig and Keith. "Take him to see Ross. I'm sure he'll have some ideas for getting a handle on the situation. Probably by kicking the shit out of him and sending him back to town with a one-of-a-kind warning. Ross kept enough shit to blackmail anyone, and if he couldn't find anything legit, he created it. "And Dig, be sure to account for your where-abouts when Ross is done with him."

"Yes, sir," he mumbled.

Alley laid curled up on the floor.

"Little dove." I brushed back her hair to check her injuries. Her lip was busted, and her right eyebrow bruised. The injuries I couldn't see were the most troubling. "Come on."

I lifted her up, but she kept her hands fisted tightly over her stomach and her eyes squeezed closed. "You'll be fine, Little dove."

When I laid her out on the exam table, her eyes opened, but she stared blankly across the room. "What happened?"

She narrowed her eyes and shook her head.

"Tell me," I coaxed, gently brushing her hair back. We only had a matter of time before Ross would finish up with the others and come in to pass judgment on her. "Just tell me."

Grab your copy...
vinci-books.com/skyinsurmount

About the Author

Skye Callahan is a bestselling author who enjoys writing fiction to explore the darker aspects of human nature and the resiliency needed to survive and overcome difficult situations. She hopes to show that even through the darkest moments and overwhelming circumstances, one can find the inner strength to adapt and eventually heal.

Skye lives in the hills of Appalachia with her husband and their feline overlords: Sassy, Knight, Raith, Dresden, and Crowley, and enjoys hanging out in the yard with all the natural wildlife (except rattlesnakes). When she's not reading or writing, she might be found in the garden, watching horror movies, or playing video games with the hubs. Prior to pursuing writing full-time, Skye earned an M.A. in History and participated in numerous local history projects, including a full-length Civil War documentary for PBS.